BLACK SWAN

CHRIS KNOPF
BLACK SWAN

THE PERMANENT PRESS
Sag Harbor, NY 11963

For information, address:
   The Permanent Press
   4170 Noyac Road
   Sag Harbor, NY 11963
   www.thepermanentpress.com

Library of Congress Cataloging-in-Publication Data

Knopf, Chris–
   Black swan / Chris Knopf.
        p. cm. — (A Sam Acquillo Hamptons mystery)
   ISBN 978-1-57962-216-9 (alk. paper)
        1. Acquillo, Sam (Fictitious character)—Fiction.
   2. Sailing—Fiction. 3. Hotels—Fiction. 4. Fishers Island
   (N.Y. : Island)—Fiction. I. Title. II. Series.

PS3611.N66B57 2011
813'.6—dc22   2011003132

Printed in the United States of America.

For the late Samuel Beckett Farrell,
Wheaten extraordinaire,
who gave me Eddie in whole cloth.
No strings attached.

ACKNOWLEDGEMENTS

In the "without whom this would not be possible" category, thanks to Tim Hannon, my friend of fifty-five years and colorful native guide to Fishers Island. Thanks to Kip Wiley for nautical knowledge and Cindy Courtney for legal language and general counsel. Special thanks to the software development demons at Mintz & Hoke: John Yeager, Don Ross, Michael Perry, Andy Turon and Mark Bonet. High fives to keen-eyed and thoughtful readers Bob Willemin, Sean Cronin and Randy Costello. Eternal gratitude to Judy Shepard, with the best editorial mind in the land (along with Marty, her co-conspirator).

As always, Anne-Marie Regish for logistical support and Mary Farrell, who has come to regard her husband's conversations with imaginary people as perfectly natural.

CHAPTER 1

I tell myself the same thing when I climb a tall ladder. Don't look down.

But I did anyway, looking over the starboard side of the sailboat as we sped up the side of a particularly steep wave. The distance from the cockpit to the bottom of the trough looked impossibly vast and untraversable. I jerked the wheel up into the incline of the wave and held on. The bow shot into the air, then drifted almost languidly down the other side, mocking my initial alarm, until the force of the next wave snatched up the stern and shoved the *Carpe Mañana* into another furious wall of water.

Only an immediate spin of the wheel to port saved us from broaching, though we hit the wave hard enough to cover the boat from bow to dodger—the canvas and plastic windscreen protecting the cockpit—in foamy green water.

With typical understatement, the nautical term for this kind of wave action is 'confused.' I'd have called it enraged, or maybe psychotic.

"That was interesting," Amanda yelled up from below.

"That's nothing," I yelled back. "We're just getting started."

She hoisted herself up the stairs that led down to the boat's living quarters. She wore brilliant orange foul-weather clothing that did nothing for her slim, winsome figure.

I reached around the wheel and clipped a tether to her inflatable harness, then gently shoved her down into the cockpit.

"So this is a milk run," said Amanda, as she wedged herself against the bulkhead. "What's a storm like?"

"Okay, NOAA got it wrong. Sometimes they do," I shouted through a spray of saltwater. "October's a tricky time of year."

NOAA, short for the National Oceanic and Atmospheric Administration (as if you could administer the oceans and atmosphere), the source of all weather forecasting, had a dirty little secret: it rarely had a clue what was happening on Long Island Sound until it was already happening, and not always then, which meant a lot less prediction than reportage.

"You've become a NOAA apologist."

"If we live through this, I'll write a disappointed letter," I said.

"I thought you said sailboats can't sink."

"Hold that thought."

I'd told her it's really hard to sink a sailboat, but not impossible. You need just the right combination of circumstances—lots of wind, sharp wave angle, a lousy boat and a lousier helmsman. The boat felt solid and responsive, which didn't surprise me, handpicked as it was by my friend Burton Lewis, who knew boats like mothers knew their kids. The helmsman was the only unconfirmed variable, and though I'd had my share of sloppy water and crappy weather, this was something different.

Amanda snatched the handheld two-way VHF radio out of its cradle and started working the controls. I adjusted my purchase on the molded teak slats that secured my butt and turned through another set of nasty waves.

The NOAA marine weather station reported, without apology, a revised forecast. The mechanized female voice said the wind had shifted to the northeast and was building to a steady thirty-five to forty knots, with gusts to sixty. Wave heights were now expected to be six to eight feet, which in my experience meant eight feet and up. The small craft advisory of the morning, when we'd set out well before dawn from Point Judith, Rhode Island, was now a somber gale force warning, insisting that whatever idiot small craft were still out on the water get the hell to the nearest port, as if we weren't desperately trying to do just that.

For the next several hours we concentrated on our individual responsibilities. Amanda was charged with staying in the boat and trying not to shriek when the boat leaned over enough to drop the rail in the water, or when a gush of sea spray hit the dodger with the force of a fire hose.

I was supposed to keep us from drowning. They say in a bad storm the people on board will wear out long before the boat, and I think that's true. It's hard to believe in the durability of your craft while a real storm is fully underway.

As I put all my strength and weight into the wheel one second, and then let it whirl between my gloved hands the next, it seemed impossible that any useful end was being served by human agency, that the boat was in some conspiracy with the sea and wanted to give me only the illusion of control.

And the water, it was everywhere: washing across the bow, blasting into the dodger, sloshing in over the transom to swirl around my feet until it drained out the scuppers on the cockpit floor. Which would have been far more bearable if it wasn't for the rain, driving in from the port bow, stinging my face and ruining my vision.

Exhausted by her efforts to sustain both emotional balance and solid handholds, Amanda turned quiet, her beautiful face a mask of taut misery.

I began to realize much of our forward momentum involved surfing down breaking ten foot waves. I'm not much of a swimmer, but I'd done my share of bodysurfing as a kid, so a sense of how to finesse the build-up to the break, and then the turbulent, barely-controllable ride down the other side of the wave was encrypted in my memory.

My back ached from standing and my arms complained with every spin of the wheel, but there was nothing to be done about it. All the while, I expected things to improve, but they kept getting worse. This is Fishers Island Sound, for God's sake, I said to myself. It's not the Southern Ocean. I wanted to check in with NOAA again, but knew it would mean nothing. Confirming that we were in a freak shit storm wouldn't help get us out of it.

I threw the boat up into another sharp rise to port, only to pull her back to starboard on the way down, barely in time to avoid a boiling mass of seawater from joining us in the cockpit.

"I guess you can't just make it go in a nice straight line," said Amanda, pulling herself up off the cockpit floor where the last set of waves had tossed her.

"If only I were a better sailor."

"You have other qualities," said Amanda. "Give me a moment and I'll come up with a few."

"It's that hard?"

"You have an unusual dog."

She meant Eddie, the midsized, shepherd-based mutt who was still below, blissfully knocked out with a hit of Benadryl and secured in a crew berth by a heavy piece of acrylic canvas called a lee cloth. It was a precaution brought on not by his fearing the storm, but of loving it too much. He was the same way in the car. The faster I went and more erratically I drove, the more he liked it. I felt a little bad depriving him of the fun, but I couldn't bear the constant barking demand that he come topside just to get washed overboard.

Another complication was the ongoing need to check our position on the GPS. It only took a few moments in that kind of weather to lose our course, costing vital time to port, or worse, putting ourselves in even more dangerous conditions.

In what amounted to a literal saving grace, the best angle on the wind also put us on a straight line directly into West Harbor on Fishers Island, a destination I'd hoped to reach at some point under less desperate circumstances. Any deviation to the north, where I'd planned to go that day, would expose our starboard bow to breaking waves, any to the south would send us into the rocks at the eastern end of Fishers, or out to sea, with only Block Island between us and a very irritable ocean.

An hour later, as I negotiated the various rocks, buoys and shoals of Fishers Island Sound, I felt a slight sense of deliverance—with the island's land mass on our port and West Harbor on our bow, it was only a matter of enduring the nearly unendurable before we reached safety.

That feeling lasted until the cable that connected the helm to the rudder decided to snap. Then all bets were off.

As I spun the impotent wheel in stunned disbelief, the boat responded as engineered, by driving up into the wind. In gentler conditions, this would be welcomed, since it would stall forward momentum and settle things into a manageable drift until help arrived. Now it meant we were brainlessly turning into the fury of the following seas, offering the broad length of the boat to whatever vindictive forces lay in wait.

As the boat pitched sideways, I went flying. Amanda screamed and grabbed at my foulies, both of us at the extreme lengths of our tethers. I hit the coaming that surrounded the cockpit hard enough to knock the wind out of me for a moment, but nothing broke. As the boat slapped over on its side, we held on to each other and strained to stay above the water pouring into the cockpit.

Then, as if by magic, the *Carpe Mañana* righted herself, as all good sailboats are trained to do, and we had a few seconds reprieve.

As the boarding seas slowly drained out the scuppers, I wrenched open a compartment in the cockpit called a lazarette and yanked out the emergency tiller, which through some bit of divine luck I'd noticed on my own during the otherwise thorough check-out of the boat when we picked her up in Maine. The next trick was to get it lodged in the fitting below the helmsman's seat. The fitting was covered by a tidy little fiberglass cap removable by unscrewing two big Phillips head screws. This would be a difficult task in the rough weather, so I chose a more expedient route and punched out the cap with a sharp snap of my right fist.

A regular person, one who hadn't had a brief career as a professional boxer, would have broken his hand with a stunt like that, and done nothing to remove the cap. I, however, obliterated the cap. And broke my hand.

Not the whole hand. Just the bone behind the knuckle of my middle finger. It hurt like hell, but I could still work my fingers, which would have to do until things improved.

Seconds before another wave had a chance to shove the boat under water, I fixed the emergency rudder to the fitting and pulled as hard as I could to port. This had the effect of shoving us to starboard and getting the bow facing the direction it needed to be if we were going to arrive at West Harbor as something more than a tangled mass of irredeemable salvage.

As we rode the hurtling seas, I felt almost airborne. I stole a glance at the GPS, which showed a speed over ground of nine-and-a-half knots, with a fleeting moment at ten point two. That the boat's maximum theoretical hull speed was eight point five told me something.

The handle of the emergency tiller was about half the length it should have been to provide the necessary leverage to steer a 46′ custom sloop in ideal conditions. Based on the tidy, elegant way it was stowed inside the lazarette, the boat designer had probably seen it as a cute accessory that would look good in the brochure under the heading: STANDARD SAFETY EQUIPMENT.

The other challenge was to adjust to the ass-backwards logic of a tiller, wherein pulling to the right makes the boat go left. The boat flirted with another knockdown as I reconciled a few thousand new operational variables, but eventually I regained the mental state that had almost brought us to safety, back in the good old days before we lost the wheel.

As the struggle continued, I was again haunted by the notion that a boat can always handle more abuse than its human cargo. I was feeling the evidence of that, in my arms, back and hands, which were steadily losing their grip. I was in fairly good shape for a fifty-seven-year-old, and working as a carpenter had actually improved my hand strength. But manhandling 32,000 pounds of displacement through the agitator cycle of a giant washing machine, for ten hours straight, would eventually take its toll on anybody.

I was fading.

My first thought was to have Amanda relieve me, but that wasn't a possibility. She was a strong girl, and ever willing to tackle whatever came her way, but this was technical sailing at its most extreme. Even I wasn't qualified to deal with conditions like this. She was just learning how to steer a sailboat, which every novice instantly learns is nothing like steering a car. And now we were running with an inadequate tiller that would have tested the patience and resolve of Bernard Moitessier. It wasn't going to happen. But there was something she could do.

"Hey, good looking," I yelled to her.

"Yeah?"

"Come over here and cozy up to me."

"Anytime, sailor."

"Stay clipped."

I switched over to the port side of the helmsman's seat and asked her to sit on the starboard. Then I explained the basic concept.

"When I tell you, push like hell against the tiller. When I tell you to stop, stop. When I tell you to pull, pull. Etcetera."

"I think I can follow that."

"I apologize in advance for yelling," I said. "Timing is crucial here."

"I won't hold it against you. As long as you don't yell, like, at me."

"Never, darling," I yelled.

This worked reasonably well, though I had to add a command, "Hands off," since she had the natural tendency to grip the tiller in anticipation of the next maneuver. The command was actually "Hands off, gorgeous" as a way of preserving civility, a prerequisite for our delicately maintained romantic entanglement.

And thus we found an effective rhythm, and Amanda earned a priceless insight into the Zen of steering a sailboat through heavy weather, a matter defined more by instinct than conscious thought.

There's no better proof that time can be slowed to a crawl. Time and space, as I watched the northern coast of Fishers Island seemingly fixed in place as we roared through the wrathful seas.

"When do I get to ask 'Are we there yet?'" Amanda asked.

"When we're there. Pull."

Soon after that exchange, I realized the grey green hump I thought was a piece of the distant Connecticut shoreline was North Dumpling, a small island just past the mouth of West Harbor. I told Amanda to keep the tiller right in the middle no matter what happened, and checked the GPS.

We were less than twenty feet from a cluster of rocks. I snatched the tiller back and shoved us hard to port. The *Carpe Mañana* groaned under the strain of the sudden course change, but then catching the thrust of the next wave, she shot off in the new direction like it was all her idea. I reminded myself that Fishers Island Sound was full of lethal obstructions, above and below water, and that God had given the world GPS so fools like me had an easy way to avoid catastrophe. All I had to do was check it once in a while.

As we passed the rocky shoal, I saw the white buoy that under normal circumstances would have given even the unobservant fair warning. It was only visible for a few seconds at a time, helpless against the battering of the big water.

Now thoroughly oriented, I looked for the giant red bell buoy that marked the beginning of the channel into West Harbor. That is, I looked when we were at the top of a wave, with a quarter-mile view across the white and grey chop. Seconds later we'd be down in a trough, facing a wall of water that any rational person would presume was within an instant of smashing us into oblivion. But then the next second we'd be aloft again, on top of a world gone mad.

I checked the GPS again, wondering if I was seeing things clearly through my exhaustion and the spray of saltwater and pelting rain.

"Where is that goddamned buoy?"

"Don't goddamned know, Captain," said Amanda. "I don't goddamn know where any goddamn thing is anymore."

So often on the water you come to doubt the evidence of your own eyes, or the accuracy of your electronics, or the reckoning of your navigation. It's not like the reality of hard ground, where things are usually where they're supposed to be, and the surface isn't a sickening mass of unpredictable undulations.

"No," I said to my senses. "It's there ahead. It has to be."

"Maybe somebody moved it," said Amanda, trying to help.

"Impossible," I said, and to prove the point, there it was, suddenly directly in front of our boat, rising up through the foam like a watery red demon, having been knocked over and drowned momentarily in the churning waves.

This time I chose to go to starboard, for no other reason than I was afraid the opposite thrust of the tiller would crush Amanda. Either way, it didn't seem possible that we could avoid crashing into the buoy. I started to make a silent accounting of life preservers, what clothing would have to come off to maintain buoyancy and how I'd keep Eddie's snout above the water. Also, calculating the odds that any of us could swim in the cold, lunatic waters to Flat Hammock, another island that helped define West Harbor, and once there, manage our way through the rocky shore to terra firma.

I closed my eyes under the strain of the tiller, and then opened them moments later to see in front of me the familiar surf, but no big red buoy. It had moved off our port stern, quickly left behind to attend to its own battles.

That was the good news. The bad news was the shoal the red buoy was in place to mark was now below the boat. I made another reckless, but essential, pull of the tiller, forcing the bow back into the channel leading to the harbor.

Moments later, the sea conditions suddenly downshifted into the merely uncomfortable. And now I could see where I wanted to be, with all the familiar landmarks, however obscured by rain and swirling wind. I knew we'd made it.

I shared that with Amanda.

"And was there ever any doubt?" she asked.

"Certainty's a rare thing here on the high seas," I said. "There's only one thing that would insure survival."

I'd relieved her of her tiller duty, and she was back in her spot wedged against the bulkhead, her proud mane of auburn hair pasted to her scalp and trailing in sodden ribbons over her shoulders and down the front of her orange foulies. Her face, daubed with rain droplets, filled with anxious wonder.

"What would that be?" she asked.

"The vodka's in a cabinet next to the galley sink. There's plenty of ice in the cooler. You know where the plastic cups are. Don't be stingy."

Amanda had wine. Eddie woke up in time to join us as we passed into West Harbor. The wind was still at our backs, but the waves had been further tamed by the surrounding land and Flat Hammock. I muscled the boat into the wind and we dropped the mainsail and fired up the motor, and the *Carpe Mañana* limped past the breakwater and into the Inner Harbor, finally safe and secure.

At least from the sea.

CHAPTER 2

Being October, I knew I'd find plenty of empty moorings in the Inner Harbor. Grabbing one was theft, pure and simple, but no decent person would begrudge a boatful of battered refugees from a stormy sea.

Since Amanda had little experience snagging moorings, it took a few passes for her to secure the buoy connected to a line that ran to the concrete mushroom sitting immovable on the seafloor.

The wind, though substantially abated, was still enough to add to the challenge. But we did it, with little damage to the boat or our social equanimity.

We were soon a pair of lumps sitting in the cockpit, drinking heavily and commenting on the beauty of the surrounding harbor. The rain stopped and blue patches opened up in the sky, allowing the sun to light up the autumnal trees, waterside homes, flagpoles, and the remaining small craft—motorized and sail—all graceful, waiting to be hauled for the winter.

Amanda wanted to discuss the fortunes of the last twelve hours, good and bad. I did my best.

"And you call that fun?" she asked.

"Fun is a wimp of a word. Doesn't describe meaningful human experience. Except those involving full body contact."

"Did you think at any time we might not make it?" she asked.

"I might have. So what? We made it. By the way, you look like a drowned Airedale."

"How many Airedales wear orange jump suits?"

I slumped down in the cockpit seat and counted my blessings to the beat of my thumping heart. I had wondered more than once if I'd be able to bring the boat safely to shore, and while I cared somewhat for my own survival, the thought of having put Amanda and Eddie at risk was unbearable. And consequently inconceivable, until we were all safe and sound, and mortal danger once again a theoretical construct.

The sun had begun to dip behind a stand of trees, backlighting the leafy red, orange and green palette. The sky above was the color of faded blue jeans, soon to be purple and rose. Typical of October, frenzied wind and sea conditions didn't always correlate with precipitation. A sailor could be consumed by a raging maelstrom, while the folks on shore enjoyed a sunny, breezy day.

"You should call Burton," said Amanda. "His boatbuilder's got some explaining to do."

I unzipped a pocket on the sleeve of my foulie and pulled out my cell phone. There was plenty of battery power, but no signal. I flipped it closed and refocused on my drink.

"I'll dinghy in and find a pay phone," I said. "After I purge about a gallon of adrenalin and bring my heart rate down closer to a hummingbird's."

Even wet and bedraggled, Amanda's essential beauty fought through. In the waning light of day, and the calming of the sea, the tone of her green eyes and olive skin had deepened, and her smile regained its brilliance.

"I think I just heard an admission of weakness," she said. "It's becoming."

"Don't pull that gender sensitivity falderal on me, young lady. I'm college trained. MIT."

"How's your hand?" she asked.

"Broken. Not yet hurting in earnest. Too much adrenalin. Though a screwdriver might have been a better idea. In retrospect."

"I should wrap it up with something," she said.

"First aid kit's below."

I've often marveled at a human's ability to move on from severe stress, at least while still in the moment. The ultimate consequences were usually held in abeyance, shoved snarling into a dark corner, ready to bust loose just when everyone thinks the coast is clear.

Amanda brought up a handful of stuff from the first aid kit to make a solid, functional brace for my damaged hand, which responded with sudden, throbbing pain.

"Perfect," I said.

"You need to call Burton. Can you manage the dinghy?"

With one hand tied behind my back, I told her. Which was more or less how it went.

All I had to do was pull the fifty-pound deflated dinghy out of the cockpit lazarette, inflate it, drop it over the side, lower the saltwater-soaked outboard from the transom mount and attach it to the back of the dinghy, hook up the gas tank and start her up.

Piece of cake.

"I'll offer encouraging words," said Amanda, always ready to do her part.

An hour later, the task was accomplished, much to Eddie's relief. He'd already lifted his leg on the mast, though with more complex ambitions in mind. It took some awkward, fur flying effort to get him down the swim ladder and into the dinghy, achieved with less eager barking and fewer blood-letting claw scratches than one might have expected.

Once in the dinghy, he scrambled to the bow and stood with head held high and tongue flapping in the breeze, a living figurehead, all prior difficulty completely forgotten.

"Pain in the ass," I said, as I clamored into the wobbly little boat.

Eddie was once again uncomfortably distracted by the clattery roar of the outboard motor, which I finally got started after pulling the cord until my shoulder nearly popped out of its socket. I clipped on his leash, half pulled him back into the dinghy and twisted the throttle on the outboard, shooting us through the dimming light of the Inner Harbor.

Eddie struggled to retain his position on the bow, and I let him, with one hand on the leash, the other on the throttle of the outboard, which nearly tore me in half, though Eddie's reckless abandon made it worth the effort.

The water fled under the boat, a foam-tipped, grey-blue blur.

Out of the fuzzy shoreline the gas dock emerged, with what I thought was an unwelcoming posture. When I got there, the thought was reinforced by a big grey-haired guy with a swollen, pocked-marked face who stood above us on the dock with hands on hips and frown fixed in place.

"Can't tie up here," he said. "Closed for the season."

"I need to use a pay phone," I said. "I'm moored out there with a busted helm."

"Not allowed to moor there neither."

"Where can I tie up?"

"Nowhere. The island's closed for the season."

I'd always known this about Fishers Island. At the east-ernmost reach of Long Island's North Fork, it's a place that doesn't want you there. Three-quarters private, gated club populated by the oldest money in the country, the other quarter a mix of merely wealthy summer people and year-round locals who fully shared in the island's rabid xenophobia.

"I know that's not true," I said. "The ferry still comes out every day."

The guy just stood there on the dock, an ugly, coveralled Horatio. Eddie waved his long mainsail of a tail and barked, the bark that meant, "Pardon me, folks, but I really got to go."

I stepped back into the dinghy and motored over to a small beach a hundred feet from the docks and drove up onto the gravelly sand. Eddie leaped out of the boat and ran over to a tuft of dune grass into which he disappeared, ever discreet. While he took care of business, the pockmarked guy strode across the beach and approached me.

"No dogs on the beach," he said.

Eddie exploded back out of the dune grass and ran up, his tail wagging, eager to make a new friend.

"Where's the closest pay phone?" I asked.

"Connecticut."

"I get the feeling you don't want us here," I said.

"You got that right."

"Tough," I said, pulling the dinghy up further on to the beach. I flipped open the cowling over the motor and with my back blocking the guy's view, used my Swiss Army knife to unscrew a part that would prevent it from starting. Eddie tried for a few moments to engage the guy's attention, but then gave up and started searching the beach for rotting sea life, one of his favorite things. I slung a rubbery sack, called a dry bag, over my shoulder and whistled for Eddie, who followed me off the beach and out to the street, which I used to reach a cluster of buildings that stood above the docks. One was a gas station, the only one on the island, that backed up to the fuel dock, another the Harbor Yacht Club—a squat near-shack where members stored bathing suits, heard race briefings and took showers in big open air stalls; and a third structure, a place called the Black Swan.

It was a neo-classic structure built a long time ago to be what it still was today—a small hotel geared to the transitory vacationer, a rare species in the hostile Fishers habitat. It was clapboard-covered, with oversized gables decorated with deep moldings covered in successive layers of partially scraped white paint. There was a battered, 90's-era Mercedes station wagon parked out front in the hotel's gravel parking lot.

The last time I'd sailed to the island, a few years before, the hotel had a bar and restaurant and a pay phone in the lobby. The sign next to the sidewalk that led through a low hedge and up to the door said "Closed"—but there was a nicely formed female rear end sticking out from between a pair of large yews that decorated the front of the building, so I had a way to ask how closed.

I cleared my throat, hoping not to startle her, which I did anyway.

"Sorry," I said. "Didn't mean to startle you."

She looked somewhere in her twenties, with long, wavy black hair and a broad, pretty face. Even in the dying light, I could see her bright blue eyes and slightly crooked grin. It was getting chilly, but all she wore was a burgundy tank top and jean shorts, both generously dabbled with paint in a variety of hues.

"You haven't seen Eloise, have you?" she asked, then looked down at Eddie, whom I was holding by the collar. "How does he feel about cats?"

"Ambivalent. But he won't hurt it."

"Won't hurt *her*. She's a girl cat."

"Haven't seen her, though I just got here. Do you mind if I use your pay phone? I've got a busted boat in the harbor and need to call the owner. I can't seem to get a cell signal."

"Service went down this morning. All the wind. We don't have a pay phone, but you can use the regular one. As long as my father doesn't mind. You can bring the dog. My brother loves dogs."

I followed her into the hotel. She flicked on a light in the lobby, which looked exactly as I remembered it, though somewhat spruced up with fresh paint and new drapes. The furniture was the original Victorian, and the rug the same oriental I vaguely remembered. The wall that once held the pay phone had a vintage poster of a woman in a long dress drinking a soda while peddling a bicycle.

She told me to wait there and disappeared through a door next to the registration counter. I peered through a pair of glass-paned doors at the bar, which looked remarkably open for business, a cheerful thought. Eddie tried to pull away from my grip, but I told him to cool it, something he was constitutionally reluctant to do.

Soon the young woman reappeared with a tall guy with a fringe of close-cropped white hair framing a bald pate, wire-rimmed glasses and large, fleshy features. I could see his daughter in his broad mouth and blue eyes. His hand-shake was dry and half-hearted.

"Your boat's disabled?" he asked, with a light foreign accent.

"Yeah," I said, "happened out there in the soup. Made for a lively trip in."

"I imagine so. We monitor channel sixteen. Sounded very bad out there. Everyone surprised."

"You could say that. I got a broken rudder," I said.

"Buchanan Marina's still open for repairs. They're good mechanics."

"What's the draft back there?" I asked, aware of the marina, located on a creek at the furthest end of the Inner Harbor.

"Four feet max."

I shook my head and used my thumb to gesture toward the water.

"Six and a half. What're the chances of renting one of your slips?"

He looked at me through his thick glasses, his face and light blue eyes registering the complex deliberation the situation apparently called for.

"That's a tough one," he said. "We're closed for the season."

"I don't need shore power. We're self-contained. I'd just rather not be moored when I'm working on the boat. And I got the dog and my girlfriend. Cash money," I added, hopefully.

He and his daughter exchanged looks which seemed pregnant with hidden meaning, then he nodded his head.

"Take the first slip," he said, "stern in. The power's still on. I can run a hose out for water. Fifty dollars a day."

His daughter smiled in a way that told me whom I should thank for the overpriced concession. I smiled back and shook both their hands.

"Sam Acquillo," I said.

"Christian Fey," said the man, "and this is Anika. My daughter. We just purchased the Swan this September, at the close of the season. We're busy with remodeling, so can't be of much help to you, I'm afraid."

"Been plenty of help already. Soon as I use your phone, I'll get out of your hair."

Anika leaned over the reception desk, dumping half her breasts out on the counter, and lifted up the phone. Then she and her father left me alone to dial Burton's cell.

"Hey, Burt, it's Sam."

"Have you changed your number?"

"I'm on Fishers Island. Cell service is down. More importantly, the cable from helm to rudder snapped on the way down from Point Judith."

"Oh dear," he said.

"Oh shit's more like it. It was kind of snotty out there. You've got an emergency tiller, by the way. Good thing."

"Terribly sorry about that. What do we do now?"

"You call the boatbuilder and have him ship the whole steering rig—cables, blocks and fittings. I haven't looked yet, but I want to change it all out. Who knows what caused the failure. Send them to me courtesy of the Black Swan. It's a hotel on the island off Inner Harbor. We secured a slip, though not without some convincing. After Labor Day this place turns into Brigadoon."

"I know the Swan. It's next to the Harbor Club. Has Fishers' only public bar. And a pool table, as I recall."

"Could be. It's got a new owner. Thinks he's doing us a favor letting us stay at his empty dock for fifty bucks a night."

"It's good you're in a slip," said Burton. "More bad weather's on the way. They're saying a whole series of storms are coming up the coast and out of the southwest. It's going to be rough for a while. I tried to call your cell phone to get your position, but couldn't make a connection."

I tried to imagine rougher water than we'd just plowed through, though I knew such a thing was more than possible.

"Until cell service is back up Amanda's computer's off email," I said. "I'll try to call on a regular basis, if I can ingratiate myself with the owners. Otherwise, you'll have to buy a house out here to get a landline."

It was quiet on the other end of the line as Burton pondered that option, one he was more than able to fulfill, being one of the fifty richest guys in the world according to *Forbes* magazine, a rating source Burton looked on with mild contempt.

"What do they know? Those numbers they publish are ridiculous."

"Too high?"

"Far too low."

We talked some more about how to proceed, dismissing several options like air freighting in the parts, mostly because of the weather. Rich as he was, Burton wasn't one of those crazy billionaires who thought natural forces—like weather, the commodities markets or the NBA—should bend to his will. He took on frustration like the rest of us, as inevitable and uncontrollable.

"I'll get you the parts," he said. "Have you heard from Jackie?"

"Huh?"

"Jackie Swaitkowski. Your attorney. She's been trying to reach you."

"I haven't heard," I said. "What's up?"

Jackie was technically my attorney because I'd once given her a dollar as a retainer against future work, which actually happened in spades, though I'd yet to increase her compensation beyond that original buck. Some day we'd have to address that, I thought.

"She didn't say, but my guess is you need to provide some guidance on the civil matter she's handling for you."

"Do me a favor, would you Burt, and tell her I'll call her as soon as I'm out of this junky weather."

"Certainly. And meanwhile, call back midday tomorrow so I can report my progress. You and Amanda try to find a way to occupy yourselves. Perhaps card games. Or philosophical debate."

After I hung up the phone, I wondered if I should find one of the Feys to thank, but decided I'd only be invading their privacy again. So I just left.

My dinghy was still on the beach when I got back, which didn't surprise me, my technical precautions notwithstanding. The pockmarked guy, now gone, had little incentive for keeping me shore-bound. I reinstalled the part and we motored back to the *Carpe Mañana,* much more slowly this time as darkness had fallen across the harbor. But she was easy to find: Amanda had put lights on in the salon and hung a lantern from the backstay to guide us home.

"Permission to come aboard," I called. Amanda climbed part way down the swim ladder to help me hoist Eddie up and over the transom. While there was still a dim glow of light along the horizon, I dropped the line off the mooring and motored slowly over to the docks at the Black Swan. Amanda sat with Eddie on the bow and swept the water with a flashlight in search of lethal hazards. The wind was still strong, but the water mostly chop-free behind the breakwater that defined the Inner Harbor. In a few minutes we were backing into the slip, and Amanda was on the dock tying off a stern line.

After the other lines were secured, Amanda went below to work on dinner. I sat in the cockpit with another drink and got a chance to look around the neighborhood. The lights were on in the Black Swan's restaurant, which looked out over the docks, and I could see three people sitting at a table having a meal. It was Fey, his daughter and another guy, young, who I assumed to be the aforementioned brother. Feeling like a voyeur, I was about to turn away when I saw the older man raise his hand as if to cuff the boy on the head. Anika leaned half out of her chair and wrapped her arms around the boy's shoulders, shouting something at her father, something I could almost hear through the glass. Fey made a brusque gesture with the raised hand, then went back to his meal. Anika cradled the boy against her chest and kissed the top of his head, then also went back to her meal, though with a deep scowl on her face.

I pulled my eyes away and looked across the channel at the Harbor Yacht Club next door. Their slips were also empty of boats, though unlike the Swan's, the docks were a type that floated up and down with the tide, now low. The tall piers that secured the docks from lateral movement stood like an orderly grove of truncated trees. On top of the pier closest to our slip, clearly visible across the narrow channel, sat a cat, lit by the club's security lights and thus unidentifiable by color, though starkly outlined, like a woodcut.

"Eloise?" I called, and as she turned her head toward me I added, "Better get home." She just sat there and stared across the water, as if urging me to apprehend a greater truth. But then Eddie barked, and Amanda called to me to come below, and the opportunity was lost.

CHAPTER 3

The first hour of the next morning was spent profitably lounging around the cockpit, drinking coffee, listening to Puccini and watching the dim glow on the eastern horizon turn into the hard light of the October sun. The wind had shifted to a dead northerly, showing little of its recent fury. I'd believed it when Burton said this was all poised to change, but refused to let that spoil the moment. I checked the local NOAA marine forecast to get more information, though their credibility hadn't emerged untarnished from the day before.

Amanda wore a blue down vest over a long, white cotton robe—like the kind religious pilgrims wear on the way to Mecca—and a baseball cap. On her feet were a pair of fleece-lined sea boots. There's something about a sailboat that even the most sartorially adept find irresistibly corrupting.

I'd met Amanda when she worked for the bank her husband ran in Southampton on Long Island. She was my personal banker, even though I had very little money to bank. The only reason I had a personal banker was because I wanted to talk to Amanda, who at the time also had little money beyond her paycheck. Her principal financial resource was her husband. His name was Roy, and he wasn't rich, but was sure trying to be. These efforts led to some complicated illegalities, with the ultimate outcome being not so great for Roy, now a resident of Sanger Medium Security Penitentiary in Upstate New York. Amanda, along the way, discovered she was an heiress, in addition to being the wife of a ruined banker, whom she eagerly divorced. While nowhere near as well off as Burton Lewis, she was still set for life, if she sensibly handled the money.

Her choices thus far had been fairly sensible, if you overlook getting involved with me.

"For breakfast we've got sautéed mushrooms and leftover shrimp ziti," I told her.

"What happened to the bacon and eggs?"

"They were to be purchased in Stonington, Connecticut, where we'd be now if the wind hadn't brought us here."

"Tell me this place has a grocery store," said Amanda.

"Surprisingly, yes. And it's within easy walking distance. Let Puccini get through the last act and we'll send out a foraging team."

It took longer than that to get underway, but neither of us felt overly ambitious, the likely residue of the day before. We finally did, with Eddie on a long retractable leash, much to his disgust. I felt he shouldn't be totally free on foreign soil. Mostly in deference to the foreigners, not yet acquainted with his distinctive charms.

I picked an indirect route so I could tour Amanda around some of the neighborhoods and tiny commercial clusters on Fishers' west end. I thought she'd like to see the buildings. Since much of her inheritance was in real estate, she'd become a developer, the hands-on type that ran the crews and battled suppliers and building inspectors. We helped each other out occasionally, but kept our construction careers separate, and thus our relationship slightly less complicated.

In keeping with the insular nature of the place, there was little to mark its place in time. The houses were mostly weatherbeaten, but well cared-for and comfortably settled within an abundance of domesticated and feral landscaping. I reckoned by the well-worn Saabs, Ford pickups, Chevy vans, Volvos and early-model Subarus, that the twenty-first century might have become established on the mainland without much notice here.

I knew a few modern architectural extravagances dotted the west end, mostly on the water, but not much of that had infected the core.

Meanwhile, Eddie's interest was fully engaged by the fresh smells and novel organic matter, some of which he sampled and occasionally spat back out. My part in this was to give him enough slack on the leash to enjoy the splendor without getting pulled off my feet by sudden, capricious changes in direction.

The grocery store, in a low-slung, wooden-floored building, also sold beer, wine and liquor, and other necessities, like bait, line and nets, and yachting caps with the Harbor Club insignia. The woman at the checkout line looked at us carefully, but likely assumed if we'd made it all the way to her store, we probably had some business being on the island, questionable though it might be. We stocked up on as many provisions as we could carry in a pair of backpacks and were about to head down the short route when I noticed the pockmarked guy sitting in a pickup truck parked at the curb.

I cinched up on Eddie's leash and gently guided Amanda out to the road. She was trying to say something to me, but I was concentrating on the pickup and didn't notice until she stopped talking. I asked her to repeat herself, which she did, though I missed that, too, when I looked back and saw the pickup back out of its spot and roll slowly down the road behind us.

"You're distracted," she said.

"I am," I said, as I informed her of the pockmarked guy who greeted me at the docks, now following us in a pickup. "Don't look," I added.

"Oh, for heaven's sake."

We walked in silence for several minutes with the truck a nearly silent escort twenty or so paces behind. Then I heard the engine's rpms rev up and watched the truck slide around us and disappear around the curve ahead.

"Asshole," said Amanda.

"I seem to attract them," I said.

"You do," she said, in a tone both sympathetic and matter-of-fact, which I didn't exactly know how to interpret. "Should we call the cops?"

"Cop. There's only one. A New York State trooper. They rotate them in and out on six-month assignments. At least that's what I'm told. I've never seen him."

"Or her."

"Or her."

◆

When we reached the Black Swan, Anika was out on the lawn, snipping with a pair of pruning shears at the hedge growing disobediently above a narrow flower garden filled with late season blooms. Like the day before, she was oddly dressed for the pursuit at hand, as young people are wont to do, something I'd learned from my daughter.

I introduced her to Amanda, who complimented Anika on her leather choke collar. I'd lived among women long enough to know this was a peace ritual, an expressed hope for boundaries to be respected and good will shared among all. Anika responded with a demure glance toward the ground, a fondling of the observed object, and a suggestion that it would look far better on Amanda, given her long, slender neck. I wondered if I should now piss on the grass at Amanda's feet, anthropologically speaking.

Instead I asked, "Did Eloise ever show up?"

"She did," said Anika. "Thank you for asking. She slept on my face all night, something she does when she's upset. Don't know why. Maybe the smell of your dog."

"Do you know a guy who hangs around the docks, a little younger than me, with a bad case of ancient acne?" I asked her.

"Track?"

"Who?" I asked.

"Anderson Track. Runs the gas station and fuel dock."

"He tried to chase me away. I wondered what his problem was."

She looked down and shook her head.

"It's what they do here. Sorry. I'll tell him you're our guest. Not that he'd care. We're still looked upon as interlopers. The last owners had nearly defaulted on the place after letting it basically crumble into the ground. But they were locals, so without fault."

She snapped the shears with a lot of shoulder in it, yielding a large clump of hedge. There were piles of faded summer flowers on the ground, and what was left cleaved to the purple, gold and red of the late season.

"Your flowers are beautiful," said Amanda. "Interesting colors."

Anika stood back and shared in the admiration.

"That's six thirty-two point five," she said, pointing to some clumps of lavender. Then she went along the narrow garden, saying, "Forty-two, seventy-six, more or less, and four ninety-six, a perfect number, by the way."

"Numbering your plants," said Amanda. "Sounds like something Sam would do."

"The owner of our boat is going to ship repair parts care of the Swan," I said. "I'm sorry for the intrusion, but if you could accept the shipment and let us know it's here, I'll get it off your hands as soon as I can."

Anika dropped the shears and rested them on her thigh. She smiled a generous smile.

"Don't be ridiculous. We don't mind accepting a package."

Amanda thanked her and pulled at my sleeve, reminding me that we were starving and needed to get back to the boat. I was about to comply when a black Lincoln Town Car pulled into the hotel's parking lot. It'd be as if a horse and buggy or fire-breathing dragon had swept up to the curb, it so captured our attention.

The driver's door swung open and a tall guy with thin legs and a bulging belly got out. He wore a dark blue suit with a light blue turtleneck and a lot of gold on his fingers. He opened the rear door and a much shorter, thinner man, with a bony jaw, fine light-brown hair and a creased face, stepped out. He buttoned his sport coat, made of soft suede, and used the flat of his hand to press an errant strand of hair back up onto his head. He looked at the façade of the Black Swan curiously, as you would the face of a nearly recollected acquaintance. His gaze drifted from the building to where we were standing with Anika. She let out a kind of sigh, of surprise or weariness, it was hard to tell.

"What brings you here?" she called to him.

The thin man's face showed recognition, but little warmth.

"Your father nearby?" he asked.

"Maybe. We're closed for the season."

The man nodded.

"Get him, would you?"

Anika turned to us, clouds forming across her once sunny face.

"You'll have to excuse me," she said, and gripping my arm, gently pushed me toward the path that led to the docks. "Got things to do."

Even I got that message. I escorted Amanda to the path and out to the boat. Halfway there I turned and walked backwards, so I could see the thin man joined by a thin woman, taller than the man, and wearing a long red leather coat. Her sunglasses hid much of her face and her unnaturally blond hair was piled up on top of her head, though none too neatly, as if bedraggled by a long trip. I turned back and wasn't able to look again until we were climbing into the boat, at which point everyone was gone, having disappeared into the hotel.

"Maybe not so closed after all," said Amanda.

◆

The next morning I woke up a little before dawn, as I often do. Amanda rarely does, so I left her and as quietly as I could slipped into jeans, T-shirt and sweatshirt and made a cup of coffee to bring out to the bow of the boat. Eddie jumped down from one of the salon settees and followed me topsides.

The sun was just heralding its arrival with a dull glow above the treetops to the east. The security lights from the Harbor Club next door cast their own yellowy glow, though the Swan was totally blacked out, a white clapboard mass, tired but elegant, braced for another day.

I was nearly through with the coffee when I saw a light flash at the back of the hotel. The wide French doors centered over the rear patio opened and Anika walked out. She wore a heavy, dark-colored bathrobe and slippers. She held what looked like a piece of paper in her mouth to free both hands to shut and secure the doors behind her. I watched her stride down the main dock toward our boat.

When she got there, she stood up on her toes to look into the cockpit, a difficult task from where she stood. She held what I could now see was an envelope between her fingers in a way that suggested she was about to flick it on to the boat.

"Good morning," I said from the bow.

She jumped and grasped her bathrobe at the throat.

"Whoa! Freak me out."

She walked down the dock and stood with her arms folded, the envelope hidden in the bunched-up fabric.

"What's up?" I asked.

She moved closer to the boat and leaned out over the water between the dock and the curved section of the hull. She gripped the gunwale to support herself as she tossed the envelope on the deck a few feet from where I sat.

"It's a dinner invitation," she said. "Tonight."

"Tonight? Good you got us early," I said.

She stood back again, and refolded her arms.

"It was my idea, but I wanted you to think it was my father's."

"He might not like that."

She used both hands to rake out her hair, stopping part way to scratch her scalp. The action released the top of her robe, exposing a deep, but gentle V.

"He won't like it, but it won't show. He's Swiss," she added, as if that explained all.

"I'm French-Canadian, with just enough Italian to explain the name."

"Your girlfriend's Italian, too, isn't she."

"With just enough Anglo-Saxon to qualify as an American mutt, which most of us are, once you dig into it."

"I'm all Swiss. Born in Zurich."

"Where's your mom?"

"Dead."

"Sorry," I said.

"Don't be. I was too young to know her. She died having my brother. You'd think by now they'd have licked the death-by-childbirth thing."

"What's wrong with your brother?"

I couldn't tell if she was annoyed or simply knocked off-balance. She had a busy face—lots of vivid expressions, bright eyes and a capricious smile, not always used to convey humor.

"I didn't know you'd met."

"We didn't. I saw him through the window. Didn't mean to. The shades were up," I pointed to the back of the restaurant. "You were eating dinner with him and your father. Once I realized what I was doing, I went below. Hard not to think of a lighted window as a TV set. Sorry."

Anika walked down the dock to the boat's gate, the space opened up by unlatching a section of the lifelines, and hoisted herself up onto the deck. She walked to the bow and plopped down across from me, her legs stretched out. Her foot touched the side of mine and gave a subtle stroke. I moved mine away.

"What's your story?" she said.

"Nothing interesting."

"People don't spy on other people, then admit to it, making the spied upon see them as honorable."

"What's wrong with your brother?" I asked again.

"What's wrong with you?" she asked back.

"Chronic inappropriateness."

Anika leaned back against a bulge in the cabin top that held the forward hatch, then sat up again, trying to get comfortable. I took another sip of my coffee.

"Want some?" I asked.

"Maybe. Have we met?"

"I don't think so," I said.

"My father's fifty-nine years old."

"I'm fifty-seven. He wins."

"Axel, my brother, can run *pi* out to ten thousand digits from memory. Then he gets bored and gives it up. I ask him why stop there, and he tells me, 'It's not that hard. What's the big deal?'"

A wayward breeze snuck on to the dock and disturbed the silken black hair that lay scattered over her brow, causing one longer strand to slide over her mouth. She puffed it out of the way.

"So Axel's the math whiz. What's your specialty?"

"I'm an artist. A painter. I've got a studio in the attic. My bed's there, too, so I have something to do when I can't sleep. You should visit sometime so I can show you my latest work."

She slid farther down on the deck and rested her head on the raised lip of the forward hatch. The maneuver caused her robe to ride up past her thigh, a situation she took her time correcting.

"Who're the people in the Town Car?" I asked.

"You are the nosiest person I ever met," she said.

"I'm sure that's true, though I know people who are far nosier than me."

"Friends of my dad. From his company. His old company. He sold out so he could retire and buy this place. And get off the bus to nowhere. You retired?"

"No. Fired. Now I do finish carpentry. And boat deliveries, though this is likely my first and last."

"That coffee is starting to sound really good," she said.

I went below and made some more. While I was there I checked on Amanda, who was a static lump in the cozy quarter berth we'd chosen as our bedroom. I brushed the back of my hand as delicately as I could across her cheek and pulled the blanket up over an exposed shoulder. She responded with a little cough, more of a snort, then lapsed back into heavy breathing. So I left her alone and brought two mugs of fresh coffee to the bow, with a pocket full of fake sugar, as Anika had requested.

She stirred in the stuff and blew over the top of the coffee mug as I settled back into my spot above the anchor locker, braced inside the pulpit, at the far forward tip of the boat.

"She *is* your girlfriend," said Anika, "not like your wife or anything."

"She's my girlfriend, though also like my wife and everything."

"Oh," she said. Then some time passed, until she said, "My dad hasn't done so well in the girlfriend department. I'd like to blame it on his kids, but the real problem is workaholia. Too busy stroking the keyboard to stroke anything else."

"Computers?" I asked.

"Oh, yeah. Co-founder of Subversive Technologies. He invented C-scale. And N-Spock. You wouldn't know, being, like, a carpenter."

Oh yes I would, I thought, not wanting to share that I'd used N-Spock to drive a wall of daisy-chained, massively parallel main-frames in the multi-million-dollar oil and gas research and development lab I ran before they fired me for socking our chief corporate counsel in the nose. There's more to the story than that, but that's the gist.

"So you're glad he's bagged it all and moved out here," I said.

"Glad isn't exactly the word, but yes, I'm glad. He's still not a happy man, but now he could be. Why am I telling you all this?"

"Because I'm nosy?"

"I have to go make breakfast," she said, standing up. "Come to dinner if you can. At least I can promise the food'll be good. Axel is the cook. No ingredient goes unloved, I guarantee you that."

She worked her way down the port side of the boat, using the shrouds—cables connecting the mast to the hull—to propel herself forward, her hips expressing a pleasant, loose roll, even under the cover of her thick bathrobe.

"Hm," I said to myself.

CHAPTER 4

I spent the next day crammed inside the engine compartment of the *Carpe Mañana*. It wasn't the engine I was interested in, but the spider web of destroyed cable dangling from where it was supposed to be neatly strung between sturdy blocks and greased fittings. Being a new boat, it lacked that smelly, corroded quality I was used to, though that was faint consolation. None of the tangle made sense; nothing indicated why the cable snapped, scything off all the supporting apparatus, leaving behind little ragged plastic parts and limp threaded wire.

I'd once been responsible for diagnosing multi-million-dollar process failures at petrochemical plants in places like Malaysia, Perth Amboy and Kuwait, but none were more perplexing than this.

Maybe I'd been out of the business too long, I thought. Maybe all that vodka had finally caught up with me.

"What time is it?" I yelled up to Amanda.

"About two thirty," she yelled back.

Too early for the first drink, goddamnit. I continued to stare at the ravaged steering mechanism. I closed my eyes and called up an image of what I thought should be a healthy steering mechanism, following the pulleys and cables as they transferred dynamic forces through a series of intermediary stages from wheel to block to rudder. With a slight jolt, I recalled the thrust of the waves out in the stormy water, and how it felt to hold the wheel against the pressure of the hurtling seas. That's when I saw the mechanics at maximum stress, and felt with my own body the strengths and weaknesses of the system.

I opened my eyes and looked back toward the transom, to where the cable curled down through twin blocks into a well that led to fittings—from that vantage point invisible—clamped to the rudder. I saw an ugly gash in the fiberglass directly above where the cable dove down into the well, which I lit up when I shot my flashlight in that direction.

My first impulse was to call the designers who'd engineered the system a bunch of lazy boneheads, but seconds later I caught myself. I couldn't know all the constraints, restrictions and overruling the design team had to endure. Something had obviously gone wrong, but responsibility was likely shared across a diverse group of designers, mechanics and accountants. That was usually the case. Disasters are almost always the result of several malfunctions occurring simultaneously, which interact with each other, causing a cascade of unforeseen consequences leading inexorably to catastrophic systems failure.

These combinations are later identified and corrected, and thus unlikely to be repeated, leaving the field clear for a new set of variables to entangle and collide.

It's impossible to anticipate all possible permutations, which is why planes will continue to crash, albeit rarely, and oil platforms will blow up and steering mechanisms on sailboats will burst apart at the worst possible moment. It's emotionally gratifying for the ignorant to blame it all on human inadequacy, but that's usually only part of the story.

Often things happen that shouldn't, but they do anyway. It was Juvenal who expressed it thus: *Rara avis in terris nigroque simillima cygno.* Or as you'd say in English, more or less: "It can be a rare bird, like a black swan."

◆

The new parts were certain to arrive soon, which was all I needed to fix the steering and get back underway. So I stopped trying to divine the root of the failure and spent the rest of the day upside-down ripping out the wreckage— clearing the work area in preparation for the new parts— and thereby casting aside further forensic study having no purpose but to satisfy my own perverse obsessions.

True to her word, Amanda provided emotional and logistical support in the form of iced tea and turkey sandwiches. She'd also reconnoitered the island and discovered a way to jack into the World Wide Web, though refused to reveal how until she had my undivided attention.

So I quit my work and squirmed back up into the cockpit where a tumbler of vodka, a platter of meat and cheese, and the sunset awaited.

"We're in for a bad storm," she said, almost wrecking the mood.

"That's what Burton said."

"It's one of those nor'easters or sou'westers, or whatever, that might as well be hurricanes, if it does what they fear. Though we don't have a lot of trust in *them*."

"When?"

"Late tomorrow, if all goes according to plan."

"Which it never does," I said.

"That's what you keep telling me," she said. "I'm just a builder. A veritable landlubber. What do I know?"

I went below and washed up, scrubbing the lubricating grease off my hands and brushing fiberglass dust off my clothes. When I came back up Amanda handed me my drink and a cracker laden with a teetering mound of pepperoni and cheese.

"We need to dig out all the fenders we can find," I said.

"The only fenders I know are on my car."

"Fenders are short, inflatable tubes that look like chubby hot dogs, or short torpedoes, that cushion the side of the boat. We'll also need a garden hose which we'll cut into sections and slip over the dock lines to reduce chafing."

"You think it'll be bad?" she asked.

"Better to prepare for the worst."

"We can handle the worst?"

"I didn't say that."

Amanda and I decided to repress concern over the coming storm and delegate preparation to the next morning. We drank, ate tasty things off platters and luxuriated in the autumnal air, the super-saturated colors born of the magic-hour light, the stalwart buildings surrounding the harbor and the inner logic of two people joined together for reasons neither quite understood, but in a conspiracy similar to the one with NOAA, choosing to ignore the dangers so to embrace the beautiful illusion.

◆

Getting ready for dinner with the Feys had its own challenges. Neither of us had packed for a social occasion, planning only to rent a car to get to Maine, pick up Burton's boat, and sail it back to Southampton, stopping along the way to buy provisions and give Eddie a chance to run around with something other than fiberglass beneath his feet.

I was the luckier one, since the boatbuilder had included a blue blazer in the hanging closet as part of the deal, fitted to Burton's lanky frame, but close enough to mine. All I needed was a black T-shirt and jeans and I was there.

Amanda had to piece together an outfit anchored by a denim skirt topped by a puffy white Mexican shirt partially concealed by a fuzzy blood red pashmina. Luckily, Amanda's a very good-looking woman, which in the end makes up for almost everything.

◆

The front door to the Swan was locked, but ringing the door-bell brought a quick response. Axel Fey opened the door, grabbed Amanda's hand and bowed nearly to the ground, where he seemed to linger, gazing at Amanda's naked ankles. She took it calmly, using her captured hand to pull him back into an upright position.

"Welcome to the Black Swan," he said. "The ever black and swanny little bed and breakfast by the Inner Harbor. Nice legs, by the way."

I took his wrist and extracted Amanda's hand.

"Sam Acquillo," I said, forcing him into a handshake. "Anika said she had a brother. That must be you."

"I did?" said Anika, swooshing into the foyer, and pulling us off the front stoop where Axel had us trapped. In the better light I got a good look at Axel, who was a younger, flimsier version of his father, with narrow shoulders, features squeezed into the center of his face and pale plastic-rimmed glasses slumped part way down his nose. His skin was pep-pered with blemishes and his light brown hair needed to be combed. As if noticing me noticing, Anika reached up and did her best to rake in a part and clear the straggly locks off his forehead. He took it with pained forbearance.

Anika's wine-colored silk dress had been applied with a paint brush. Her figure was a type of near zoftig that rarely held up past a woman's forties, but at this stage, was close to a modernist platonic ideal. My tastes had always run toward the soft-edged ectomorphic, as exemplified by

Amanda Anselma, though I could imagine how others might see the appeal.

Anika herded us into the main dining room at the back of the hotel where they'd set a single large table. A sideboard was covered in trays filled with chicken skewers, broccoli and shrimp. I snatched a small plateful and headed to a small service bar. A little table-tent sign told me to serve myself, something I was highly equipped to do. Halfway through pouring a vodka on the rocks, Christian Fey approached the bar and ordered a bottle of Spaten beer.

"Pretty tricky," I said. "Get the guests to handle the bar."

"I apologize for my daughter's presumptuousness," he said, pouring the beer into a heavy glass mug. "But please feel at home. We are, after all, a welcoming small hotel, season or no season," he added, with a sincerity that might not stand up to a gentle breeze.

"Are your friends coming?" I asked.

He paused before answering.

"You must mean Derrick and his entourage," said Fey. "He's my ex-business partner, though we've had our friendly moments."

Amanda joined us and I poured her a glass of pinot noir after Fey had a chance to make her feel at home as well. Like his son, he bowed, though with less depth and shorter duration. He also complimented her outfit, which was probably the most diplomatic thing he'd do all night.

I made it out from behind the bar right before Derrick and company arrived on the scene, saving me from another round of bartending. He was still in his suede sport coat, but his companions had freshened their looks, with the big meatball now in a white polyester jacket over a flowered shirt and tan slacks, and the blond in a turquoise dress that lent an opportunity to examine key features of her anatomy. I was tempted to ask where they'd parked the cruise ship, but Fey was talking, trying to explain what we were doing there.

"Sam Acquillo," I said, offering my hand. "And this is Amanda Anselma. What Mr. Fey is trying to say is we washed up on shore in a damaged boat and he's been a prince about letting us stay until it's repaired."

"Looks that way," said Derrick, now behind the bar assembling a pair of martinis for himself and the woman, and snapping open a Budweiser for the guy. In the course of this I learned her name was Del Rey, after the big marina in Los Angeles where her parents proudly owned a condo, and the big guy was Bernard 't Hooft, who like Fey, spoke with a European accent, I surmised Dutch. Del Rey helped me get the spelling right.

"Imagine if the first letter of your name was an apostrophe," she said, giving 't Hooft a friendly swat on the arm.

Derrick ignored the interplay and focused on asking about the *Carpe Mañana*—where it was built, the trip down from Maine, the nature of the failure. As I spoke he seemed to deliberate over the answers, as if comparing them against a list of unexpressed criteria. Despite the creases in his face, I guessed his age to be late forties at most. His hair looked a natural light brown, and his eyes were pale blue, pale enough that pupils and whites nearly merged into one.

"So who owns the boat?" he asked. "Custom jobs are big bucks."

Burton liked to protect his privacy, so my first impulse was to keep that information confidential. But then I thought of how we'd imposed on the good graces of the Feys, who were outside the conversational circle, but close enough to overhear. It seemed somehow impolite to be that secretive, so for their sake, I gave it up.

"Burton Lewis," I said. "A friend of mine in Southampton."

"Burton Lewis as in Lewis and Straithorn? The law firm?" asked Derrick.

I nodded. He nodded back.

"Good friend to have," he said.

Del Rey waited to be filled in, but he ignored her.

"I never had time for gentlemanly sports," he said.

"Too busy conquering the world," said Anika.

Derrick toasted her with his martini glass. Christian took Anika's elbow and used the long sweep of his other arm to herd the group toward the table.

In both the unconscious and overt maneuvering for seats I ended up between Anika and 't Hooft, with Amanda across from me flanked by the younger and elder Feys. Derrick and Del Rey anchored the opposite ends. Nobody seemed entirely happy with their seating, but the dice were cast. I tried to cushion the disappointment by offering to schlep another round of drink orders. As always, a good idea.

"So what do you do when you're not delivering boats?" Derrick asked me, speaking across Anika.

"Installing crown molding, baseboard and window trim," said Amanda. "He can also handle tricky shopwork, like mantelpieces and built-ins. Very proficient. And affordable, especially for me, since I've yet to pay him a dime."

"Sounds like tit for tat," said Del Rey.

"We could use you around here," said the elder Fey to me. "Sometimes I think surface tension is the only thing holding this place together."

"Rethinking the investment?" asked Derrick, a little too quickly.

"Not for a moment," said Fey.

Del Rey polished off half of her second martini before all the drinks had cleared the tray. She was about to finish the job when 't Hooft slid his meaty fingers through the stem of the glass and anchored it to the table. Del Rey shot him a glance of equal parts fear and reproach, but kept her hands in her lap.

Meanwhile, Amanda was holding her own inside the brace of Feys. Axel was in and out of his seat as he checked on various servings, carried out to us by his sister. This benefitted Amanda, who otherwise had to endure a continuous violation of her personal space. When he crowded into her, she was forced to lean into his father, who looked just as pained by the imposition.

As a distraction, she asked Derrick how long they'd be staying at the Swan. The meager burble of conversation at the table suddenly ceased.

"That depends," said Derrick, before the dead air became unbearable.

"Indeed," said Christian Fey, tilting back his head to chug the ample remains of his beer.

"I'm thinking of launching a reality show," said Anika. "'*So You Think You're Dysfunctional!*' What do you say?" she asked me.

I said something about the dysfunctional management of the Yankees infield, and the room settled back into a tentative equilibrium. Another distraction was the food, which as advertised, was delicious. Axel studied each of our faces as we ate, and only picked at his own food, arranging the portions into geometric shapes, further sorted by color and composition.

I caught myself staring at his plate and returned to general awareness in time to notice the sensation of fingertips tracing the top of my thigh. I reached down and gripped Anika's wrist, returning her hand to her own lap. I shook my head in a way I hoped conveyed a message to her alone. Amanda didn't notice, thankfully, still engaged in a contest with Axel Fey for the airspace rights around her chair.

"You might not know there's an airfield here on Fishers," said Derrick. "I'd be happy to fly you to Long Island and arrange to have your boat towed to a larger marina. The one in Greenport, say."

I told him I appreciated the offer, but felt I owed it to Burton to bring his boat home on my own. And if I had to capitulate, I'd let Burton foot the bill.

"Your choice, of course," he said, holding his wineglass up to the light, on the lookout for impurities, I guessed.

Christian Fey overheard the talk about the airport, and leaned toward me so I could hear him over the other conversations.

"The man at the airport called and said they can't deliver your parts. He's down a man and it's too late in the season to hire another. We could, of course, drive you there."

I couldn't let him do that.

"Don't worry about it," I said. "We'll figure something out. You've done way too much already."

The evening staggered to completion about an hour after that. Amanda was the first to rise from the table, ostensibly to stretch her legs, but actually to escape the persistent attentions of the young Fey. I was next up for similar reasons.

As soon as I was on my feet, I felt a pull on the sleeve of the blue blazer. I looked down as 't Hooft took my hand and opened my fingers, then lodged a cold metal thing into my grasp. I said thank you, even though we'd exchanged not a single word all evening.

It wasn't until we were back on the boat, with the cabin lights ablaze, that I had a chance to look at the Dutchman's gift.

It was a fork taken from the Black Swan's silverware, crumpled into a ball.

CHAPTER 5

The next morning we mounted another expedition to the mainland. Amanda gave away the destination by tucking her laptop into her backpack.

"Broadband hunting?" I asked.

"Already found. Just follow me."

Happily for Eddie, the route was over untrod territory, redolent with fresh smells, each of which he lingered over with intense interest. So the journey across the island toward the southern coast was accomplished at a polite pace, which was fine. The humans in the party were in no particular hurry.

We filled the unhurried time by dishing on our dinner companions of the night before.

"I think Fey senior could be an okay guy," said Amanda. "At least he wants you to think so."

"I think that's praise too faint to damn."

"Better than his creepy kid."

"Autistic kid," I said. "Not the same thing."

"Oh, thanks. I get to be creeped out *and* politically incorrect."

"You're right. He's creepy. But he doesn't want to be, and has no way to know for himself that he is."

"So now you know how insensitive I can be—Del Rey's boobs, what do you think? Fake or real?" she asked.

"Fake as a twenty-dollar Rolex. At least based on what I could see, which was nearly everything."

"Del Rey? By that naming standard I'd be Oak Point Anselma."

"I like it. Oaky to your friends."

"Derrick, on the other hand, no read. Seemed cocky and edgy at the same time. And condescending, though he didn't know I noticed, which is typical of condescenders. So he sells some freaking software. So the hell what."

"N-Spock revolutionized large-scale computation. I loved it. Saved me huge time and money. Very robust analytical application. Jillions of if/thens a minute. Way ahead of its time. Can't imagine what they can do now, given the speed of modern platforms."

"I keep forgetting you weren't always a dumb carpenter. Is that insensitive of me?" she asked.

"Why would it be?"

"So what's their story? Derrick and his entourage? Can you have an entourage with only two people?"

"Don't know, on either count," I said. "But it doesn't smell right."

"I'll be glad to be out of here," said Amanda. "I feel like we're in some third world country and on the verge of getting thrown into a squalid prison filled with rats and Peace Corps volunteers. Unless we pay some huge ransom. Or worse. 'Money eez not the only currency we accept from women such as you, Madame,'" she added, in a generic foreign accent. "Grrr."

"Stay cool. Burton's sending the letters of transit."

We were interrupted by a pair of West Highland terriers who raced around Eddie as they tried to decide whether to attack or cavort. Eddie settled the question by doing a doggy-down and running out the length of his very long tether as the Westies joined the game. Lots of chasing, wrestling and slobber ensued.

We waited it out.

Ten minutes after resuming the trek, we crested a hill and walked down to a ragged row of shops behind a white picket fence that looked handmade by a team of drunken colonial artisans. The last store in the row was on its way to dissolving back into the earth. It had a sign that said SALUBRIA, ANARCHIA, HEONIA. YOU DECIDE.

"Let me guess," I said.

"Keep an open mind."

The first trick was to step over the bulldog lying in the middle of the front door. We let Eddie break the ice, while holding the tether slackless for quick extraction. No need. The bulldog hardly acknowledged he was there. Eddie hopped over and we followed.

Inside was a wall of incense complemented by the smell of decaying carpets and scented candles. Abba was on the stereo and the lighting made the room feel like there was no outside, no brilliant autumn sun nor azure sky. The store's trade seemed to be a random display of ragged crafts, sandals made from recycled beach debris, esoteric books, voodoo dolls wearing three-piece suits, healthful fruit drinks with handmade labels and a desktop Apple MacIntosh computer on a desk against the wall. The sign above it said, THE WORLD AWAITS. TEN BUCKS AN HOUR.

"Cover your ears," said Amanda before ringing the ship's bell hanging in the middle of the room. My hearing was saved, but I felt the sound in the pit of my stomach. A few moments later a woman came out of a door behind the counter at the back of the store.

"Oh goody," she said. "Company."

"Customers," said Amanda.

The woman's age was hard to pin down, given her pure white hair, pulled back into a lavish ponytail, clear, pinky complexion and straight posture. She wore a heavy cotton shirt under a pair of overalls, and motorcycle boots.

"Even better," said the woman. "Buy anything you want. Even me. Hey, I know you," she said, pointing at Amanda.

"I was in before," said Amanda. "I used your computer and bought a set of salt and pepper shakers in little crocheted cozies."

The woman reached up with both hands and scratched Amanda's head.

"I remember you," she said. "The hair. Thought it was a wig."

Amanda, a private person, took the affront with grace. She gripped the woman's hands by the wrists and gently disentangled them from her hair.

"We'd like to buy some more computer time," said Amanda. "Cell service is still down and we need to connect with home."

"With reality, you mean," said the woman. "Won't find that here. Who's the hooligan?" she added, looking at me.

"Sam Acquillo," said Amanda. "Don't let him fool you. He's worse than he looks."

"I'm Gwyneth Jones. Welsh witch, part-time, so don't try any of your peccadilloes on me."

"Noted," I said.

"I take Visa and MasterCard. And cold cash, or trade, though I doubt you folks have a set of brake pads for a '69 Citroën Deux Chevaux."

"I can get them," I said. "And do the installation. I just need a garage bay and the tools. Metric. And a manual. Prefer it in the original French. Can't trust the translations from those days."

She looked at me for a moment, then waved us over to her computer.

"Go ahead and log on," she said. "We'll discuss little French lemons later. Coffee anyone? I have Nigerian and Chock full o'Nuts."

I sat next to Amanda and watched her log on to her email. She sent a message to Burton's private mailbox asking when he thought the parts would arrive. Then I asked her to go to the NOAA marine forecast site, which featured, in brilliant red letters, a small craft warning beginning late the next day, Tuesday, and running through Thursday afternoon. She went deeper into the site and found speculation that we were in for a full-out gale. Most big winds came out of the northwest or northeast that time of year, but this was a rare sou'wester.

The commentator included a link to a climate change site called itstoolatebaby.com. I clicked on it for the hell of it. They said we were in for a series of big storms, in rapid succession, and that the corporate executives responsible should be tried in the world court for crimes against humanity. I thought I probably wouldn't go that far, though I might make exceptions for a few, not for the same offenses.

We heard a little ding. It was the email program telling us Burton had written back. He wrote that the plane he'd chartered would be delivering the goods the next morning, in time to get back to Maine before the storm hit.

"Put up more vodka. You'll be pinned to the dock for a few days," he wrote, signing off.

Gwyneth brought us our coffee orders.

"Your friend told me you're staying at the Swan," she said.

"At one of their docks."

"They have the only rentable rooms on the whole island," she said.

"Get out of here," said Amanda, not looking up from the screen.

"I'm surprised the town didn't buy the place so they could shut it down," said Gwyneth. "Not the worst thing. I've got a sleeping porch with a fold-out cot. I could corner the market. What happened to the nose?" she asked me.

"Rene Ruiz, the Filipino Phantom, took advantage of a moment's distraction and busted it with a right jab."

"You could have that straightened out."

"Not without losing a daily reminder to pay attention, especially in a boxing match," I said.

"Those Swissies who bought the Swan, what do you think?" she asked.

"They'll try to make a success of the place," said Amanda, rescuing me from having to dodge the question. "What do you think?"

"I thought they'd already thrown in the towel and you two were the next owners."

"Really," said Amanda.

"Are you?"

"No," said Amanda. "We want what everyone else wants of us. To leave here as soon as possible."

"Not me," said Gwyneth. "You can stay forever far's I'm concerned. Improve the gene pool. Though you're a little old for that. I'm forty-two. Tell me I don't look a day older than seventy-five. What's your position on cannabis? Stuff grows like Topsy on the island."

"We're all set, but thanks," said Amanda, vaguely, her attention still thoroughly absorbed by what she had on her screen.

I didn't know much about the Internet, not owning a computer or committing much time to learning the ins and outs. What little I did know I'd learned from Jackie Swaitkowski, my lawyer friend, who like Amanda, seemed to have a remarkable facility with the thing. I realized much of the world's information was now literally at your fingertips, an alluring concept. Maybe after I finished all the books at the Southampton Library I'd give it a shot.

"Subversive Technologies, headquartered in Weston, Massachusetts and developers of the software N-Spock, has a market capitalization of one point five billion dollars. Golly," said Amanda, reading off her screen. "That should help cover the Swan's new paint job."

"And Fey sold out?" I asked.

She scrolled down the page. "Apparently. The other co-founder, CEO and CFO Myron Sanderfreud, now holds the controlling shares, followed by Derrick Hammon, formerly head of sales and marketing, who succeeded Fey as Chief Technology Officer. He's in charge of the next big release, N-Spock 5.0, projected for the 1st Q next year."

"What's a Q?" asked Gwyneth.

"Quarter," I told her. "We're now in the 4th Q of this year—October, November, December."

"N-Spock is the dominant application for massive analytical processing, serving notably scientific research, securities trading and industrial R&D," read Amanda off her screen. "Though in recent years a number of competitors have eroded this position with applications that take better advantage of Next Gen processors and cloud computing. Whatever the hell that means."

"The march of progress is catching up to them," I said. "Happens to everybody."

"It's more drag race than march," said Amanda.

"I wouldn't feel too bad for them. Dominant share is still dominant share, and it'll be years before people are willing to chuck their proven N-Spock platforms for the flavor of the month."

"Throwing in the towel on the Swan will not be a financial decision," said Amanda. "The Feys are crazy rich."

"They're in the right place," I said.

Gwyneth scoffed.

"New money means nothing here, folks. No matter how much you have."

"According to the corporate press release, Fey simply announced his retirement, apparently in keeping with a succession plan, and that was that," said Amanda. "There's not much else on Subversive that makes any sense to me. If you want to savor the technical enhancements to N-Spock 5.0, I'll go do a little shopping."

"We have some nice things on sale," said Gwyneth.

I was actually tempted, but since the N-Spock of my day was version 2.5, I didn't think I'd understand the technical specs any better than Amanda. So we left after she bought a book on divination strategies from the *I Ching* that Gwyneth insisted was the only reliable way to keep track of the impending storm.

"A lot more dependable than the official weather report," she said.

We took another circuitous route back to the Swan, stopping along the way at the general store to take Burton's advice and stock up on essentials, like breakfast food, batteries, water, paper towels, ice and Absolut. There was no sign of Anderson Track, the surly gas station manager, and made it all the way back with no further incident.

In the small parking area to the right of the Swan a silver Lexus was parked next to Derrick's Town Car. It had a Massachusetts vanity plate that read SUBVERTECH.

"What is this, the company party?" said Amanda.

We walked around the hotel and out onto the docks. I unclipped Eddie and he made a dash for the boat, considered for a moment leaping up on the deck, then thought better of it. He looked back at us and barked.

"Keep your fur on."

We spent the next several hours securing the boat. I stripped off the sails and stowed anything that could blow off in the wind. Being a brand new boat, there was a minimum of gear hanging off the railings that tends to accumulate over time. Still, I went around with a screwdriver and pair of pliers and a box full of cotter pins and rings, tightening anything remotely suspect.

I used bungee cords to pull clanging halyard fittings away from the pristine white mast and cleated off the running rigging. I hoisted the dinghy's motor up and into a deep lazarette, then pulled the dinghy itself onto the dock where I deflated and folded it, then stowed it with the motor.

It took a while to retie the lines, doubling up and estimating the necessary slack. I looked with envy across the inlet at the yacht club's floating docks, which would have made so much fiddling unnecessary, inured as they were against the rise and fall of the tides.

Amanda stowed and re-secured all the provisions, put fresh batteries in the lanterns and flashlights, and filled the refrigerator with ice against the possible loss of shore power. The boat's main battery banks were topped off—good for a few days—and we could always start the engine if needed. Not being at sea, we had less concern about flying objects below, and it would be about twenty-four hours before the worst of the storm was scheduled to hit, but overpreparation was never a bad idea in my mind. The mind of an engineer. Frequently disdained and usually blamed the first time anything goes wrong.

"Now what, Cap'?" asked Amanda when I went below at the end of the afternoon.

"We eat, drink and rot in the cockpit. What else?"

It was after dark and in between uncounted rounds of cocktails and wine when a tall, broad-beamed guy with an unruly head of long curly hair and a skinny white-haired woman half his size strolled down the center dock toward our boat.

They paused to admire the *Carpe Mañana*, then spotted Eddie trotting down the deck, and subsequently Amanda and me in the cockpit.

"Hello," I said.

They walked down our dock, with Eddie following along on the boat.

"We didn't see you there," said the man.

"We're keeping a low profile," I said.

"Christian said he had unexpected guests in the marina."

"That's us. Sam and Amanda. And Eddie. He's the dog."

"Grace and Myron Sanderfreud," said the woman. "We're also unexpected."

Myron smiled down at her.

"Grace would rather be home winterizing her garden, but I can't do without her company. I uprooted her to come racing down here. Is this a pleasure cruise or impending voyage?"

"Delivery. Broke a steering cable. We're only here till the parts come, then we're on our way to Long Island. To winterize her."

"She has a beautiful sheer," said Myron, looking down the boat's hull. "We're on a Hinckley 59. When I can get away, which isn't often."

"Never," said Grace.

"We did when we were younger."

"And smarter."

"Care for some wine and Italian breadsticks?" asked Amanda.

Myron looked interested, but looked down at Grace for the go-ahead.

"If you want," she said. "It is a pretty boat," she added to Amanda, so we wouldn't think her reluctance was any fault of ours.

"How do you feel about dogs?" I asked.

"We love dogs," said Myron.

He stood behind his wife and grabbed her below the armpits. Her look of alarm turned to embarrassment as he lifted her up and onto the deck, where I helped her through the gate in the lifelines and down into the cockpit. She used a hold on Eddie's scruff to balance herself. Myron followed on his own, noticeably tipping the boat with his sizeable bulk.

"This is why I married her," he said. "She came in a handy, easy-to-carry package."

"For Lord's sake," said Grace, though not without a trace of good humor.

Amanda took care of her wine and I went below to rustle up a beer for Myron. I could hear the click and scratch of Eddie's claws on the deck as he bestowed on our guests the dubious pleasure of a hearty welcome.

It was hard to stick to small talk when both Amanda and I were itching with curiosity, though the Sanderfreuds made it easier by engaging in the kind of boat-talk that can absorb sailors for endless hours. Despite Grace's initial carping, they'd racked up considerable experience cruising the Eastern coast and more exotic seas like the Greek and Polynesian archipelagos. Though not as much recently.

"Why is it the more successful you are, the harder you have to work?" asked Grace, nearly unsettling the social equability we'd just established.

Myron seemed either annoyed or defensive, or both.

"Work ebbs and flows," he said. "We're just in flow-mode at the moment."

"He's talking about how busy he is. Not how much money he's making."

Myron's good-humored composure lost its hold on his face.

"I don't think these folks are interested in that sort of talk," he said, still indulgent, but terse.

Grace looked chastened.

"I'm sorry," she said, "you're right. It's just that I worry about him."

"She thinks software is a young man's game. She's right," he added, the avuncularity back in place. "I can still work the twelve-hour days, but the stress doesn't get any easier. How about you guys. Ebbing or flowing?"

I pictured Amanda in dust-covered T-shirt and jeans, stalking around one of her work sites with a worried sub-contractor in tow, pointing out shortcomings and praising achievement in equal measure. Later that day, she'd be sweeping floors, salvaging useable materials and writing instructions on the open studs and walls with a black Sharpie. With her money, none of this was strictly necessary, but she'd been a regular girl for most of her life, and only felt like herself when under life's load, however manufactured.

I didn't have her wealth, but shared her point of view. I had to work to pay the bills, but I would have done so anyway, having come to the realization that work was what kept you connected to the world in ways that were impossible for the leisure-prone, and disenfranchised, alike.

"We go with the flow," said Amanda, the question both answered and ambiguous. Myron seemed to enjoy that.

"We should let you people get back to work," he said. "It looks arduous."

They disembarked using the same procedure, in reverse. Grace seemed more receptive to the idea, now that she had some warning. Some pleasantries concluded with Myron inviting us to visit them the following evening for cocktails. Make it a storm party.

"We'll stay by the windows so you can keep an eye on the *Mañana*," he said.

Now that we'd established a history of being invited to Christian Fey's hotel by people other than Christian Fey, I told him to expect us.

"As long as we can bring the dog."

"Better yet."

We watched the two morphological opposites walk back down the center dock and disappear into the hotel. We sat in the quiet of the night, or what I thought was quiet.

"You're making those sounds," she said.

"What sounds?"

"The ones you make when something's bothering you but you don't want to talk about it."

"I'll stop."

"Just tell me what you're thinking."

"Nothing," I said. "It's none of my business."

"Those are two different thoughts," she said.

"I don't want to talk about it."

I got her off the topic by plying her with more wine and Italian breadsticks, and tales of adventure on the high seas, or low seas, if that's how you'd describe the beloved and capricious Little Peconic Bay, into which thrust Oak Point, where our houses stood side by side at the water's edge. It's where I'd learned to sail—on little boats worth less than the box of Eddie's dog food stowed under the galley sink. Leaky clinker-built dories and skiffs usually salvaged out of the marshland and powered by sails also scrounged, this time from the dumpster behind the sail loft in Sag Harbor, modified to fit their reduced circumstances. Luckily, the principles behind these makeshift craft and boats like Myron Sanderfreud's million-dollar Hinckley were essentially the same. They all had sails, keel, rudder and the rigging needed to control it all, to the extent nature allowed anything to be controlled.

Sailing is both an engineer's nightmare and dream. The dream part is the endless potential for tiny mechanical variations to dictate the success of the enterprise. That's the nightmare as well. Though less so for me, an engineer as besotted with the beauty of random circumstance as with the elegance of flawless precision.

And an engineer whose attention was often seized by happenstance falling somewhere uneasily in between.

CHAPTER **6**

The next morning's dilemma was determining when the plane was going to land and how to get there and back again with the boat parts. My reluctance to bother the Feys with additional logistics meant we'd have to take the more difficult, yet less socially awkward approach of getting up early and walking with Eddie to the airport, a solid five miles away, with hopes of discovering a better course along the way.

The airport was deep within the confines of the Country Club, the private reserve that made up three quarters of the island. The single road that accessed the club had a gate and a stern guy in a uniform during the season, roughly Memorial Day to Labor Day. During other times, the territory was patrolled by private security teams who were legendary among the transient sailors who anchored out in West Harbor, though none of us had ever seen one.

The day was grey and windy, the high-contrast clarity of the prior day's colors replaced by a soft fuzz, the air now thick with moisture and portent.

None of which dampened Eddie's mood, or enthusiasm for snuffling under leaf piles and marking every available object.

I took us on a route that passed by Gwyneth Jones' emporium of the peculiar. We were rewarded by the sight of her in a burgundy velour sweatsuit doing stretching exercises on her front lawn. The bulldog and Eddie sniffed at each other through the fence slats.

"Hale to thee," she said, when she saw us looking over the morning glory-enveloped white picket fence.

"You're probably not open yet," said Amanda.

"The computer never sleeps," she said.

"How 'bout a land line," I said. "Can we use that?"

"You could, but why?" she answered.

"Is the cell tower back up?"

"As of ten minutes ago when I called my sister in Seattle. I love waking her up."

Through a typical act of over-preparedness I'd dropped my cell into the pocket of my jeans before we left the boat. I pulled it out and speed-dialed Burton.

"This must be you," he said, answering. "Or someone who's stolen your phone."

"We're an hour from the airport, by foot," I said. "What's the prognosis?"

"Your parts are already there in the possession of a Mister Lee Two Trees, the man in charge of airport administration, which essentially means mowing the airstrip and keeping the wind sock from fouling."

"That's great, Burt. How much cargo are we looking at?"

"You said to send the whole array, so you'll need some sort of vehicle."

"How 'bout a '69 Deux Chevaux?" I said, glancing over at Gwyneth. She shook her head.

"Two real horses would be more suitable," said Burton.

He gave me the airport guy's cell phone number and sincere words of encouragement. And envy. Burton loved to stick his head into a messy knuckle-busting repair. What he

lacked in formal training, he made up for in gusto for whatever project was at hand, mechanical or otherwise.

I signed off and called Two Trees, but only reached his
voice mail. I clicked the phone shut and asked Gwyneth if
she knew where I could rent a truck.

"I don't know," she said, sadly. "Let's brainstorm. Who
drives trucks?"

"Contractors," said Amanda, a contractor who owned a
sprightly little red pickup.

"Don't know any."

"Subcontractors," I said.

"What're they?"

"Framers, electricians, plumbers . . ."

She snapped her fingers.

"I know a plumber. Vince Foley. Family's been on the
island since Adrien Block ran into it. A little touched in the
head, but he's got a truck. Couple of them, actually."

"We'll pay his hourly rate, but he's gotta come right
away," I said. "It's already getting breezy."

We all looked at the sky, which was filling up with dark
grey balls of wool. The trees, still full of red, green and
orange leaves, rustled in short, syncopated bursts of unsea-
sonably warm wind. A sou'wester, a summer storm that had
stumbled blindly into the late fall.

Gwyneth disappeared into her shop, and barely a few
minutes later, a black Dodge pickup skidded to a stop at the
front gate. A bearded man stuck his head out the window
and asked us what the hell the big hurry was all about.

"The man's got a load of spare parts waiting for him at
the airport," Gwyneth yelled back at him.

I was glad she didn't say, "And a storm's a-comin'!", true
as that was.

"We'll pay your hourly rate," I said. "Pretend you're
driving out to fix a leaky pipe without doing the actual
work."

I probably should've left that last part out; Vince was already confused enough by the situation.

I never believed in having dogs ride in the back of pickup trucks. Eddie would love nothing better, but his ability to assess personal risk was limited at best. Before Vince could raise an objection, I had Amanda jump into the middle of the bench seat and I followed, pulling Eddie onto my lap.

"You're good to do this," I said, pre-empting possible complaint.

It was an intense five-minute ride to the airport. Having rarely sat on a person's lap, Eddie experimented with a variety of positions, only settling down when I opened the window so he could stick out his head, a practice he'd perfected driving around Southampton in my '67 Pontiac.

The airfield had changed little in the years since I'd been there. The pay phone was gone, but the little shed which constituted the airport's ground facilities, still stood. Parked next to it was a banged-up Toyota Corolla with the trunk open. Vince swung his truck around so the driver side windows of the two vehicles lined up. He rolled his down.

"Dude," said the driver of the Toyota, a grey-haired man of indeterminate racial composition whom I assumed was Mr. Two Trees.

"You got some packages for these people?"

"I do indeed. Shipped here all the way from Maine. That pilot was none too eager to hang around. Never shut down the motor."

"Storm's a-comin'," said Vince.

"That'd be right."

"So, fellas," I said, as Eddie dug a forepaw into my thigh, "let's make the transfer."

The makers of the steering gear had their name printed on four boxes in a variety of sizes that we pulled from the car's trunk and dropped into the truck bed.

Probably out of some sadistic impulse, Vince took his time driving us back to the Swan. He also felt obliged to predict the hotel's certain failure in the not-too-distant future. Amanda asked him why.

"They're not from the island. Know nothing about it," he said.

"Neither would their guests, presumably," she said. "Who better to make outsiders feel welcome than other outsiders?"

This thought was of a conceptual nature that eluded Vince's ready powers of cognition. So he dropped the matter and slowed the truck to a near crawl the rest of the way to the Swan.

After piling out of the truck, to our great relief, I commandeered Anika's wheelbarrow from inside the hedge and used it to haul the gear out to the boat, where I spent the rest of the day deciphering the manufacturer's installation instructions. In the face of their best efforts to confuse and misdirect, and while in a semi-upside down contortion inside the engine compartment, I made the repair.

The only hitch was the need to run the cable through an enclosed channel right above the rudder. This feature had apparently been added by the hull builder as a tribute to the steering gear maker's love for unnecessary complication. I tried a variety of means for about an hour, and was about to call Vince Foley back and ask if he had the needed piece of equipment, appropriately called a snake, when Amanda handed one down to me.

"How did you know?"

"I assumed the words, 'A fucking snake. Where am I gonna get a fucking snake?' had nothing to do with herpetology."

"Where did you get it?"

"I called Vince Foley. You owe me a hundred bucks."

"Expensive snake."

"It's a seller's market."

Buried as I was in the belly of the boat, I hadn't noticed the wind picking up until I felt a sudden tremor and heard a whistle coming from the mast, the sound transferred from somewhere above down into the bilge. By then I was done with the installation, a good thing. For the last hour I'd been choosing between loss of circulation in my left leg and loss in my right. Meanwhile, the experience had reversed the healing process in my broken hand, trading a dull ache for knife-like jabs of pain.

Thus in a complicated mood, I emerged from the deep lazarette that led to the engine compartment with an immediate need written all over my face.

"Vodka?" asked Amanda.

The air had warmed up considerably and the sky was now mostly a uniform grey. According to NOAA, the system moving in from the southwest was scheduled to plow into a cold front drifting down from Canada, with the battle line forming across Connecticut and Rhode Island. In other words, right on top of us.

The wind had continued to pick up, though still nothing extraordinary. It felt good, actually, rustling around the cockpit and swirling Amanda's hair.

"So we're seaworthy again," she said, pulling her hair through the hole in the back of her baseball cap, which was clipped to the collar of her flannel shirt.

"We won't know for sure until the sea trial, but I'm reasonably confident," I said, spinning the big chromed wheel from where I sat in the cockpit and feeling it move smoothly from one extreme to the other. "Better yet, I could see the failure point, which I've corrected. For want of a pair of stainless steel screws we could've gone ass-over fin keel."

"If we hadn't had so adept a helmsman."

"Exactly."

"So now what?" she asked.

"We wait out the blow, then get the hell out of here."

There's one thing you'd think I would have learned by then: never project current circumstances indefinitely into the future.

◆

I heard a hoarse scream coming from the hotel. Moments later, I saw Anika running down the dock. Even through the gloom of the early evening, barely relieved by the dock lights, her face was an inflamed mask.

"Oh God, oh God, oh God," she repeated, gripping the gunwale to steady herself as she looked into the cockpit. Amanda and I stood up in alarm.

"Please come with me," she said to me. "It's terrible."

"What?"

"Myron. Oh my God, what're we going to do?"

I told Amanda to secure Eddie and stay in the cockpit, then jumped to the dock and followed Anika as she ran ahead, her open denim shirt flapping behind her. Lights started coming on along the eaves of the hotel. Shouts and calmer words joined the screams, now more a low, wet groan. I followed the sounds around the left side of the hotel. Flashlights crisscrossed through the darkness and lit up a rough cedar booth built against the wall that I assumed was an outdoor shower. Anika grabbed my sleeve and pulled me toward the scene.

Bernard 't Hooft suddenly loomed in front of me and blocked my way.

"We don't need the help," he said.

I shoved past him, not an easy task, and looked in the shower stall. The floodlight from above down-lit the massive corpulence of Myron Sanderfreud, his neck cocked at an impossible angle, a white nylon line tucked below his jaw and leading up and over the wall of the stall.

CHAPTER 7

Christian Fey held a flashlight up to Myron's face with one hand and tentatively sought a way to undo the line with the other. I reached over his shoulder and took his hand, pulling it back.

"Don't," I said. "Wait for the police."

He spun around angrily.

"We can't leave him like this," he yelled.

"Yes we can," I said. "Don't touch anything."

He resisted me when I tried to pull him out of the stall. When Grace started to shove her way in, he relented and gently forced her back out to the brick path. She was soaking wet. He gripped a wad of her shirt and moved her tiny frame away from the stall. In the process I snuck away his flashlight.

"Nobody touch anything," I shouted behind me. "And stay off the soft ground."

"By whose orders?" asked 't Hooft from the darkness.

"You explain to the cops why you contaminated the crime scene," I said in the general direction of his voice.

"Crime scene?" wailed Grace.

"We don't know that," said Derrick Hammon, who was hidden by the glare of the flashlight in his hand.

"That's why you should all back away and wait for the police to get here. Somebody called, I hope."

"I did," said Axel, sticking his flashlight directly in my face. "She said not to touch anything."

Somehow Anika had worked her way into the booth and stood next to me, clutching my biceps with both hands.

"Who found him?" I asked.

"Grace," said Anika. "I turned on the water for him. We'd shut it off to avoid freezing, but he was so into the idea. He was gone an hour before Grace came looking. That scream is like in my head forever."

I ran the flashlight around the stall. The concrete floor pan was littered with soap fragments and tiny bottles of shampoo brought out from the hotel. Myron was barely in a standing position, his knees bent akimbo and his feet rolled up on their sides. Without a tape measure it was hard to be sure, but the distance from where the line was attached to his neck and the top of the wall seemed enough to hang him, and then settle him part way back into the stall. I tried not to look at the naked folds of his body drooping down from his chest and over his midriff, the thick wet mats of hair on his chest and forearms and blackened blotches on his cheeks where the blood had been squeezed, then left behind when his heart stopped.

"He has such a little thing for such a big man," said Anika, almost matter-of-factly, which made the comment that much more jarring.

"What the hell is going on?" came a vaguely familiar voice from out of the dark. I leaned out of the stall and shot my flashlight in that direction, lighting up Anderson Track.

"Stay where you are," I said to him. He stopped and tried to squint through the brilliant light. "We have a situation here," I said, "If you want to help, stay out of the way."

"What sort of situation? Who the fuck are you anyway?" he said.

I saw Christian Fey move in between me and Track, but didn't hear what he said. But Track moved back, his hands aloft in a sign of capitulation, which was all I cared about at that point.

A few moments later, another flashlight came erratically down the path from the front of the hotel. I caught the glint of steel from the lights shot in the newcomer's direction.

"Please stand clear of the area," said a woman's voice.

I held my ground as the others fell away, including Anika, who let go of my arm with a light sweep of her fingers.

"You, too, sir," said the statie, her hand supported comfortably on the top of her holster.

"I could describe the scene if you want," I said.

"You police?" she said.

"No. Mechanical engineer. And former defendant in a murder case. You learn some things."

She held her flashlight in my face for a moment, then moved it toward the ground. I did the same. She was a small, slender-waisted woman with longish dark hair that fell in pin curls to her shoulders. Dwarfed next to Amanda's five eight, she looked either misplaced or completely comfortable in her statie uniform—it was hard to see in that erratic light. Her face was serious, a good cop face, and her posture assured.

"Okay, go ahead."

I did my best, adding detail as it came to me, occasionally asking Anika to chime in. The others just stood around and listened, everyone but Grace, who Christian Fey held to his chest with both arms and rocked from side to side. Amanda came down the path, after seeing the light from the cruiser.

"Sam?" she said, moving to my side and taking the part of my arm recently vacated by Anika. Her grip tightened as she heard the account I was giving the cop, whose name plate read JENNIFER POOLE. She wrote briskly in a little case book pulled out of the back pocket of her slacks, her flashlight held under her arm.

She was clearly rattled, but to her credit, acted like she wasn't.

"So no one's touched the body since it was discovered," she said.

"Grace hugged him," said Anika.

"And Christian Fey tried to release him from the noose. Both understandable reactions," I said.

Trooper Poole took a cell phone out of a holster and walked away from the gathering to make a call.

"We have no coroner on the island," she said when she came back, looking at me darkly. "And minimum forensics. Plus the ferry just stopped service due to the weather. I called the closest CSI team, which is at the state barracks in Riverhead. The coast guard can get them out here, but it'll take a while, since they have to sail over to Orient Point from Connecticut."

"Are we talking hours?" I asked.

"We are."

"Seems pretty grim to just leave him there," I said.

"They said I could take him down as long as I cleared that part of the scene."

"Do you know how to do that?" I asked.

She looked at me, sizing me up.

"Mostly," she said.

"You have a digital camera?" I asked.

"I do."

"At least we can record everything," I said. At my request, Anika retrieved a tape measure and a box of surgical gloves Axel used in the hotel kitchen. I took the box and pulled out a pair for me and handed another to Trooper Poole.

"Before we do that, leave me alone with him for a few minutes," she said. She put on the gloves and went in the booth, then closed the door. Ten minutes later she emerged with a look that said, "Don't ask."

The brilliant pop of Trooper Poole's camera aided my careful recording of the body's position relative to the house and the wall of the shower stall, and the distance from the noose around his neck to the top of the stall. Then I brought her around to the other side of the wall and showed her where the line had been tied to a cleat bolted to the hotel's foundation. It was used to secure an extravagant canopy that shaded the walkway. A foot above the cleat two loops were tied in the line.

Poole shot more pictures and I made a dozen more measurements.

After that, with the young cop's help, I uncleated the line and lowered Myron's body to the ground.

Anika had sent her brother to retrieve some bed-sheets that we used to cover Myron's body, for the sake of his dignity and the witnesses' fragile hold on personal composure.

Then Poole shut the shower stall and put a piece of tape across the jamb. It was a type that would shred if you tried to remove it. She used the same material to tape off the top, supported by a ladder also fetched by Axel Fey. When she was finished, we all went into the hotel and settled in the lounge, all but Grace who demanded to go to her room. Amanda volunteered to go with her, which Grace accepted with minimal resistance. I whispered in Amanda's ear.

"See if you can get a sleeping pill into her, if she has any. Put the rest in your pocket."

Amanda nodded and put her arm around the tiny woman, helping her up the narrow old stairs to her room.

Trooper Poole asked for a room where she could take each of our statements in private. I looked around and counted a full contingent, minus Anderson Track, who'd apparently slipped away. Derrick leaned against the bar with his hands in his pockets, with one of Del Rey's arms through one of his. 't Hooft was behind the bar pouring beers for himself and the Feys. Nobody argued with Poole's request that we all stay put, and she went off with Christian to find a room and do her first interview. I joined 't Hooft behind the bar and poured myself a tall Absolut on the rocks.

"Makes no sense," said Derrick.

"What doesn't?" I asked.

"Killing himself. He had his challenges, but Christ."

"He didn't kill himself," I said.

"You know a lot for a guy who delivers boats," said 't Hooft.

"There was too much slack in the line," I said. "Serious suicides make sure there's no turning back. To do a proper job, he would have cleated off a shorter line, stood on the seat inside the shower, jumped off and that'd be it."

"People who seem happy are sometimes the most depressed," said Del Rey. "Who's to say Myron wasn't one of those?"

"There you have it," said Derrick. "A phenomenally trenchant psychoanalysis, explaining all."

Del Rey jerked at his arm.

"Just a theory," she said. "No reason to get fresh."

"Never argue with a theoretician," I said. "Sometimes they're right."

"See?" said Del Rey, with more emphasis than was necessary.

"I'll take that under advisement," said Derrick.

"I knew Myron better than most people," she said, looking at Hammon. "He talked to me."

"What about?" I asked.

"Nothing he'd want you to share," said Hammon. Del Rey snapped her mouth shut and looked away.

As we waited for Poole to come back, the room settled into a pair of loose confederations. Me and Anika cleaved to the bar, while 't Hooft, Derrick and Del Rey sat around a small cocktail table, none of them looking entirely comfortable. Axel rocked back and forth on one of the bar-stools, which he'd moved to the center of the room. Anika kept one eye on him and the other on Derrick's contingent.

A general gloom had gathered about the group at large, which Del Rey seemed slightly desperate to lift. She waved at me and Anika.

"Hey, people," she said, "how's the weather over there?"

"Mixed and variable," I told her.

A brief burst of wind clattered the window at the other end of the room. I watched everyone's eyes shift in that direction—everyone but Axel, who seemed to be staring at Derrick Hammon.

Who, in turn, was staring at me.

"So, Mr. Acquillo," he said. "What's your deal?"

"Everybody's got a deal?" I said.

"No. Just some people. What's yours?"

"Finish carpentry."

"Why is your name so familiar?"

"The world's lousy with Acquillos," I said.

"Of course."

Trooper Poole and Christian walked into the room. He had his hands in his pants pockets and she was writing in her little case book. She looked up and around the room, trying to figure out the next victim.

"Me, me," said Anika, raising her hand. "I got there just a few seconds after Grace. I want to get this out of the way."

When they left, I sat on one of the bar-stools, keeping my distance from Axel, but suggesting a shared experience. He noticed and briefly stopped rocking. I smiled at him and he smiled back.

"So, Axel," said Derrick, "the dad still have you developing?"

"He looks pretty developed already," said Del Rey.

"He means coding," said 't Hooft, jumping in front of Derrick's impending response. "Computer programming."

"Oh."

"We're in the hotel business now," said Axel, looking down at the floor.

"Of course you are," said Derrick.

't Hooft took a long sip of his beer, looking at the kid over the lip of the mug. The room was silent after that, until Poole and Anika came back. It was two hours before Poole had taken everyone's statement, including Grace, in her bedroom while Amanda waited outside. I kept Amanda company.

"I don't know what the officer expects to learn from her," said Amanda. "The woman's in complete shock. Who wouldn't be."

"Did you tell anyone I was finished with the boat repair?" I asked.

She shook her head.

"I just said you were working on it."

"Good."

The CSI team called Poole on her cell phone to announce their arrival. She was just leaving Grace's bedroom, and Amanda offered again to stick around and look after the distraught woman. Poole thanked Amanda and asked me to come outside with her so I could give her my version before she left to pick up the CSI's.

When we reached her cruiser, she stopped to talk.

"You're known," she said to me.

"By whom?"

"My boss. Semple's a friend of his."

She meant Ross Semple, the Town of Southampton's chief of police. I wondered what being a friend of his would be like. She had to mean a professional friend, because who could be both smart enough and weird enough to be on personal terms. I said as much.

"Semple thinks you're dirty. But he likes you anyway. My boss said you could help, but to keep an eye on you."

"Whatever that means," I said. "You've got more serious issues than me. Sanderfreud was murdered and unless it was some ninja that swam ashore, did the deed, then swam back to a submarine off the coast, it's somebody on the island, and likely in that house."

"Semple thinks you killed someone yourself," said Poole, "but he could never prove it."

"Nobody's perfect."

"Sanderfreud's friends all think he hung himself. What do you think?"

"Simple. Wait until Sanderfreud's busy taking his shower. Put a ladder next to the stall and climb up until you can see over the lip. Stick your foot in one of the loops tied in the middle of the line, slip the noose over the guy's neck and jump off the ladder. Then just wait until the thrashing stops, cleat off the line and step out of the loop."

"That's what I think, too," she said, as if I'd just passed a test. "Clever bit of engineering. Isn't that your specialty? Clever engineering?"

"You'd have to prove Amanda's lying about where I was."

"Semple's not so sure about her, either."

"If you want my help, you can knock off the innuendo," I said. "Besides being insulting, it's a waste of time you don't have."

It was hard to see her face in whatever light was reaching us from the hotel. And harder to read her thoughts by the way she stood with her right hand resting on top of her holster.

"You'll be here when I get back," she said, part question, part command, though she shook my hand before getting in her car. I said I'd be there and watched her drive away.

Back in the house, I bypassed the bar where everyone still congregated and went upstairs to Grace's room. I gently knocked on the door and Amanda answered. She slipped quietly out into the hall and shut the door.

"I did what you asked," she said. "She's out cold and I've got her sleeping pills and a full bottle of aspirin. There were some other prescriptions that I didn't recognize, so I had to leave them."

"Poole's on her way to collect the crime scene people from the town dock. They aren't going to want us hanging around while they work, and I'd be just as happy to get back on the boat."

"Eddie'll be happy to see us."

"We can check out his alibi."

We stopped off at the bar only long enough to tell the Feys we'd be on the boat if anyone needed us. Anika was the only one who looked unhappy about it, but didn't say anything.

Even a less sensitive pup than Eddie would have known something in the world had gone amiss. So, as predicted, he was full of joy when we opened up the companionway.

As Amanda fussed around the galley I went out to the bow and called Burton Lewis. When he came on the line, I briefed him on the current circumstances, starting with the boat repair and ending with the appearance of the CSI team from the mainland.

"I've met Sanderfreud and his wife," said Burton. "And Christian Fey. Sanderfreud was the money guy. And professional manager. Fey's the programming genius. We had a hand in the IPO. Strictly tax consulting. Terrible thing."

"Any more on the storm?" I asked.

"Severe thunderstorms and high winds reported in Pennsylvania. Headed your way. I was checking while we talked. How are you set for dock lines?"

"We're good. I'll check in later. Keep your cell handy if you can."

"Have you talked to Jackie Swaitkowski?" he asked. "She's hounding me about getting in touch with you."

"I'll call her. Promise."

I went back down below and sat on one of the settees so I could watch Amanda putter around the serenely beautiful galley, a natural cherry and Corian masterpiece of efficiency and craftsmanship. LED lighting fixtures in chrome and glass shades cast a gentle light on the counters and throughout the salon, the settees resplendent in tropical upholstery. Eddie, a product of scrub oaks and sea grass, looked a little out of place lying on bamboo shoots and palm fronds, though it didn't seem to bother him.

A small built-in space heater had warmed the cabin to the point that Amanda could get away with one of my T-shirts and a baggy pair of running shorts. Her legs were lean, muscular and still dark from the recent tanning season. She'd brushed out her mass of hair, which in the last year had started to show strands of grey. She'd asked me if I cared, and I said what she did with her hair was entirely her concern. One of the things I loved most about Amanda was she preferred those kinds of answers, never leaping to subtle or sinister interpretations.

Like Ross Semple, I was never entirely sure about Amanda. She'd done some things in the years we'd known each other to which words like subtle or sinister might easily apply. But we'd survived it all, a tribute to the powers of forgiveness, or selective amnesia, or both.

Our connection was not a conscious thing. To me, it was an act of random happenstance, a natural phenomenon, never to be repeated. I'd decided early on that whatever Amanda was or wasn't had nothing to do with how I felt about her. Which was a vast and unquenchable longing and desire, a fantastical admixture of delight and gratitude. Not just that such things could be felt, but that she could have her own version of these feelings for me, which I knew were manifestly undeserved.

I might have been brooding over these fancies that evening, because without turning around from the galley stove where she was pouring two cups of green tea, she said, "What."

"What do you mean, 'what'?"

"What're you thinking? I can hear it all the way over here."

"How little I like green tea."

"It's good for you, and no you weren't."

The wind picked that moment to whistle in the rigging of the boat, a sound we'd last heard out on the water, only now more spectral and portentous in the dimly lit cabin. The boat pitched slightly to starboard, causing a pan in the galley stowage to bang against the cabinet door.

"What does that mean?" asked Amanda, looking up at the cabin ceiling.

"In my experience, over twenty knots of breeze."

"Storm's a-comin'."

"Indeed."

"So what're you thinking?"

"That we need to get some sleep tonight, because tomorrow could be lively."

So, after forcing down the tea, we did just that, serenaded by the hum of the quivering shrouds that anchored the stalwart mast, and the slap of tiny, wind-borne bay waves against the bow, insistent and merciless in their need to be heard.

CHAPTER 8

In the misty realm of emerging wakefulness, an oncoming storm is a pleasant thing. Especially if you're on a boat, wedged agreeably next to a naked woman in the made-for-two coffin-like enclosure called the quarter berth. There was a bigger bed in the bow called the V-berth—an apt name, contrary to nautical custom, shaped as it was in a flat-bottomed V. But I didn't like it as much. Too ample and fussy.

It was light out when I opened my eyes and saw the dull grey sky through the nearest porthole. The boat vibrated from the steady wind and the ghosts were back cavorting in the standing rigging. I looked around the cabin for Eddie, then spotted him up on the starboard settee, on his back with his rear legs splayed and tongue lolling out of his mouth. Mr. Sea Dog, impervious to the menace of natural forces.

Recollections of the night before arrived unwanted, disrupting my unrealistically peaceful mood. Images crowded into my mind—of Myron Sanderfreud and the female cop, Derrick Hammon's studied stare, Axel Fey's inexpert use of a flashlight and Amanda leading Grace Sanderfreud up the antique stairs.

And then I started to think about dock lines and fenders, our only points of defense against the clamor outside. A few seconds later, I was too agitated to lie still, and thought only of extracting myself without disturbing Amanda and getting on with the day.

"Don't worry," said Amanda, reading my mind. "I've been awake for an hour. It's getting breezy out there."

"What do you think's going on?" I asked her.

"A storm?"

"No. At the Black Swan."

She settled deeper into the bed and shoved up against me.

"Hammon and his crew came here for a reason. They were unexpected and unwelcome. As were the Sanderfreuds. The Feys are hiding something. Actually, lots of things. Axel is in la-la land, much to his father's disgust and shame, which doesn't say much about his father. 't Hooft is more than muscle and not as committed to Hammon as it might appear. And Del Rey isn't as clueless as she pretends to be. Hammon is very angry, I think at Fey, but I'm not sure. He showed little remorse over Myron's passing, only puzzlement. In fact, none of them seem as upset about Myron as they ought to be. Except for Grace, who hates Hammon, which is no great insight, since she told me so in terms that would embarrass a sailor. Wait a minute, you are a sailor, and you're never embarrassed. She thinks he killed her husband, even though he was deep in conversation with Christian Fey for at least two hours leading up to her discovering his body, which makes that a physical impossibility. When pressed, as gently as I could, she wouldn't offer up a motive other than to call Hammon a snake in designer clothing, whatever that means, along with a few other choice things. I like Trooper Poole, even though she treats me like your trashy girlfriend, and I wonder why you're avoiding Jackie Swaitkowski, who clearly needs to talk to you, since she called me on my cell and told me in terms that would embarrass a former banker that if you don't call her today you'll be forfeiting certain treasured parts of your male anatomy."

"That's all?"

"There might be more after I'm actually awake."

I got into a pair of shorts and T-shirt and I took Eddie for a jog along West Harbor and around the northern curve of the island, eventually heading west toward the ferry dock. I hadn't run for a week, and felt it, especially running against a strong headwind. Eddie trotted at my side, a habit formed over years of jogging the sand roads around the Little Peconic Bay in Southampton, where this seemingly attentive obedience would be punctuated by mad bursts into the sea grass and piney scrub growth in pursuit of God knows what. That day I still had him on a leash, an affront he took with barely contained forbearance.

For both our sakes, I slowed to a walk when we reached the ferry dock, where as hoped, a red and gray coast guard patrol boat was tied up against the tall dock walls. There was no one on the deck, so I resorted to yelling, "Anybody home?"

The cabin door opened and a long-haired guy with a heavily bearded face and wire rimmed glasses popped out.

"Depends," said the guy.

"On what?"

"What you want."

"A conversation. I was at the Swan last night when they found the body."

"We don't discuss open cases."

"What if I possessed vital information?" I asked.

"What information?"

"I can't tell you if you won't discuss the case."

The guy was young, the thick curly hair that covered most of his head a deep, dense black. I think it was a signal to the rest of us that he was the intellectual sort.

"I'm a crime scene investigator," he said. "You need to talk to the regular cops."

"Over your head. I get that."

The guy's glasses were too thick to clearly see his eyes. Instead, the refraction made him look like a confused bug. A very hairy bug.

"Okay, what kind of information," he said, after a long pause.

"The killer knew boats. And ropes."

"Who said there was a killer?" he asked. "We were sent out here on a suicide report."

"You're kidding, right?" I asked.

"Haven't seen a hanging yet that wasn't self-inflicted."

"In the shower?" I said.

"Still possible."

"Is there somebody on board who's ready to take this seriously?" I asked.

"If you mean another CSI, no. I'm it."

"Ah, crap," I said, kicking the ground like a ten-year-old. Eddie looked up at me, vaguely unsettled.

"Listen, sir, I appreciate your eagerness to help, but everything is under control. Let us do our job and we'll sort this all out."

"You don't appreciate me at all. And what you're doing is guaranteeing you'll never figure out what happened here. The police are sending in the Rockville Little League to play the Boston Red Sox. You're already fucked and you haven't even finished your report."

"I beg to differ. And as of right now, this conversation is over," he said, then popped back into the boat.

Nicely done, Sam, I said to myself.

"Hey, sorry," I yelled at the boat. "Come on back. I apologize."

A different guy came out, this one a foot taller in height and wider at the shoulders. A coastie.

"Something I can help you with?" he asked, in a flat, dead voice.

"I was trying to talk to the CSI."

"Not on my boat you aren't," he said. "Please step away."

Eddie looked ready to jump aboard and make some new friends, but I used what little sense I had left, and after giving the captain a quick salute, turned and strolled back down the tall breakwater and out to the street. As I tried to remember the location of the state police office my cell phone rang. The little screen said it was Burton Lewis.

"Hi, Burt."

"Hah!" said Jackie Swaitkowski, "I knew it."

"Ah, shit, Jackie, I don't want to do this now. How'd you get Burton's phone?"

"He handed it to me. We're here in my office. It's decision time and I can't hold them off much longer."

I'd known Jackie since she was a real estate lawyer working out of her house, and then a screwball office in Watermill, a little village within the Town of Southampton. During that time she'd switched over to criminal law, providing her the opportunity to defend me on several occasions, successfully, through no fault of my own. Now she ran the East End office of Burton's free legal defense operation, which he'd started in Manhattan and slowly built out across Long Island and into Upstate New York. This particular matter, however, was strictly civil, in the legal sense.

"Yes you can," I said. "Rushing you is just a legal tactic. If stall ball was in their favor they'd be doing that. Anyway, I'm busy right now. Geez, Jackie, show a little backbone."

"You're impossible," she said.

"Since Burt's right there, could you put him on the line?"

I couldn't hear what she said when she handed him the phone, but I could guess.

"Say, Burt, remember when you told me seeking help from friends was good for the soul?" I asked.

"I do. It still is."

"Then could you do me a favor? Get one of your minions to do a little research on Subversive Technologies. What's their financial and operational status? What's the public story and what's going on behind the scenes, the extent to which we can figure that out."

Ordinarily this was the kind of favor I'd ask of Jackie, but now didn't seem the ripest time. Anyway, I'd asked Burton for help along these lines once or twice before, and he was always gracious about it. Having a few thousand tax lawyers at his disposal was particularly handy. They not only knew numbers, they knew people in every corporate office in the country.

"Already underway," he said.

"Really."

"I knew you'd want to know. And take your time with the boat. I was only going to pull her out for the winter anyway."

I almost got off the phone feeling nothing but warmth and gratitude toward Burton Lewis, when he spoiled it by putting Jackie back on the line.

"I don't understand your reluctance over this," she said, using her reasonable-girl voice. "There's a lot of money at stake. Have you been broke for so long you don't remember what lovely things money can buy?"

She was referring to the lawsuit against my old company Con Globe, brought by a group of people in the engineering department. It involved an intellectual property claim on some technology they developed, the rights for which Con Globe had done a lousy job retaining solely for itself. I'd assumed I forfeited all such claims myself when they shit-canned me, and had me sign things in return for ignoring that I'd punched our corporate counsel in the nose.

But in the following years a lot had happened, like the prosecution of Con Globe's senior management for fraud and the take-over of the company by one of their competitors. I had a hand in making some of that happen, in the midst of which Jackie found a way to void my severance agreement and get my name added to the settlement, which was soon to be wrapped up by the courts.

When Jackie got on to something she could be a mixed-breed bloodhound and Staffordshire terrier, and this was no different. What got her particularly exercised was learning that the technology in question, an octane-enhancement device, had been developed by a research team led by the director of R&D, who was credited with some of the key design features that made the thing work, and whose name appeared prominently on the patent. That director being me.

"Get the best deal you can without taking anything from the others and I'll sign the papers," I said.

An unfamiliar silence formed on the other end of the line.

"Just like that?" she asked. "After stalling and wheedling and avoiding me at every turn?"

"I just hadn't figured out what to do with the money," I said.

"And now you do."

"Just now. Thanks to you," I said.

She asked for an explanation and I was going to give her one when Officer Poole pulled up next to me. Jackie didn't believe me, but I told her I really had to go.

Poole looked unhappy when she climbed out of her car.

"I just had to have a coast guard patrol boat captain surgically removed from up my ass," she said.

"Sorry," I said. "I shouldn't have let that CSI get to me."

"You shouldn't have left your boat. Listen up. I appreciate the help you gave me last night, but you're now busted back to full-time civilian. Any more bullshit and I'll charge you with impeding an investigation."

"You don't actually think it was suicide," I said.

"I don't. But Jeffrey doesn't want to rule it out."

"Jeffrey's the CSI? He's a dick."

"And you mean that respectfully," said Poole.

"Can't you get him back to the Swan so I can go through what actually happened?"

"They're pulling out now," she said, nodding toward the harbor. "His boss wants him back before the storm. So do the coast guard."

"The loops in the rope were made with a bowline. And the end was cleated off in a standard figure eight. That's a sailor," I said.

"Like Myron Sanderfreud."

I don't usually let my face share what I'm thinking, but not always.

"Don't glower at the police," said Officer Poole. "It's our job to consider every angle. You'd understand that if you weren't a civilian."

I closed my eyes and breathed, collecting the bits of myself that were flying freely through the air. When I opened them up, she was still standing there.

"Sorry," I said. "I do know how hard a cop's job is. I've seen a lot of it up close, more than I ever wanted to."

She studied me, as if to determine the authenticity of my apology.

"I'm actually headed for the Swan now. Do you want a lift?"

I demurred, disappointing Eddie who clearly wanted to ride in the cruiser. Instead, I forced him to jog with me the long way back to the boat, hoping the extra miles would soak up some of my frustration. Which didn't happen, though the black clouds gathering along the northern horizon and the lighter grey swirls streaming overhead started to become a distraction. The sun was temporarily shining through a clear spot, lighting up the autumn foliage against the backdrop of a darkening sky. I noticed the leaves flipping over, exposing a pale delicate underside, a telltale of big weather on the way according to my old man, who was occasionally right about things like that.

Eddie noticed it as well, pausing to sniff the air and letting the ground-hugging gusts back brush his fur.

When I got to the hotel, Poole had apparently come and gone. Only one of the gleaming cars that had brought the unheralded guests was in the parking lot—the Town Car. Anderson Track was standing in front of the gas station that served as the land-based fuel dock. He had his hands on his hips and a smirk on his face.

"That dog ain't no jogger. Can hardly run in a straight line."

"You're right about that. Nothing straight ahead about him," I said.

Disappointed that he hadn't insulted me, he tried again.

"Runnin' around in your underwear seems like a stupid waste of time to me."

I stopped jogging and leaned on my knees to catch my breath and feel the freshening breeze cool the sweat off my back. I looked up at him, standing about twenty yards away, forcing us to almost shout back and forth.

"That's why you're fat," I said. "And these are jogging clothes. I only run around in my underwear on Saturday nights."

"You are truly begging to get your ass kicked," said Track.

"And you're truly welcome to give it a try."

He stayed where he stood, deferring the ass-kicking to some future date, which was fine with me, tired as I was from the run around the island and concerned about Eddie getting caught up in the fray.

I walked the rest of the way to the Swan and was about to head down the path to the docks when Anika stepped out from behind a hedge, appearing suddenly as she often did from the dense foliage she scrupulously attended to.

"Your cop friend was here," she said. "She wanted to look over the shower again. Took a bunch of pictures. Wouldn't let me talk to her. A hearse took Myron over to New London on the last boat before they closed for the storm. He's going to the medical examiner. Grace wasn't happy about it, but the cops have all the say, apparently. She followed the hearse to the mainland. You think somebody killed him, so I guess that's alright with you."

I looked around the property.

"Make sure everything's tied down," I said. "Could have a bit of wind."

"Oh, geez, you're right. Never thought of that."

In fact, the area had been scoured of unanchored objects and the shutters on the first floor of the hotel closed and latched.

"Sorry," I said. "I'm projecting boat anxiety."

"You should go look after her," she said.

"I should."

"But not before I show you my painting."

"Your painting."

"Up on the third floor. In my studio. I told you I'd show it to you and this is probably the last chance I'll have before I turn into Dorothy and get blown out to sea."

She wore a pair of paint-splattered denim overalls over a white tank top that made only a weak effort at containing her upper body. Sweat gathered on her upper lip and across her forehead—despite the cooling winds—and dampened the hair at the edge of her scalp. As if noticing me noticing, she used the back of her arm to wipe it clear.

"As long as I can bring the dog. Never look at art without a critic by your side."

The ceilings were high in the Black Swan, so the third floor was more of a climb than expected. The last leg was up a steep and narrow enclosed staircase that building codes had disqualified fifty years ago. It was a true attic, unfinished and rich in woody mothball smells. Anika asked me to hold Eddie while she put Eloise in a travel case.

"Your dog might be okay with my cat. Not sure about the other way around," she said.

She was gone a few moments, then came back and let me in the door. She flicked on a switch that fired up a bank of bright can lights that exposed a huge canvas running parallel with the ridge of the hotel and standing nearly as high. I voiced my first thought.

"How're you going to get it out of here?"

She walked to the end of the attic and patted the wall.

"Through the gable between these studs. With a crane."

"That's okay with your dad?"

She gave me the same look I got when I suggested she properly prepare for a big storm. A friendly blend of insulted sensibilities and patient tolerance.

"I own half the joint, pal," she said. "It's okay with *us*."

I only half heard her, since I'd already been swept up by the painting itself. It was a rectangular concoction of precisely rendered swirls, each formed by a slightly different palette of colors and shades. Taken as a whole, it was an orderly composition, but as you moved in closer, greater variation was revealed, especially where seemingly separate swirls intersected.

"Interesting," I said.

"Doesn't that usually mean something sucks?"

"No. It means the painting's interesting. I like looking at it."

"You an art lover?" she asked.

"Not exactly. I just like the stuff I like. How did you get half the Swan?"

"Nosy, nosy. Axel and I sold the Subversive stock my father gifted us when we were born, when it wasn't worth so much. The Swan was my idea, so I put my money where my mouth was."

"You're a programmer, too?"

"I did a little as a kid. Nothing like Axel, who was all in. It was the Fey family's version of fun. Other girls played dress-up and went on vacations. I wrote code."

"And painted pictures," I said.

"And painted pictures. Axel joined Subversive. But I found art a better way to express an analytical creation than i's and o's. Left brain, right brain. The only part of me that's in balance."

"Balance is over-rated."

"Maybe by your standards," she said. "I know your whole history. I think imbalanced and out-of-control were two of the more flattering adjectives applied to you."

"Don't believe everything you Google," I said, pointing over at a flat screen monitor hooked up to a CPU.

"You didn't tell me you ran a big lab, and that the lab ran on N-Spock," she said. "You missed out on the later versions. They're a lot more robust."

"Can't say the same for me. My earlier version had a leg up."

"That's not what I see," she said, moving closer. "Design engineers really do it for me."

"Anika," I said, "no go. One woman at a time is complicated enough."

"That's entirely no fun at all."

"You should have thought that through when you marooned yourself on an island."

To punctuate the point, a gust of wind slapped the window at the gable end of the attic. We both looked over.

"It's just a sou'wester," said Anika. "The Swan's been through a lot worse than that."

"I should get back to the boat."

"Next time a girl invites you up to look at her paintings, you'll know what to expect."

Before I could react, she kissed me on the cheek. Her lips were fuller and softer than Amanda's and her smell a rougher sort, though more than pleasant enough. I headed for the staircase and she followed.

Back out on the docks, I could see that conditions had continued to deteriorate. There were now white caps out in West Harbor, which generally meant about fifteen knots of steady wind speed. The breakwater was still holding the worst of it back, but the chop just outside the docks was hardly restrained. I re-checked the dock lines and the placement of fenders around the *Carpe Mañana* and made a few adjustments. There's an unwinnable debate among sailors over where to weather a storm—out of the water, in the water, at a mooring, tied up at a dock, and so on. Unwinnable because you only knew the right answer after your decision proved to be disastrously wrong.

When the light drizzle that had greeted me when I came down from the attic turned to solid rain, I climbed aboard and went below, where Amanda had a late breakfast waiting. She looked a little nervous, but wouldn't admit she was. I ate my food then took Eddie out for what could be the last time for a while. As confirmation, the rain fell harder, now slanted by the force of the wind.

I got us below again as lightning lit up the sky, and a crack of thunder followed seconds later, betraying the lightning's proximity. Eddie had spent the first two years of his life living in the pine barrens of Long Island, a feral dog directly connected to the natural world. I think that explained why he gave little notice to things like thunder and lightning, or heavy rainfall. I couldn't say the same about his human shipmates, as we anxiously battened down the hatches, entombed in the luxurious yellow-lit cherry cabin, hunkered down to wait it out.

CHAPTER 9

There wasn't much to do after that but listen to the roar outside and try to distract ourselves by reading books pulled from the boat's library, pre-stocked with hardbound classics, and playing the calmest music we could find on Amanda's iPod, which was jacked into the boat's sumptuous audio system. Predictably, the shore power flicked off to the accompaniment of a huge blast of lightning and thunder. There was no immediate effect on us, since everything we needed, including the lights, ran off the battery banks. Even with the battery charger off-line, we had at least twenty-four hours of reserves without firing up the engine.

I opened the companionway hatch, which was protected from the rain by the canvas dodger overhead, and looked down the docks at the Swan. With the sun still up it was hard to know for sure, but it was likely the whole neighborhood, if not the island, was off the grid.

Before poking my head outside, I'd turned on the anemometer—the gauge that read wind speed. It was mounted on an instrument array at the helm, so I had to climb into the cockpit to read it. A steady thirty-five knots, or roughly

forty miles per hour, with gusts to fifty. Enough to be uncomfortable, but not so dangerous there at the dock. I examined all the lines—the ones on the windward side were taut
enough to play a bass line, but doubled up as they were,
staunchly held us off the pilings.

I was about to duck back out of the rain when I saw a
guy in full rain gear running toward us down the center passageway. He yelled my name.

"You gotta come with me," said Mr. Two Trees, his dark,
rain-streaked face looking through the tunnel formed by the
hood of his jacket. "It's Poole."

"What happened?"

"You gotta come now. Bring water and blankets. It's bad."

I went below to break the news to Amanda. She took
it as she always did, alarm in her eyes, but her face set in
false equanimity. I ignored Eddie's pleas to come along and
put my foul weather gear over my wet T-shirt and jeans. I
gathered up some blankets and threw several water bottles
into the dry bag. I looked at my cell phone, which had lost
service. I grabbed my handheld VHF radio and turned on
the more powerful version built into the navigation panel.

"Keep it on sixteen, the universal distress channel. Monitor whatever's going on out there, it might include a message from me."

Two Trees was waiting for me in the Swan's parking lot
in his old Toyota.

"Since she's a one-man band out here, so to speak, I like
to check in whenever there's a storm or other emergency,"
he said, gunning the engine and tearing out into the slippery
street. "The cell service is down and I couldn't reach her
on the radio, so I drove over there. Found her on the floor
with the shit kicked out of her. Can't talk. Wrote out how
to fire up auxiliary power, but somebody's taken the generator. Dropped it in the drink is my guess, since her barracks are right there on the ferry channel. Then she wrote

out, 'Get Acquillo at Swan's dock.' Good thing I knew who she meant."

As we drove I tried to reach the mainland with my hand-held, but it didn't have the range.

"I tried all that," said Two Trees. "We need a beefier radio, like the one in Poole's office. Or at the ferry dock, though we'll have to knock down the door, since the pussies are all in New London."

I called Amanda on my handheld. When she came on I told her to switch to channel sixty-eight. Then I asked her to try to reach the coast guard.

"Roger that," she said. "What do I tell them?"

"Poole's been attacked and needs medical attention. If you get the coasties it'd be nice if they brought along another state cop or two."

"I'll only call you back if I get through," she said.

"Got it," I said, signing off. "Any doctors on the island?" I asked Two Trees.

"Not off-season. In July you could staff a hospital off the golf course and yacht club. And the Swan's bar."

As described, Poole's barracks was a small, clapboard-sided building perched high above the mouth of the ferry channel. I was out of the car before Two Trees had it fully stopped and into the little building. Poole was lying on the floor, on her side with her knees drawn up, her soft ringlets spread out on the carpet as if arranged by a stylist. There were blood marks on the floor around her head, her face an unrecognizable mash of cuts and welts.

I dropped to the floor and spoke her name. She opened her eyes. I gently took a small pad of paper out of her hand and checked her pulse. I didn't know what I was checking for, but it seemed neither too fast nor too slow. She pointed to the pad, which I gave back to her. In her other hand was a pen. With both hands pressed closely to her abdomen, she was able to write, "Sit up."

I got one hand under her shoulder, and with the help of Two Trees, pulled her up and turned her so she could lean against the front of her metal desk.

"Who did it?" I asked.

"Didn't see," she wrote. "Cold-cocked from behind."

"How about internal organs?" I asked.

She nodded and wrote, "Gut kicked."

"Does the ferry dock have a generator?"

She shook her head and wrote, "Battery backup for the radio. A day's worth."

I looked at Two Trees, who also nodded before leaving the building.

"Just don't bust him for breaking and entering," I said.

She smiled a tiny smile and shivered. I went back out to the car and retrieved the blankets, draping one over her shoulders. I opened a water bottle and handed it to her. She winced when it touched her swollen lips.

"Any guess at all?" I asked.

She shook her head.

I looked around her office as if some explanation resided there.

"Gun from holster gone. Others locked up," Poole wrote, then wrote the number for the combination lock on a separate sheet and handed it to me.

I touched her sleeve and told her I'd be right back. Then I went outside the building and radioed Amanda, bringing her up to date. I told her I had no idea how long it would take to contact the coast guard or when they could have a boat out to the island.

"Take your time," she said. "We're fine here. Eddie's passed out on his berth and I'm reading *The Sun Also Rises*. Seems appropriate."

I signed off with Amanda and went back in the building. Poole had her head back, resting on the front of the desk. I squatted down next to her and she opened her eyes. She handed me her little pad, on which she'd written, "Take my picture. Camera in desk. Evidence."

I did as she asked, not enjoying the experience. Then I squatted back down and asked her if she felt any worse, and in what way, but she shook her head.

"But I have felt better," she wrote.

I sat down next to her and squeezed the hand holding the pen. She smiled another little smile and nodded her head, and there we sat in silence until Two Trees burst into the building with news that the coast guard was only ten minutes away. It was the same patrol boat that had brought over the knuckleheaded CSI, so he knew exactly where to go. At the captain's request, I tuned my handheld to channel seventy and we discussed docking below Poole's barracks—how and where to tie up lines and how to secure the ladder he'd raise to scale the breakwater.

After the boat arrived, extreme professionalism took over and all I had to do was watch, be impressed and stay out of the way. In a few minutes they had Poole strapped in a rugged rescue stretcher and lowered into the boat. While this was happening, another seaman took statements from me and Two Trees, captured by a video recorder. The only sour note came when I asked about a replacement cop.

"We put in a request to the New York State authorities," said the captain. "They said it would be a day or two before someone could be assigned."

"To protect and serve. When they get around to it. You realize whoever did this is still on this island."

"Noted, sir. We'll try again. The important thing now is to get the police officer to a hospital."

I didn't argue with that, and watched as the muscular little patrol boat spun around in the ferry channel and threw herself back into the clamorous seas.

"Take me to the ferry dock," I said to Two Trees, who drove us down a narrow street between houses built when the country club was still cheap farmland, to a building only slightly larger than the state police barracks. Two Trees led me through the front door, stepping over the glass he'd punched out, and over to the radio room behind the ticket counter. He sat down at the desk and flicked on the radio, which looked like a relic from the Second World War.

"Here's a list of people to hail in case of an emergency," he said, pointing to a printout taped to the instrument panel. "Who do you want to call?"

Since we'd already connected with the coast guard, I picked the Suffolk Police Marine Bureau, under whose jurisdiction the waters surrounding Fishers Island theoretically fell. After a dozen tries on channel sixteen, a voice came back.

"Go to nine."

When I did, the voice told me that all their boats were pinned to the docks, and to call the coast guard. I asked him if there was a state police barracks nearby I could radio. He said if our signal reached JFK airport, I'd have a shot. Presumably the patrol boat captain had relayed the information to them that one of their troopers was down, but I asked the marine bureau guy to do the same. Any engineer will tell you, redundancy rarely hurts.

"I'll pass it along, but no guarantees," said the guy.

"Do what you can. As far as I know this is the only contact we have with the outside world. The power's out, phone and cell service are down, ferries aren't running, and someone's eliminated the only police presence on the island."

After signing off, I tried to extract the ferry dock's radio from where it was mounted on the antique instrument panel, but the wiring was impossibly entangled and indecipherable. So rather than destroy what we had, I left it there and had Two Trees drive me back to the boat, backtracking on the way to retrieve Trooper Poole's cache of weaponry, which consisted of a Remington police shotgun and a pair of Glock 37's.

The beat-up Corolla took the further buffeting from the wind in stride as we drove over narrow roads filled with leafy debris. Large branches and whole trees were down everywhere, but we managed to wind our way through. When we got to the Swan I told Two Trees he could stay if he wanted, presumptuously confident of Anika's largesse—if not her father's—but he said he had to get home to his wife and dog, one of which he was sure would be glad to see him. I started to thank him for what he'd done, but he cut me off.

"You do what you do. Call me if you need a hand with anything," he said, then shooed me out of the car.

The rain had died down a lot, but the wind was still in a fury. I struggled as it caught hold of the Remington and bag of blankets, now laden with the two Glocks and several boxes of ammunition. I could see light through the portholes of the *Carpe Mañana* at the end of the dock, and made for it.

"Oh my," said Amanda when I opened up the companionway and handed her the shotgun.

"It's Poole's. I didn't want to leave it at the barracks. There're also a pair of semi-automatics in with the blankets."

I gave her as thorough a briefing as I could, filling in what I hadn't had a chance to convey already. Then I went back outside with Eddie, who was smart enough to run to the end of the dock, take care of business in the foliage around the Swan, then run back again. This bought us at least another eight hours. Wild dog heritage aside, he seemed happy to get back below where it was dry, lit and equipped with comfy berths and Big Dog biscuits.

"I think I solved the communication problem," said Amanda, handing me my first vodka of the day.

"Oh?"

"You told me to stay on channel sixteen, which I did, mostly. That got boring, so I checked to see what was happening on all those other channels."

"And?"

"There's a lovely retired man who lives in a town called Groton in Connecticut where they apparently make submarines, of all things. He's a radio enthusiast with a very powerful setup. He was chatting with a friend on channel seventy-two, and was gracious enough to allow me to break in. I asked him if he wouldn't mind relaying messages for us, and he was delighted. But then he did one better. He has a way to take our signal and transfer it directly into the phone network. It's a new system that they're beta testing and he's apparently one of their betas."

"This is what happens when you ignore my instructions."

"It is," she said, lifting the handset off the radio. "Who would you like to call?"

The process took a while, which included some friendly back and forth between Amanda and Mr. Berman, the retired radio fanatic, then a few failed tries to make the relay to the telephone interface. But finally we had a dial tone, immediately followed by the sound of Mr. Berman dialing Burton Lewis's cell phone number.

Burton wouldn't usually answer if he didn't recognize the number of the caller, but we caught him in the right mood.

"Who is RadioLink International?" he asked, answering the phone.

"It's me. Sam. Long story I'll make as short as I can."

Which I did while Burton listened to silently.

"What would you like me to do?" he asked, when I wrapped up.

"Lean on whoever could lean on the state police to get a cop on a coast guard boat headed for Fishers as soon as possible."

"I'll do what I can. Do you still want intel on Subversive Technologies?"

I'd almost forgotten about them.

"Yeah. What have you got?"

"I have a report in front of me from one of our analysts. Eighty percent of their revenue flows from the high-volume analytical software N-Spock 4.0, which has a large installed base in industrial, government and academic research labs," he said, reading from the report. "Though dominant, they're feeling intense pressure from competitors who are using more modern platforms to leapfrog over N-Spock's speed and volume limitations. It's the classic software dilemma— keep upgrading your program based on the operating system and hardware you've always used, or scrap the whole thing and jump to the cutting edge. The first option can work if the users are satisfied with the product, and it's a hell of a lot cheaper. On the other hand, investing in a whole new technological approach may be the only way to preserve their base, maintain their brand image and prepare for future competition."

"So what're they going to do?"

"They're working on the next version, N-Spock 5.0, which is said to be based on the absolute latest development principles, which take advantage of the most current processors, web-based applications, cloud computing, fourth- and even fifth-generation programming language, which gets frighteningly close to artificial intelligence."

"They made the investment."

"They're making it. N-Spock 5.0 is over a year late and the rumor is they're stuck. It's only a rumor, since Subversive has done an excellent job keeping a security lid on the project, but if this version fails to launch they're in huge trouble. They become a legacy application, which will take years to dwindle away, providing continued revenue, but their stock price will tank and private equity will flee, meaning the end of the big money flow, and that's what everyone ultimately cares about. It hasn't helped that Christian Fey, the head of development since the founding of the company, has opted out. It's not much of a stretch to interpret that as jumping off a sinking ship."

"Wait till they hear the CFO was found hanging in the shower."

I heard a beep on the line, followed by Mr. Berman.

"Terribly sorry to interrupt, but I've lost power. There's quite a storm going on out there. I only have an hour of reserve power, and have to do an orderly shut-down of all the systems. You understand."

Burton and I talked over each other thanking Mr. Berman for the time we had. He replied with a few equally gracious comments, then unceremoniously cut the line.

Since our entire conversation played on the radio, I didn't have to brief Amanda.

"What are you thinking?" she asked, in the light, seemingly unconcerned tone she often used when she was the most concerned.

"I need another drink."

"The ice won't last forever."

"We'll run the engine and make more."

"Do you think Sanderfreud's death has anything to do with Poole's beating?"

"The word 'death' implies there's a possibility it was an accident or he committed suicide. It was murder."

"Okay, murder," she said. "Is there a connection?"

"I don't know."

"So there could be."

"Yes," I said.

"What kind?"

"We could guess all day, but that's a waste of time. Not enough data to go beyond conjecture."

Amanda didn't challenge that assertion, having heard once too often about the importance of achieving a critical mass of data points in order to reduce the number of thesis-killing variables. She liked that I'd been a technical trouble-shooter at the company before taking over R&D, but her interest in the particulars of the trouble-shooting process wasn't limitless.

"So what are you going to do?" she asked.

"Get more data. After I have this drink."

CHAPTER 10

The clock read 7:30 PM, but it looked like the middle of the night. I brought a little pocket flashlight to guide my way down the center dock and around the side of the Black Swan to the front door. It was open, so I walked in.

There was a glow coming from the bar, along with the burble of voices. I announced myself before entering the room.

"Hey, Sam," said Anika. "What's up?"

The bar was well-lit by dozens of candles. It looked like the whole crowd was there, sitting around the tall bar tables which were covered in drinks and plates of food. Anika was wearing a little black dress and heels. Del Rey, on the other hand, now wore jeans and an oversized men's sweater. Her hair was in a ponytail, which would have revealed her whole face if she hadn't left a tuft of bangs to hang over her forehead and right eye.

't Hooft and Hammon wore short sleeved shirts, Hammon's a supple silk and 't Hooft's a polo with the logo of a Connecticut casino on the chest. Both had muscular arms, attached to contrasting body types. Hammon was all veiny sinew and 't Hooft resembled a long-legged sumo. They sat away from the others at a table with Christian Fey, with whom they were locked in deep conversation when I entered the room.

"Just checking on everyone," I said to Anika. "Heading for the disco?" I added, looking at her outfit.

"I can only get away with this when the lights are low," she said.

I was glad the lights weren't all that low, and would have said so if I hadn't wanted to discourage what that comment might elicit.

"We'd planned on installing a generator," she said. "Just hadn't gotten around to it. How're you on the boat?"

"Fine. Plenty of battery power, and there's the engine. As long as we have fuel, we're good to go."

Axel, who'd been sitting with Del Rey, walked over.

"The worst of the storm is over," he said. "The wind's now dead east, and slipping toward the north. That'll pull in more high pressure air as the storm front moves off the coast."

"And that's your weather report from WAXL, Fishers Island, New York," said Anika.

"She thinks I'm a dork," he said.

"You are a dork. Dorks rule the world."

He smiled. They'd had this exchange before.

"They do," he said, convincingly.

"Sam's a dork himself," said Anika, "he just doesn't want you to know it."

"Hardly ruling the world. Quite the contrary."

"Okay, former dork," she said.

"I could never memorize *pi* beyond a few dozen digits," I said.

Axel looked at his sister.

"I could go on forever if I wanted," he said.

"Good memory," I said.

"I don't memorize, I calculate."

"So why don't you want to, go on forever?" I asked.

"I'm done with the freak show," he said. "It's no different than the boy with two heads, or the bearded lady. They stare at you in horror."

"Axel can do things like tell you which day of the week you were born on. Rain Man stuff," said Anika. "For which people call you an idiot."

"Must come in handy when you're writing software," I said.

"You don't 'write software,' " said Axel, disgusted. "You *develop code*. The words matter. All software is code. It's not a fucking story that you write, like *Alice in Wonderland*."

"Watch the language," said Anika, frowning at Axel.

"You're not a freak, Axel," said Del Rey, joining the conversation. "You're a genius. I heard the whole thing," she said to me. "Got ears like a cocker spaniel."

Axel looked pleased by her defense.

"Chris had him working at Subversive when he was just a little boy," she said. "Ultra-illegal of course, though it's not like child slavery. Axel loved being there. So did Annie," she added, using the long 'a' as in Anika. "We all babysat for them, at work and home. Made it feel like a family business. We were like family," she said, in the insistent way you do when someone had once disputed your assertion.

"A family like in Addams," said Axel.

"Del Rey still works in the shop," said Anika. "She does quality assurance for the boneheads in development. Catches all their screw-ups."

"Not all," she said. "I can be pretty boneheaded myself. Good thing the boss's sleeping with me."

She looked at Anika and Axel as if expecting to be refuted, but they were silent.

"This is the longest I've ever spent in conversation without a drink. Do you still have ice?" I asked Anika.

She smiled at me and strolled over to the bar, narrowly avoiding multiple collisions between her hips and the bar furniture. I got the feeling that little black dress had seen its share of underlit rooms.

"She's so cute," said Del Rey. "And Axel, stop looking. She's your sister."

Axel spun 180 degrees on his bar-stool and folded his arms like a rebellious child. Del Rey shook her head and whispered in my ear, "A mother would've helped."

Anika brought me a vodka on the rocks in a half-gallon cocktail glass. Then we all toasted the Black Swan and its steadfast defiance of inclement weather.

"It got moved off its foundation in '38, so they just dug a new one where she sat," said Anika. "Better than the old. Since then the water-line's risen, so we might be moving her again."

"You call her 'she'—like a ship," said Del Rey. "I like that."

"She might be a ship if the water keeps rising," said Anika.

The conversation from there wandered a bit, as did my attention, which was drawn to the three men in the corner. Even in the candlelight it was clear a serious topic was at hand. Fey and Hammon both leaned out over the table till they were barely a foot from each other's face. 't Hooft sat back a bit, but listened intently.

According to the commentary we read at Gwyneth Jones' place, Derrick Hammon had contributed to the original N-Spock application. But soon after the company was established, he'd moved to the business side, leaving Fey to focus on technology. Sanderfreud had always been the financial guy, which included liaison with public and private investors. Watching the two men bend into their conversation, I wondered how big a hole the oversized Sanderfreud had left in the structure of their relationship.

This thought was interrupted by Anika handing me a stack of plates.

"I know you didn't get any of the food," she said, "but since you're standing there . . ."

I followed her with a large load of used dinnerware down a hall guided only by the penlight I held in my mouth. In the kitchen, lit by dozens of candles and a few electric lanterns, she showed me where to unload.

"There's plenty of tenderloin in the big 'fridge," she said. "We'll only have to throw it out if the power doesn't come on by tomorrow."

"I'm all set."

She handed me another vodka, mysteriously transported in with the dirty dishes. She had a full glass of red wine.

"Tricks of the waitress trade," she said, toasting me.

"Do you know what's going on?" I asked her.

"There's a storm outside?"

"Why Hammon's here. Why Sanderfreud was sent for after Hammon arrived. What he's talking to your father about."

"Now there's a new level of nosiness. No, I don't know any of those things, but I have a guess or two, which are none of your business."

"It's about N-Spock 5.0," I said. "They're not ready to launch in January and they need your father's help. Or advice. Or something."

"How would you know that?" she asked.

"I'm not a professional interpreter of body language, but Hammon looked like he was trying to press a point and your father looked like he was resisting. He shook his head ten times to every one of Hammon's."

"Were you really innocent, or did you kill that guy in Southampton?"

"Googling are we?" I asked. "Nice try, but I'm impervious to distractions."

"Oh yeah?" she asked, taking one of the shoulder straps of the little black dress and slipping it over her shoulder, causing most of the supported breast to come into view.

"I didn't kill him," I said. "The real killer confessed. That's a settled matter. Did Axel work on N-Spock 5.0?"

She frowned and pulled the strap back over her shoulder. "My brother's off-limits."

"Jennifer Poole, the state police trooper who was investigating Myron's hanging was beaten nearly to death today. The coast guard had to evacuate her off the island, leaving us without a local police presence. In a storm. Poole was convinced Sanderfreud was murdered. Don't pretend you aren't sophisticated enough to grasp all the implications."

She cleared a space to sit on the counter where we'd dumped the dirty dishes. It took a couple hops, restrained by the tight dress, but eventually she made it. I leaned against the opposite wall and nursed the vat of vodka.

Anika used her fingers to brush back her shiny black hair.

"My father created N-Spock and knew everything there was to know about the application. But as you well know, the people who create things are rarely the ones who benefit financially from their creativity. That goes to the people who buy and sell their work. The business people, the money people. Still, my father is a rich man, richer than he needs to be to live the way he wants. So what's the point in being some asshole's workhorse for the rest of your life? Why not get out while you can still enjoy the fruits of your labor? That's what he did."

"Obviously not out far enough," I said.

"You'd have to ask him about that. He's still my father. Only tells me what he wants to tell me."

I downed most of the heroic glass of vodka, and put the glass on the counter.

"I need to get back to the boat. If you need me for anything, don't hesitate."

"You realize the irony in that statement."

I crossed the distance between us and kissed her on the cheek, then left the hotel by the French doors in the back.

It was still tempestuous, but true to Axel's prediction, the corner was turned. The part of me on edge because of the storm let go, filling me with a soothing calm. Looking back on the Swan, it was still dark and uneasy. Ahead, the portholes of the *Carpe Mañana* were aglow, and I caught just the hint of movement aboard, probably Amanda fussing around the cabin, fixing up plates of unannounced delectables, scrunching around Eddie's sensitive jowls and otherwise enjoying an existence that was far from predestined and the source of constant revelation.

I headed in that direction.

The next morning was sharp and brilliant as the edge of a razor. At 7:00 AM the sky was a deep blue, cloudless and unperturbed. For some reason, the wind had missed the memo, and was still blowing with unabated wrath. I'd seen this before with autumn storms, beautiful deceptive killers.

I pulled myself out of the quarter berth and checked the instrument panel. Shore power was still out, but the batteries were barely tapped. I flicked on the gas valve and fired up the stove for coffee. When I poured the boiling water into the plastic French press, over a mound of Costa Rican select, Amanda stirred.

"Could you pour some of that down my throat?" she asked.

For Eddie, the smell of coffee portended a different experience. He waited patiently at the bottom of the stairs that led up to the companionway while I put on whatever clothes were within reach. Now familiar with his surroundings, he made a beeline to a cluster of hydrangea at the back of the Swan, into which he disappeared just long enough to take care of things, then ran back down the center dock.

Back on board, I used the radio to check the NOAA weather report, which foretold a slow decline in wind speed during the day, with the promise of gentle winds tomorrow.

The storm was all but over.

We celebrated with a large breakfast, recklessly depleting our provisions on the assumption that we'd be shopping at the Southampton delis long before we ran out of food.

I dug the dinghy and related equipment out of the deep lazarettes and put it all back together again. After that I took Eddie over to the pebble beach so he could run around for a while and get out the kinks. I brought my coffee with me, which I would have enjoyed more with a cigarette, but I'd quit, for the second time in my life. The first time was when I was around twenty-five, never having quite acquired the habit. In those days I was trying to sustain a career as a professional boxer, and the training was hard enough with clear lungs. I took up smoking again about twenty-three years later, the day I lost my job, left my home and wife, lost all my money and essentially burned my life to the ground. Adding a deadly habit didn't seem like such a big deal at the time.

Things had improved since then. The route had been circuitous, but I was better for the trip. When I was living on the bottom of a ditch, self-reflection had seemed a meaningless endeavor, so I sought a blank calm, an unknowingness that would decouple waking consciousness from all that aching sadness and regret. To maintain this state of mind in the face of undeniably improved well-being seemed churlish and vain.

Instead, I'd begun to count blessings the way I once catalogued guilt and remorse. While not what most people would consider an ideal romance, Amanda and I had found an equilibrium capable of sustaining the relationship. We lived together at the end of a peninsula, albeit in separate houses. We were both in the building trades, though in separate ways—she a general contractor and me a journey-man carpenter and cabinetmaker. She tolerated the few friends I'd made (with the exception of Burton Lewis, whom she adored), and they tolerated her, but she never begrudged time spent with them and I never asked about times away from me, frequent occasions that were unannounced and rarely explained.

I knew from my daughter Allison that some of these episodes involved the two of them cavorting around New York City. This constituted the greatest and most mysterious blessing of all. Allison had spent the first twelve years of her life trying to engage my attention, exerting the full force of her yearning will, and yielding the most meager of returns. She'd spent the next twelve, give or take, hating me for it, an inclination aided, abetted and reinforced at every opportunity by her mother. I got to it late, and only when there was almost nothing left of my life, but we'd more or less brought our relationship back from the dead. But then to have her magically connect with Amanda was astounding.

And I'd lived to see it, an outcome that was far from an eventuality. In fact, on several occasions the odds were heavily weighted the other way. So whatever time I had left I decided to treat as a bonus, out of respect for which I'd make some effort to support the cause.

CHAPTER 11

I didn't have the heart to put Eddie back on the leash, but we were still in an untested environment. So I compromised by forcing him to heel, something he would do if convinced I really meant it. A few carefully chosen words were usually all it took.

Thus configured, we were nearly at the boat when I heard someone running up from behind. It was Anika.

She gripped my arm with both hands and said, "I'm not ready to panic yet."

"Over what?"

"I can't seem to locate Axel."

"Does he like to disappear?" I asked.

"No. That's sort of the point. He likes to cling."

"What about your dad?"

"He's pretending to be unconcerned, but he took off in the car a few minutes ago to search the roads. I've already looked all over the hotel and around the Harbor Club. I don't think Axel's been anywhere else on the island by himself."

"It's not that big an island," I said.

"Big enough. Though he can't get lost. He has a map of the place in his head."

"We could report a missing kid, but there's no one to report to."

"Technically, he's not a kid. He turned eighteen last month. Of course, if you say he's autistic, there's no problem. As if he's retarded or something, which he's anything but. I hate that label."

I pulled her along to the boat as we talked so I could deliver Eddie to Amanda. I asked Anika to wait for me, and went below to explain things.

"What's next?" said Amanda. "Are you going to lead the local militia against an invading horde?"

"You remember how to start the engine and drive the boat?" I asked.

"I do. Why?" she asked, stretching 'why' into two syllables.

I pulled a detailed chart of Fishers Island out of the navigation table.

"We're here," I said, pointing to the waterway beyond the breakwater. "Up here on the eastern shore of West Harbor, there's this little lagoon. The charts tell you it's too shallow for our draft, but that's not true if you follow this course."

I used a pencil to draw a route from the Inner Harbor, through the breakwater, around a buoy and a cluster of rocks, and then through the narrow inlet, favoring the southern shore.

"I've been there with Burton on a bigger boat than this. I've been tucking in there since I was a kid. It's part of a big estate and there's nothing on shore, no access roads or houses."

"Why are you telling me all this?" she asked.

"Unless I radio and say to head straight for New London, this is our best bet. Don't make a big deal of it, just start the engine, untie the lines and slip away. I'll tie the dinghy off on the dock before I go, and meet you there as soon as I can."

"You'll never stop scaring the hell out of me."

"I'm just getting started," I said, pulling the shotgun out of the hanging closet. "Ever used one of these?"

Before I gave her a lesson, I poked my head out of the companionway and reassured Anika I was coming. She had her arms clenched across her chest, holding herself. She said to meet her back at the hotel and to take my time, though she didn't mean that last part.

Down below Amanda was staring incredulously at the Remington's long black barrel. As I loaded it, I gave her the essentials of safety and proper use. I don't like guns, and have never owned one. But as a young mechanical engineer, I'd made a study of their inner workings.

"With a shotgun, you don't have to be a very good shot. Just aim the barrel in the general direction and pull the trigger. Try to stay on your feet. This model has a reduced recoil so a cop can get off a few shots at a time, but it still has plenty of kick."

"You're saying this as if it's going to happen," she said.

"Better to be ready."

"For what?"

"I don't know, but we're in the realm of three."

"The realm of three?"

"A term coined by a guy who taught me how to trouble-shoot process applications. Two simultaneous coincident failures could easily be unrelated. The likelihood of coincidence drops dramatically after you hit three. Sanderfreud is killed. Poole beat up. Now Axel's missing. All in a short period of time. It's got my attention."

Amanda and I had been through a lot together, so she wasn't completely unfamiliar with moments like these. Though past events never involved sailboats, hidden lagoons or pump-action shotguns. Or beautiful young artists.

"This will make Anika happy, "said Amanda.

"Her happiness isn't my concern," I said.

"It isn't?"

We stood and looked at each other, stopped in our tracks by a topic neither of us had ever broached.

"It's not like that," I said.

"When you asked me what I thought was going on at the Swan, I almost told you that Anika was trying to seduce you, but thought better of it. You might realize it, or you might not. You can be pretty oblivious about that sort of thing."

She was right about that, having little experience with the romantic dance. But this time, Anika had left little room for ambiguity. None, actually, which I shared with Amanda.

"I've never asked you to be faithful," said Amanda, her voice stripped of inflection, "and I won't now. I just don't want to feel like a fool."

"I have no intention," I started to say, but she stopped me by putting her fingertips on my lips.

"Don't say it. I know your intentions are good. But things happen. Let's leave it there."

I didn't want to, but she stuck the backpack in my hands and hustled me up the companionway. I knew her well enough to leave without further protest.

I tied the dinghy off under the dock with a mixture of confidence and dread. There were no guarantees Amanda could drift off unnoticed, or that I hadn't been seen separating the dinghy, or that either of us wouldn't be followed, but since I had no reason to think any of these things would happen, it felt reasonable to ignore unsubstantiated fears, which I almost did.

Christian Fey was pulling his Mercedes station wagon into the hotel parking area as we reached the end of the dock. The car jerked to a stop, a small cloud rising around the wheels where they dug into the sandy gravel. His normally placid face was alight with angry worry. I hung back when Anika approached him so I didn't hear what they said to each other, but it was clear she was pushing him hard and he was fighting back. When he saw me standing there, he walked over.

"I don't know why my daughter involved you in this," he said. "I appreciate your concern, but it's a simple family matter."

"I sure get a lot of appreciation on this island and not much else," I said. "Has your son done this before?"

Fey shook his head, then stopped himself.

"Really, Mr. Acquillo," he said. "We don't need your help."

"It's Sam, and yes you do. Where're the boys and girls from Subversive Technologies?"

"They said they were going sightseeing."

"That's a short morning's work. I don't suppose you'll tell me what's really going on," I said.

Fey's quizzical look was almost convincing.

"What do you mean?" he asked.

"Quit the bullshit. Hammon and 't Hooft aren't here to go bird watching. Something's going on with Subversive that caused them to make a surprise visit. Something big enough to drag in Sanderfreud. They want something from you, but so far the trip hasn't paid off too well."

Fey struck an imperious pose of a type only a European can achieve. Chin up, lips pursed, hauteur leaking out of every pore.

"You seem to know an awful lot for a boat deliveryman," he said.

"I watched you guys in the bar last night. My dog could have figured that one out."

"Sam used to be senior vice president for R&D at Consolidated Global Energies. The third largest hydrocarbon processor in the world," said Anika, "before they imploded. Not his fault. He was long gone."

To his credit, Fey shook that off, though the tenor of the conversation took a different turn.

"Buyouts are always messy things," he said. "We're still haggling over silly details."

"I don't believe you," I said. I could feel Anika stiffen, the reaction communicated across three feet of breezy Long Island Sound air. "Not that it's any of my business. But I might be able to help you out if you let me in on it."

He glowered at me, his hands on his hips, his broad shoulders squared off. Anika reached out and took his forearm.

"If you don't," she said to him, in a soft, firm voice, "I will."

Suddenly distracted, Fey looked over my shoulder toward the Inner Harbor.

"Isn't that your boat?" he asked.

I didn't bother to turn around.

"Amanda has to get back to Southampton. She's leaving *Carpe* in New London. I'll take the ferry over and pick up the boat when I can. Your daughter said I could have a room."

Anika nodded, even though this was news to her.

Fey did his best to maintain a manly resistance, but something about seeing Amanda float away undermined his resolve.

"Come inside," he said to me. "I need a cup of tea."

We went into the woody darkness of the Swan's lobby, then through the sitting room and out to the dining area that overlooked the docks, the brightest part of the building. Fey went into the kitchen to get the tea while Anika and I waited at a round table. I started to ask her a question, but she cut me off and pointed toward the kitchen.

"Let him tell you," she said. "It'll be good for him."

So I kept quiet until we each had our teacups and saucers in front of us. Of all the beverages I might pick to drink at any moment, regular tea would barely make the list.

"So how does this work?" I asked.

Anika helped me through the mechanics, which I found ridiculously more complicated than building a simple cup of coffee, though I kept my criticism at a minimum.

"Didn't drinking tea cause the fall of the British Empire?"

Despite the aspersions, the first sip seemed to calm Anika and Christian alike. The elder Fey leaned his head back and closed his eyes.

"Children are the best and worst thing that can happen to a person," he said, opening his eyes.

"Not sure how to take that one," said Anika.

"There's no better example than Axel. A mind like a Formula One race car with the maturity of a go cart."

"Interesting metaphor," I said.

"Thank you. I've used it before. With the therapists who've tried to help me cope with this delectable dichotomy. With the constant joy and sorrow."

"That's great, Dad. How're we going to find him?" said Anika.

"Maybe we're *not*," he said, his voice rising several decibels above appropriate.

Anika sat back in her seat, both hands turning her teacup, her eyes frustrated and patient, fixed on her father.

"Did you say something to him? Do something to him?" she asked, her voice low, but firm.

Fey looked down and shook his head.

"I've barely spoken to him since Hammon and his minions arrived. And even if I had, he's not that sensitive. Lord knows," he said, looking over at Anika for confirmation. She nodded her head.

"Another blessing and a curse," she said to me.

"How much did Axel contribute to N-Spock 5.0?" I asked.

The Feys looked at each other.

"He helped around the edges," said Fey.

"So what's the problem?" I asked. "Why the delay?"

The two Feys sat back in their chairs as if pulled by invisible strings. Anika crossed her legs and Christian folded his hands in his lap. They looked at each other, then back at me, then back at each other.

"We don't know," said Christian, finally.

"Yes we do," said Anika. "They can't transfer essential data from the existing version into 5.0. What they don't know is why."

Fey was unhappy, but couldn't resist further explanation.

"Let's pretend you're still running your lab and you're on N-Spock 4.0," he said. "You have a vast—too small a word—a galactic amount of data that you'll need to transfer when you upgrade to 5.0. For some reason, when they try to do this in beta test, it gets three quarters of the way through and then suddenly turns chaotic and the whole program crashes. This doesn't happen with fresh data, only during the mass conversion of an existing database. Therefore, they can prove the program is light-years ahead of anything they developed in the past, or any competitor could conceive of today, but when they try to make a legitimate conversion, the application blows itself up. And it's not a virus, or a glitch you can isolate and reverse. It's in the body of the code itself. Inextricably intertwined."

"Who wrote the code?" I said.

After a long pause, Anika nodded toward Fey.

"My father owns the heart of N-Spock. The other developers, Axel included, just played around with the fingers and toes."

"And it can't be reverse engineered," I said.

"No. Impossible. They don't call it code for nothing," said Fey. He turned to me. "You didn't tell us you had experience with N-Spock. I probably sounded quite haughty."

"I'm a private person, Mr. Fey," I told him. "What you might have said to me is my problem, not yours."

It was my turn to sit back in my chair and take a sip of tea, but I could barely get the stuff down my throat.

"What's the Swan's policy on coffee?" I asked Anika.

She smirked at me, and left for the kitchen.

"Is that why they were all here, Hammon and 't Hooft, and Sanderfreud? To pressure you to solve the problem?" I asked.

Fey sat in the chair with his elbows resting on his knees, his eyes staring down at the carpet.

"Hammon and I had a fundamental disagreement on how to migrate to 5.0. He had this notion we could fast-track the development process, his terms, leaving out crucial testing and documentation phases. He based this foolishness on our prior transitions from 1.0 to 4.0, not appreciating that these were refinements of our base code, not the ground-up creation of a new application, which needed all new underlying systems, hardware, servers and networks—the technological superstructure people like Hammon disdain, not understanding the challenge in coordinating such vast complexity and still making it look preordained."

"I thought he helped create the original N-Spock."

Fey huffed.

"He had the good sense or good luck to support my ideas, which were unproven in those days. And the chutzpah to convince people like Myron to come aboard and help sell investors. His reputation for technical prowess was a creation of the media, which Hammon never disavowed. I didn't care, as long as I was given the resources needed to establish proof of concept. Which I did with C-Scale, our first commercially viable program. That paved the way for N-Spock."

"So are they blaming problems with 5.0 on you?" I asked.

His smile held little humor.

"Who else can they blame? It's my program at the core. Except that they didn't let me design it the way I wanted to. Now they think I can wave a magic wand and make the problem go away. Can't be done."

As I listened to him, a certain perverse pleasure competed with an anxious twist in my guts, a genuine reaction to phantoms of my past. I knew exactly what he meant and its significance. I'd lived the experience daily, battling people with power over me who had no grasp of the sensitive interdependence of millions of variables, the most important of which was the arch of time. Certain things have to be done thoroughly and in the right order. I knew now what Fey had been arguing, and why his position was anathema to Hammon. The only solution to curing N-Spock was to start at the beginning and essentially rewrite the code, this time applying the proper testing protocols at each stage before moving on to the next. Not going to happen in the next three months.

I shared with Fey what I was thinking, including a few examples from my own experience. He nodded, his posture softening, aware now that I was part of the brotherhood.

"So you know. Speaking truth to power is child's play compared to speaking common sense to the willfully ignorant," he said.

Anika came out of the kitchen with a mug and a small carafe of coffee, her face creased with worry. I was reminded of how I came to be sitting there.

"Had Axel been acting strangely in any way in the last few days?" I asked her.

She shook her head.

"No, but he might have been thinking strangely. Thinking and acting are two different things with Axel. I also hadn't spoken with him very much since our guests showed up. There was so much going on, I was distracted."

I'd never been a cop myself, but I knew a few of them, for better or worse. One of them was even a friend, of sorts, a guy named Joe Sullivan of the Southampton Town police.

I knew what he would do when he had to find someone without a single clue as to where they were. He'd get off his ass and start looking.

"Do you folks have a VHF radio?" I asked.

"Of course," said Fey.

"Monitor channel sixteen, if you can," I said. "Can I borrow your car?"

Fey put the keys to the Mercedes in my palm. Anika took my bag and gave me a key to one of the rooms. I went out into the wind, which might have calmed, but it didn't feel like it. The sky was a deep blue, with the only clouds a few puffballs racing overhead.

I walked over to the gas station on the other side of the yacht club. Track was in the grimy office, his feet up on the desk and his nose stuck in a soft-core men's magazine. The walls surrounding him were covered in calendars, notices, self-made ads for local services, ferry schedules going back to the prior century, and posters supporting products that were once new, but now largely forgotten.

"Ever clean this place up?" I asked. "It stinks in here."

He looked up from the magazine, but kept his feet on the desk.

"Maybe I could use your face as a mop."

"When was the last time you saw Axel Fey?"

"Who wants to know?"

"He's missing. His family is worried. It wouldn't kill you to do a favor."

"Wouldn't help me, neither. They'll be gone by next season," he said.

"Okay, why not pretend you're a regular human being and help them find an innocent kid."

"A whack-job kid. I haven't seen him since that guy was hanging in the shower. The kid don't come outside much. Afraid of the sun. Not like his sister, who's out all the time, which is the only good thing about having those foreigners around."

"Who owns this gas station?" I asked. "Can't be you."

This disturbed him.

"None of your business."

"I can find out in five minutes once the power comes back on. Why not just tell me?"

"Fuck you," he said, almost cheerfully.

I thanked him for his valuable time, and went across the street to where a pair of houses sharing a common driveway were built into a hill. One had a car in the driveway, so I picked that one to knock on the door. A tall, thin, stately looking guy answered. This impression was enhanced by where he stood on his screened-in front porch, a tall riser-height above me.

"Yes?" he said.

"Do you know Axel Fey, the teenaged kid who lives in the Swan?" I asked, jerking my head in the direction of the hotel.

"Not personally," he said, "but I know who the people are."

"He's gone missing. You didn't happen to see him last night or this morning outside the hotel, maybe walking down the street?"

"I did," the guy said, "early this morning, about six, walking down the street. I was eating breakfast here on the porch."

"No kidding. Which way did he go?"

He pointed toward the east, away from the public end of the island toward the private country club.

"As you can see, the road curves right after the Black Swan, so I have no idea where he went from there."

Ah, I thought. This is why Sullivan keeps harping on the value of routine police work. All you have to do is ask and people will just give you the information.

"What was he wearing? Was he carrying anything?"

The guy thought about it.

"He wore a backpack, I think, though I may be wrong since all young people wear backpacks. You're the one with the dog and the custom sloop. Has a lovely sheer. I race little boats myself. Hereshoff Bullseyes. Too lazy to cruise. Where have you put her?" he added, looking out across the Inner Harbor, much of which you could see from his elevated location, though not past the breakwater to my secret lagoon, much to my relief.

"My girlfriend took her back to the mainland. Had to get home and the ferry's not running."

"Must have been a rather raucous voyage."

"Not for her. She loves that stuff."

I was about to leave him, when I had another thought.

"Do you know who owns the gas station across the street?"

"That would be Desi Arness. Of course, there isn't much on the island he doesn't own."

"Really. Does Lucy know about this?"

He spelled Desi's name.

"The Arness family has had an estate here since the mid-1800's. With a first name like Luther, the nickname was inevitable. Damn fine sailor. He bought the fuel dock to prevent development next to the yacht club. Would have bought the Swan if the prior owners hadn't detested him, unfairly I might add. That donnybrook in the bar was not his fault, inebriated though he was. I told them that myself, though my own condition during the occasion might not have served my credibility."

"Do you think Desi might be around?" I asked.

"He's never not around. He's lived on the island his whole life. Third generation to do so. Though you won't get to see him unless he wants to see you. Very friendly chap, but keen on his privacy."

He used the British pronunciation of the word 'privacy'—a pretension so effortlessly delivered that it felt entirely sincere.

"So you, too?" I asked. "Year-'rounder?"

"Since retirement. Wharton, professor of economics. This was my parents' home. I don't go as far back as Desi, so as you can see, my privacy is of less concern."

I got the feeling the professor was actually a little lonely, comfortable as he seemed standing there in the doorway being interrogated by a complete stranger. He had wavy, dark-grey hair that spread from a hairline starting about mid-scalp, and a weather-beaten face. It wasn't hard to see him bending to the pull of a long-handled tiller, or standing in front of a classroom full of über-capitalists.

"Sam Acquillo," I said, sticking out my hand.

"John Featherstone," he said, accepting the hand-shake. "If I see the young chap again, I'll let you know. You're a friend of the Feys?"

"I'd like to think so."

After leaving Featherstone, I drove down the road to the next house and knocked on the door. No answer. The same was true of the next three houses. At the fourth house, a young mother said through a crack in the door and over screeching children that she hadn't seen anyone go by her house that morning.

I realized I hadn't thought to bring along a photograph of Axel Fey. Some cop I'd make. I thought about going back to the Swan to get one, but decided to press on. Despite my reverence for disciplined methodology, backtracking was something I was never any good at.

The next two hours of door-to-door activity yielded nothing. Most of the houses were empty, and the people in the others were no help. As I reached various intersections, I chose a route that took me in the direction of Gwyneth

Jones' place. When I got there she was in the yard with her bulldog, looking up at the sky.

"What's your prediction?" I asked.

"Clear for a day or two, then there's another wingdinger headed this way."

"Do you see the signs?"

"No, I hear the marine forecast from those dunderheads at NOAA. But I think this time they're right."

"How come?" I asked.

"I see the signs."

I asked her if she'd seen Axel Fey, describing him as best I could. She regretted telling me no.

"Tell me more about him," she said. So I did, in detail, not sparing his family's privacy. She listened carefully, then shook her head.

"I'm thinking runaway, and I'm thinking there're a few dozen houses within easy walking distance that're empty and at least somewhat stocked with things you can eat."

"That's what I'm thinking," I said. "Axel's no survivalist, so forget the woods. He'd be one to find a comfortable location and hole up. Without a cop on the island, we can hardly search house-to-house."

"What do you mean, no cop?"

I told her about Trooper Poole and my efforts to secure a replacement. She looked very unhappy.

"This doesn't happen here," she said. "No matter how ornery or mental we can get over the winter, the state cop is untouchable. I like that woman. Reminds me of my mother. No nonsense. What happened to your pretty girlfriend?"

"She had to go. Took the boat over to New London and caught the big ferry home."

She seemed to ponder that for a moment.

"Lovely hands for a rough-water sailor," she said.

"It's all in the gloves."

I asked her to keep her eyes out for Axel and to tell her friends and neighbors to do the same. I was about to continue on when Hammon's Town Car pulled up behind me. He and 't Hooft both got out.

"Fey just told us about Axel," said Hammon. "Any luck?"

He looked genuinely concerned, though I didn't know him well enough to judge how genuine.

"Not so far. All I know is he headed east after leaving the Swan at about six this morning."

"Helluva thing. Kooky kid," said Hammon, more exasperated than angry. "We need to call the cops."

"Cop," I said. "Can't do that now. She's indisposed."

"Fine time for that," said Hammon. "So what do we do now?"

"Drive around and look," I said. "I'll go east, you go west. The odds are just as good that he went that way after hitting the first intersection. I'm banging on doors and looking for witnesses, but that's a personal decision. You do what you want."

Hammon nodded and looked around Gwyneth's front yard, trying to make sense of the buoyant eccentricity.

"Interesting," he said.

"Not to the enlightened," she said.

"Of course," said Hammon, as he and 't Hooft climbed back into the big, black Ford and swooped off down the narrow, light-dappled street.

"Hoodlums?" she asked.

"Entrepreneurs," I said. "Close enough."

CHAPTER 12

I drove around, knocked on doors, refined my presentation till I was bored with it, and got nowhere. When I started hearing from people that two other strangers in a Town Car had already asked the same questions, I gained some confidence that Hammon meant what he portrayed—the legitimate concern of a family friend.

I soldiered on until dusk, after which it seemed imprudent to further test the xenophobia of the island's residents. As I drove back to the Swan, I was cheered by the sight of lighted windows, however sparsely distributed. The Swan itself was lit up from stem to stern, as if celebrating the return to normalcy. I parked the Mercedes out front next to Hammon's Lincoln. The hood was hot to the touch, so he'd only beaten me home by a few minutes.

Inside the hotel there was no one to be found until I checked the rear patio, where everyone had assembled. The evening was cool, but after the stormy mess of the last few days, I could understand the impulse to get outside. Strings of white Christmas lights hung above the tables helped the atmosphere, though the main work was done by the floods up under the eaves. A rolling tray had been filled with cold snacks and another held beverages, among which I was delighted to count a bottle of Absolut.

Expectant faces turned toward me as I walked between the tables, but I quickly shook my head.

"No dice," I said. "How 'bout you guys?" I asked Hammon.

"Nothing," he said. "A few people in town reported seeing a teenager or two, but they were likely locals. Tomorrow we need to pass out copies of his photograph."

Two great minds, same thought.

"Do you think he's still on the island?" asked Del Rey. "I mean, he could've grabbed a boat and gone ashore."

"That's certainly true," said Hammon. "As I could have grabbed a rocket and flown to the moon."

"Axel can't swim," said Fey. "He's afraid of the water."

"Oh, yeah," said Del Rey. "I forgot that."

I helped myself to the vodka and sat down next to Hammon. His slight, spidery frame looked ill at ease in repose, as if anything less than soaring flight was inherently unnatural. His long fingers rotated his cocktail glass in quarter turns. He looked over at me with a look both curious and bored.

"Fey tells us you're an N-Spock aficionado," he said.

"That's not exactly it," I said. "I used to run an R&D shop that used the application. Back when you were only at 2.5. We liked it."

"That's nice to hear," he said, though not quite bowled over by the niceness of it all. "How many users in your operation?"

"About a thousand. More if you count Lucerne and Dubai. I had a woman who kept track of it all. The point for me was what the computers did, not necessarily how they did it."

"That big," he said. "What was the company?"

"Con Globe. The late and great. I would have thought the Feys had told you."

"Oh," he said, his cool poise slightly undone. "They were one of our largest customers. I sold it in myself."

"I wouldn't know," I said, taking a casual sip of my drink. "I left that sort of thing to procurement."

His fingers stopped spinning the drink and started tapping on the table.

"The successor company has yet to sign up for 5.0," he said. "Know anyone there?"

"Not anymore, but I know a few guys at East End Building Supply. I'll put in a good word."

"Amusing."

He went back to looking around the hotel grounds.

"Any guesses on Axel?" I asked. "You knew the kid when he was growing up."

"Not really. Del Rey and Sanderfreud took an interest, but I'd rather play golf. If I wanted a pet I'd get a goldfish."

Del Rey's face tightened up and she got out of her chair and left.

Charmed as I was by him, when I saw Anika enter the patio I thought I should join her. I excused myself and caught her at the drink trolley. I asked how she was doing.

"I'm too shook-up to know," she said.

"Any theories? About Axel?"

"I'm too shook up for that, too. You might think all the scary excitement would have driven him away, but that's not Axel. The more anxiety he feels, the closer to home he wants to be. I was surprised he hadn't just locked himself up in his room, though with the power out, there wasn't much he could do in there."

"No computer."

"Sometimes I wonder if computers made him the way he is. It's all he's known for his whole life. The digital environment is his natural habitat, the only place he's utterly at home."

A good case could be made for that, once I thought about it. A motherless child with a distant computer genius for a father, socially isolated, slightly agoraphobic, touched by savantism—who could know where cause and effect started and stopped.

"I still don't own a PC," I said. "Though I've tried out a few. I can see the appeal. And the seduction for information junkies."

"It's more than that," she said. "When you write the code, you don't just process information, you control it, and by extension, the people who use it. You rule over the thinking and behavior of anyone ensnared in your application. You own their minds."

She said this so calmly, so matter-of-factly, that I almost missed it. She looked up at me, as if suddenly aware that I hadn't.

"That sounded horrid. Sorry. I'm only trying to explain what it's like to be Axel. Lost in the delusions of computer-land."

The lights that lit the patio from above spread enough to render the docks beyond in a colorless outline of piers and walkways. I could see all the way to where the *Carpe Mañana* had been docked. The empty space gave me a fearful little jolt. Once again, I excused myself, and walked back out to the street where I could radio Amanda without being overheard.

This strategy wasn't fully realized, since Del Rey was out on the lawn smoking a cigarette. Her left arm held her midriff and supported her right, and one hip was slightly cocked, locking her in place.

"Sorry about Derrick," she said when she saw me approach. "He can be a creep sometimes."

"Sometimes?"

"I can't think like that if I have to live with him," she said.

"You don't have to. The world's a big place."

"I used to believe that. Now the world's shrunk down to peanut-sized. No big career. No youth. No kids, no family."

She took a deep pull off the cigarette.

"You made it sound like the Feys were family. It must have been tough when they moved away," I said.

She brushed her hair with the back of her arm, the cigarette in her hand trailing smoke like a festive ribbon. I breathed it in through my nose.

"The kids, yeah. Christian's no big treat. Got the sense of humor of a tree stump. And zero parenting skills, which worked out for me, since I got to have so much quality time with Anika and Axel. Like a maiden aunt, though that's okay. Better than nothing."

"Sounds like you weren't the only one who chipped in."

"Myron was always eager to look after them, even though he had a daughter of his own. Bought things for them, took them to the park, out to eat, that kind of thing. Grace didn't like it so much, so a lot of the looking-after happened at the office. Or on his boat. He kept a little day sailer on a lake nearby. Anika loved it, but Axel stayed with me on those days. Afraid of the water. Myron was such a good man. I can't understand why he'd want to kill himself."

"You think that, too?" I asked. "I don't get it."

She leaned in toward me so I'd hear her lowered voice.

"Things aren't so peachy keen at Subversive these days. It weighed on him really bad. All he'd done was green light 5.0, but when things started going haywire, he took it all so personal. He kept it all bottled up inside and put on a good front. But I knew, because he talked to me."

"Having the kids move away must have been hard on him, too."

She shook her head, impatiently, then dropped the exhausted cigarette on the ground and toed it to extinction.

"Right about the time Anika hit puberty she totally rejected poor Myron, and for some reason, got attached to me. You know how teenaged girls get. She went from talking to Myron every day to ignoring him completely. I don't think she even saw him again until he showed up here. Axel had to go along, too. I asked him, 'What's up with Anika and Myron?' But he didn't know."

"And he didn't have a say?" I asked.

She responded with thinly veiled ridicule.

"Axel doesn't take a pee-pee without Anika's permission."

"Headstrong girl," I said.

"Worse than that," she said, then seemed to regret it. "Don't get me wrong," she said, touching me on the arm to make sure I was listening carefully. "I love her, like a daughter. Which she's been to me."

"I've got a daughter of my own, so no reason to explain," I said.

"Good," she said. "So you understand."

With that she left me and went back to her peanut-sized world, a swirl of mystified disappointment following in her wake. I watched until she disappeared into the shadows and pulled out the VHF.

"Hello," said Amanda, returning my hail. "Nice to hear your voice. Scratchy and garbled though it may be."

"So you made it."

"It's a lot choppier in West Harbor than it looks from back there. But yes, we made it fine. Cute little spot. No lights anywhere around. And now that the wind's down, the water's like glass. I pulled the shades and just have one little lantern going. Eddie and I swam to shore. The water's actually quite warm. He found a tennis ball. We brought it back to the boat. He's so proud."

I told her about meeting Professor Featherstone and my fruitless canvas of the west end of Fishers Island. She asked me what I asked Anika—any theories on Axel?

"It's pretty sure he left on his own, which is contrary to his normal behavior. He's a house cat, but a very smart one. Other than that, there's too much I don't know."

I gave her a rundown on the status of Subversive Technologies and the status of N-Spock 5.0. Amanda was a patient woman, never more evident than in the way she listened to me when I'd launch into an intricate tale of technological imbroglio. Mindful of that, I trimmed the story to its essence.

"I have no idea what you're talking about, but it sounds problematic," she said.

"It is," I said, then asked if everything was okay on the boat. She mentioned a few things, which I talked her through, adding some additional advice and gentle cautions. She complimented my attention to operational detail and asked me if I'd be returning to the boat, or should she be researching funeral options. And if there was a will.

"Whatever it takes for Eddie to live out his life on Oak Point. The rest goes to my daughter."

"You're not kidding, are you."

"I never kid a kidder."

◆

After signing off with Amanda, I spent a while walking around the hotel grounds and the Harbor Yacht Club next door. The moon was big in the sky, turning everything colorless and cool. I had to arbitrate between competing impulses. Part of me, the more insistent part, wanted to get in the dinghy and ride out to Amanda, board the sturdy sloop, greet the gregarious mutt and sail back to the South Fork. I could see them anchored in the lagoon, motionless, the stars reflected on the surface of the black water. Nocturnal chirps and chatters on shore, the occasional flip of an insect-hunting fish.

I had no stake in this fight. There was nothing in it for me. I didn't know what was really roiling below the surface, but for sure it wasn't any good. I had no reason to care, no percentage in trying to care, no upside whatsoever. I was on the cusp of getting my own unruly life somewhat under control. There were blessings there I couldn't deny, but they were on loan, with permanent status contingent on responsible possession.

I brooded over what Amanda had said about Anika. I'd never put much of a premium on being honest with myself, preferring to let avoidance and denial work their soothing charms. But standing there in the chill October night, I let the walls fall and asked the hard question.

The answer was more felt than heard.

"Dammit," I said out loud, and wishing I had a cigarette, walked back to the Swan to try and get some sleep.

❖

Somewhere around four in the morning, Anika crawled into my bed. As my dream-addled mind swam through the muck toward consciousness, my body contended with the shock of softly silken female nakedness.

"Goddamnit, Anika, would you knock it off," I mumbled, turning away from her. She put her arm over my shoulder and squeezed into me, spoon-style.

"You're right about marooning myself on an island. I'm so horny my eyeballs are starting to float out of my head."

"I'm not the solution."

"I don't understand why not," she said. "I don't care how old you are."

"I don't care how old I am, either. You don't know this yet, but people can decide that the person they're with is the person they're with and that's that."

"You're right," she said. "I don't understand that."

She pressed herself into me and worked her hand in a southerly direction. I caught her wrist.

"So go put some clothes on and come back and I'll explain it to you, as long as you stay on top of the sheets."

"No one will know," she whispered.

"I will."

"You're in great shape," she said. "I knew it." She moved her hand within the range permitted by my grip. "I know you want it."

Part of me did, including the part Anika was trying to reach for. I squeezed her wrist.

"I do," I said. "But I'm not gonna."

She shoved herself even closer, got close enough to my ear to nibble on it before saying, "Not yet."

Then she got out of the bed and left the room.

She was gone longer than it took to get dressed, though there was no danger of going back to sleep before she showed up again, wearing white panties and an oversized sweatshirt with CARNEGIE MELLON INSTITUTE OF GIZMOLOGY written on the chest.

"Tell me why you got fired from your big-shot job," she said. "And why you never tried to get another big-shot job. Corporate politics, I bet."

I waited for her to get settled on top of the bed before answering.

"Politics is too weak a word. For some people, the purpose of an organization is to provide an environment within which to wage internecine combat. Whatever product or service the firm sells is secondary to the goal of personal enrichment at the expense of one's fellow human beings. It's not enough to succeed. Someone else has to fail in the process."

"God, that's cynical," she said.

"You asked."

"I just can't stand it."

"Why'd your father leave Subversive Technologies?" I asked.

"Nosy again."

"You teed it up."

I sat up in bed and used the pillows to support my back. Anika sat cross-legged at the foot of the bed, her hair, unbrushed, hanging to either side of her face. A faint glow appeared outside the window, calling an end to the night and any hope of further sleep.

"Politics?" I asked.

"All he ever cared about was code. The beauty, the sublime elegance of lines of alpha-numeric commands. He told me when I was a little girl that he could judge the quality of a programmer's work by the shapes his lines of code formed on the screen."

"And he left running the business to Hammon and Sanderfreud," I said.

"Are you suggesting that might have been an itty bit foolish?" she asked.

I almost said, "Doesn't the guy who controls the product control the company?" But I already knew the answer to that. The powerful who don't make anything assume they can always find plenty of makers out there to replace the ones they have, and they'll be just as good. Maybe better.

"But your father is set for life," I said. "He can afford to shake it off and move on."

She smiled at me, with that weary, patronizing smile I got used to seeing on my daughter's face.

"When they forced him out they may as well have murdered him. He'll never be the same."

"Forced him out."

"Hey, thanks for making us rich, buddy. Now get the hell out of here."

She described how Hammon brought in a team of consultants to assess the viability of N-Spock 5.0, over Fey's

adamant objections. They concluded that it was fully functional, and ready for release. A millisecond later, Hammon
and Sanderfreud exercised a forgotten clause in the corporate agreement. Forgotten by Fey, anyway. The one that
said at any time a two-thirds majority of the founding share-
holders could purchase all the stock of the remaining third,
at a value set at the end of the preceding fiscal year, which
for Subversive Technologies had been suppressed as rumors
about 5.0 circulated around the financial markets.

They brought Fey into a conference room, and while
corporate counsel explained what was going down, security
packed up his office and the consultants installed new passwords on the development servers, locking him out of his
own creation.

"But they were wrong," she said. "Nobody'd bothered to
fully test the data conversion from 4.0. Oopsies."

Seemingly unfazed, they stuck to their deal with Fey. The
consultants poured into the building and went to town on
the application, secure in their belief that a fix was but a few
keystrokes away. A month later, reality set in. The failure
point was inside a small but critical region of the program
that had gone missing. It was a black box, a black hole, a
dense fortress that no external assault was able to breach.

What happened was the unthinkable. The most powerful
application ever written for its stated purpose was unwork-
able, unusable, worthless.

"A lot of money was at stake, so you can imagine, people
got upset," said Anika.

A lot of money, for sure. Billions as it turned out. Oopsies
is right.

"So now they need your father to come back and fix
things. He should be in the power seat."

"He should be, that's right. But he's telling them what
he's told me. Without the missing code, he'll have to start
at the beginning and run through the entire application,

stopping along the way for testing and QA, in order to isolate the glitch and allow him to write in a patch that will solve the problem. This will take most of next year, not the next three months, which Hammon doesn't want to hear, but that's the deal."

"Why should he help them at all, after getting heaved out?" I asked.

"You wonder that, too, eh?" she said, wagging a finger at me, but this time without the condescension. "Why was he so docile when they gobbled up his stock? Why was he so deferential when they all showed up unannounced on our doorstep? This should be his moment of triumph and he's acting more like a hopeful lover. What is up with that?" she asked, stringing out each word.

The light on the bedside table came on. I reached down to the floor and dug my cell phone out of my jeans. I turned it on and saw that service had returned. For some reason, all this revival caused in me a craving to be outside in the morning air. I shared those feelings with Anika, who suggested we freshen up, get dressed and retire to the patio with sliced fruit and toasted bagels, which she'd happily prepare. Not a hard sell.

Not long after we were out there, watching the sun warm up the island. Anika still wore the Carnegie Mellon sweatshirt, though she'd added jeans and orange Crocs.

"We keep talking about your father," I said, "but the real issue at this point is Axel."

She sat back in her chair, mug in hand.

"Fucking Axel," she said. "I love him with all my heart and he never stops driving me crazy."

"No ideas?"

She looked at a loss.

"How can I explain this? Axel is a creature of habit. He's filled with inconceivable anxiety, and the only thing that keeps that in check is routine and familiar surroundings. So what do we do, leave our home in Newton, Massachusetts, where he's lived his entire life, and move into a broken-down hotel on Fishers Island, New York. All the professional people said this was a terrible idea, but it's actually gone pretty well. Until Derrick Hammon, Master of the Universe, shows up. And then Myron is, like, naked and dead. That was the straw. Flipped him out completely. You wouldn't have seen it, probably, but I knew."

"So that's why he ran away?"

"I don't know. Axel is a routine freak who can surprise the hell out of you by breaking routine. I admit this is a big break, but he's done stuff like this before."

She bowed her head and used both hands to scratch her scalp, causing her long, shiny black hair to tumble over her face. When she threw back her head, it somehow knew how to fall into place. I didn't know how old she was, but likely younger than my own daughter. It was hard to think of her as the mother of an eighteen-year-old boy, but that's essentially what she was. Her father probably had even less interest than skill in being a parent, so the upbringing of an odd child had fallen to her, while still a child herself.

"It must have been tough when he was little. Del Rey made it sound like you had some help from her and others at Subversive."

Anika was one of those people who reacted to things you said as if you shared inside knowledge of the situation, even when there was no way you could.

"You call that help? That's funny."

"Really," I said.

"I wish I hadn't said that. Now you'll want to pry."

"I do."

She looked away, as if to organize her next thought.

"Del Rey did a lot for us, that's true," she said. "It wouldn't be fair to say otherwise."

"Not Myron?"

"Let's just say Myron Sanderfreud had an interesting interpretation of the word help."

I turned my attention back to the sunrise, which we couldn't see directly, but was doing its best to light up the eastern horizon. There was a sturdy breeze out of the northwest roughing up the surface of the water in the Inner Harbor. With the sun so low, the chop looked like molten metal, decorated with shards of light, some refracted into random evanescence. I'd seen a lot of mornings like this from an Adirondack chair that sat at the edge of a break-water on the Little Peconic Bay, the outer limit of my back-yard. The show was familiar, yet never exactly the same.

I rubbed my face, the beard stubble coarse enough to abrade my palms. My eyes stung with interrupted sleep and the coffee burned on the way down, but I was getting ready to move out, impatient with inactivity.

"What're the chances of borrowing your car again?" I asked.

She studied me.

"You're going to look for my brother. His own father has already given up. From what I read about you on-line, I wouldn't have taken you for a philanthropist."

"I do things for my own reasons."

"Am I one of those reasons?"

"If you were, I wouldn't tell you," I said, and left her there at the table, with her plate of citrus fruit, her seeking eyes and fragile grin.

CHAPTER 13

Before I drove out of the parking lot, I called Amanda.

"Another country heard from," she said, answering the phone. "I guess the power's back on."

"How was your night?"

"Not bad. I kept busy, swimming with the dog, drinking martinis, cleaning the shotgun. How 'bout you?"

I shared the high points of my conversation with Anika, keeping the setting entirely on the patio, seeing nothing gained by a more complete description.

"So what are your plans?" she asked.

Good question.

"I'm going to hang around until they secure another cop, then dinghy out to you so we can get the hell out of here."

"That's a good plan," she said.

"Keep your powder dry."

◆

My first destination was an easy call. When I rang the bell at Gwyneth's place, she came out from the back wearing a trench coat and a towel on her head.

"You're still here," she said.

"Apparently. Do you know Desi Arness?"

"Mediocre pool player who can afford to lose four out of five games. One of my better sources of revenue. Though only during the season when the Swan's open. Assuming your Swissie friends haven't ditched the pool table."

I didn't have the heart to tell her they apparently had.

"Do you know where he lives?"

She went behind the counter and pulled out a worn map of the island.

"We're here," she said, putting her finger on a spot just west of the entrance into the country club. She ran her finger along the route to the Arness estate, deep inside the reserve, on a cliff above Fishers Island Sound.

"He's here. The folks in there aren't too keen on interlopers," she said, looking up at me. "Even off-season."

"Maybe you could put a spell on me. Make me invisible."

"Don't be so sure I can't," she said. "Here, take the map. I've got plenty more."

"If you were a teenaged runaway this time of year, where would you hide on Fishers?"

She used the finger that was still pointing at the Arness estate to circle the island.

"A few thousand people in the summer turns into less than three hundred off-season. Plenty of room to hide," she said. "There're a lot of empty houses in the club. The only trick is knowing who's got an alarm system and who just relies on the club's security squad. Got any more questions? I need to get dressed."

"Can you set up that thing so I can write some emails?" I said, pointing at the Mac.

"That's what they're there for, buddy."

I sent the first one to Jackie Swaitkowski. It took about a half an hour to detail my instructions on how to conclude the negotiations with my former company's lawyers, and then, assuming there were funds out of the settlement, how they should be handled. I sent her the email and copied Burton Lewis.

Then I wrote Randall Dodge, the owner of a computer repair and help desk operation in Southampton Village. Randall had worked in digital security in the navy and had acquired skills and capabilities that far exceeded those of Jackie and Amanda, especially when traversing decidedly extra-legal territory.

I put "This is Sam Acquillo. Are you awake?" in the subject line.

"Yup," came back a few moments later.

"I need to talk. What's a good number to call?"

He sent me his cell phone number, which I called after I left Gwyneth's place and climbed back into the Mercedes.

"What're you doing on Fishers Island?" he asked when he came on the line.

"How did you know that?"

"From your IP address."

"That answers my first question. You can trace messages back to the originating computer."

"Sure. The only serious security level is at the access provider. But I have ways around that."

A Shinnecock Indian, Randall could be lyrical in describing his daring journeys through other people's networks and databases. The key, he'd tell me, was to look, but not touch, to pass like a ghost, silent and ephemeral. He acknowledged the pursuit had an intoxicating effect, even addictive if one indulged too much. And while he conceded to voyeuristic thrills, he said he never succumbed to outright theft, however easy it might have been.

"What if you wanted to get into the development servers at a big software shop, say Subversive Technologies," I said.

"Whoa, sharp right hand turn into no-no land. Tracking down IP addresses goes both ways. I'm good at evasion, but people in places like that are very good at security. One slip up and they catch me and put me in jail."

"That'd be bad," I said. "I like having you around."

"I like having me around, too."

"Let's pretend you really wanted to hack into Subversive, how would you do it?"

"I'd bribe one of their developers to give me an administrative user ID and password. Once in, I'd scramble to unlock their security measures, which would likely include rolling updates of user IDs and passwords. These are difficult things to do, but possible if you're on the inside."

"So then let's pretend you're safely inside, can you look at whatever they're working on?"

"Unless it's on a completely standalone box, unplugged from the net, yes. Probably. Though I wouldn't know what I was looking at. Programming is not my thing."

"How about their emails?"

"That I can do. If I'd lost my mind and all sense of self-preservation. Do you really want to hack Subversive or are they just an example?"

I told him what I could about the situation with N-Spock, including the unfortunate tendency of blowing itself up at critical junctures. I also told him about the Feys, Sanderfreud and Poole.

"That's one creepy little island you got yourself stuck on there, Sam."

"Don't say that to the Chamber of Commerce."

"The problem with N-Spock could be like an immunological disorder. And because the application turns on itself, not in response to a virus that has commandeered the program, it's very hard to isolate."

"How would you?"

"Shy of starting over and rewriting the whole thing, if you knew what was happening you could write a subprogram, a patch, that nipped the destructive cycle in the bud."

"An inoculation," I said.

"Sort of, yeah, if we keep stretching the analogy. Though like I said, this ain't exactly my bailiwick."

I hung up after thanking him and refocused on finding Desi's house. The gatehouse for the country club was empty as expected, as were the winding streets lined with trees and open fields, interrupted occasionally by unmarked driveways that disappeared into the foliage. I counted these off as I followed Gwyneth's map, which was well adorned with place names and landmarks, including the Arness mansion itself.

Reasonably sure I'd found it, I drove down an unpaved drive that had an overgrown meadow on one side and a stand of hardwoods on the other. There were several curves, the last of which saw the driveway flow into an oval parking area in front of a three-story brick and stone house. Really, more like a central house, flanked by two smaller versions. At the far end of the circle it opened up in front of a free-standing five-car garage. I parked in front of the house and was about to get out of the Mercedes when the head of a giant black dog appeared at my window. It didn't bark or snarl, but neither did it blink. I heard a sound on the other side of the car and saw an identical head peering in the passenger side window.

I reassessed the value of my visit to Desi.

I lowered the window a crack and shared with the Great Danes my deep respect for all dogs, especially very large ones. This had little impact on their posture, which seemed poised for anything, including an attack. Since the path ahead was clear, I started the car and slowly moved forward. The dogs held their positions at the windows, but allowed me to proceed. I waved goodbye and was about to accelerate around the circle when a man stepped out in front of the car. I put on the brakes.

He looked in his early forties, of medium build, though he carried extra weight in a face that was smiling broadly. He wore a red hunting shirt, tan vest and khakis that bunched up at the top of a pair of rubber boots. He walked over to the Mercedes, and bent down until his eyes were at the same level as the Great Danes'. I cracked open the window again.

"I see you've met Sacco and Vanzetti."

"Cute pups."

"They're my security detail. Cheaper and more effective than the human variety."

"Agreed. Sorry to bother you. I was just looking for some information."

"Calling ahead would have been smarter," he said, though he still wore a jovial expression.

"Did you know that Trooper Poole was assaulted a few days ago? They had to evacuate her and haven't replaced her yet."

His face darkened.

"I heard that. Damn awful thing."

"This happened right after a man was murdered at the Swan."

"I heard that, too."

"You hear a lot. That's why I want to talk to you."

"What are you, a cop?" he asked.

"Engineer. No official standing, just happened to get mixed up in this."

He flicked his hand in the air and the dogs moved away from the car. He backed away and they trotted over to him and lay down with haunches up in response to a second hand signal. He told me I could get out, but to keep at least ten feet between us.

"Not a problem," I said. "I've got a mutt of my own, though the only hand signal he knows is when I reach for his bowl."

"You can ask me what you want, but it doesn't mean I'm going to answer."

The Arness place lived up to the designation "estate." In addition to the big house, the grounds featured a salad bowl of luxurious green growth—giant flowering bushes, viney wooden arches and moss-covered brick patios. At the center of the circle was a huge stone urn, looted I guessed from some ancient city by one of Desi's ancestors. It was filled with an assortment of unidentifiable plants continually freshened by a central fountain.

"I heard you tried to buy the Black Swan. I was curious how the deal ended up with Christian Fey."

"What's your name again?"

"Sam Acquillo. A boat I was delivering was docked at the Swan while I made some repairs. I sent her on with the crew and now I'm staying at the hotel."

I filled in some more detail, including news of the missing Axel.

"So I was also wondering if one of the private security outfits around here could check on the houses in the club. The human kind," I added, looking down at Sacco and Vanzetti. "Though I don't want him frightened or hurt in any way."

"If that's a requirement, it's a good thing you asked me first. Some of my neighbors have a taste for thuggery. The security guys would be the last people you'd want involved in this."

I thanked him.

"As far as the Swan goes," he said, "the previous owners are distant cousins of mine. Though not exactly the Hatfields and McCoys, our families have never gotten along. It didn't help that I had to break their bartender's arm when he tried to bounce me from the place. I was in Special Forces during the first Gulf War and I don't like people touching me without my permission."

"So that's what killed the deal?" I said.

"Hardly. The greedy bastards would never let principle stand between them and a U.S. dollar."

"So what happened?"

"Outbid. The other side offered twice as much as I did, and I offered twice as much as the place was worth. I didn't want it that badly."

"Obviously Fey did."

"If by Fey you mean Christian Fey, that's not who we dealt with," said Desi, reaching down to scratch one of the Great Danes between the ears.

"His lawyers?"

Desi shook his head.

"It was the girl. Anika. Can't call it a bidding war since it was over after the first skirmish. What the hell, her money."

"Literally hers?" I asked.

"According to my dopey cousins, though who knows with a family like that. Whose boat are you delivering, if you don't mind me asking."

"Burton Lewis. I owe him a lot of favors, and there're worse ways to pay down the debt."

He made another subtle hand signal and the dogs jumped up and galloped away. He walked over to me and offered his hand.

"Luther Arness. I've known Burt since the regatta days," he said, proving the suspicion that all old money rich guys belonged to the same fraternity. "Good sailor, poof or not."

"A good man, poofness and all," I said.

He held up both hands.

"Sorry. You're right. No offence intended."

"None taken. I asked him if he could pull a string or two and get some cops over here. Maybe you could do the same. I'm told you're the king of the island."

He chuckled.

"Only when they're looking for something from me. Doesn't matter. Somebody's got to preserve this place."

"That meatball who runs your fuel dock thinks it's his job."

"Track? He is a meatball. He was part of the deal when I bought the place."

"If you want him healthy enough to keep running it, tell him to back off," I said.

"You ex-military?" he asked me.

"Ex-juvenile delinquent."

He let me go after I described Burton's boat as well as I could in the face of daunting technical questions.

"Marine architecture's a hobby of mine," he said, as a form of apology. "I'm thinking of building myself a boat in the garage over there. Once I find a place for all the cars. Or maybe I should just build a workshop somewhere else," he said, looking around the vast property, his voice falling off as the thought circulated around his mind.

"Good thing I'm not married," he added. "Workshops are the kind of things wives hate."

I almost suggested he get to know Anika Fey as more than a reckless spendthrift, but didn't know how to frame the concept. Instead, I just thanked him again and drove off in the Mercedes. Sacco and Vanzetti came out of nowhere and followed me to the curve in the drive, then peeled off and loped back out of sight.

I spent another two hours of unmolested time wandering around the country club, holding to the faint hope that I'd spot Axel or some clue to his whereabouts. Though the odds were long, I didn't see it as entirely fruitless, remembering what my cop friend Joe Sullivan said about professional detective work: "Most of our success comes from the ability to withstand the kind of boring crap that would kill an ordinary person."

At the end of those two hours I'd gotten nowhere, but the boredom came to an end when a little blue and white car plastered with insignias and flashing a roof-mounted yellow light careened around me and put on its brakes. I slowed as the car slowed and stopped when it pulled to the side of the road. I waited until a guy got out, then went around him and continued on my way. In my rear view mirror I saw him scramble back into his car, which quickly sped up behind me again, its headlights blinking along with the yellow bubble-gum machine. I ignored him.

This continued until we came to a relatively straight patch of road, which he used to race past me and then skid to a stop, the rear end of the car swinging around until it effectively blocked my passage. I considered ramming him, but I wasn't driving my own car. I watched the guy leap out and stalk over to my door, which he rapped with his knuckles.

He was a young guy, with a pale, blotchy and almost hairless face. He wore a generic security guard's uniform, including a military hat, out from which sprang sprigs of thin red hair.

"What the hell are you doing?" he said, when I rolled down the window.

"Driving down the street. What the hell are *you* doing?"

"This is private property."

I looked around.

"Looks like a street to me," I said.

"It's a private street."

"So what?"

"What are you doing here?" he asked.

"Joy riding."

He looked into the back seat where the Feys had left some plastic bags filled with who-knows-what.

"What's in the bags?" the guy asked.

"None of your business."

"I need to examine those bags," he said.

"Not a chance."

"Get out of the car," he said.

"No."

He reached in the window and grabbed my shirt collar.

"Get out."

I shoved the door open with my shoulder, crashing it into his knees. He let go of my shirt and staggered back a few feet.

"Touch me again and I'll break your face," I said.

I saw him reach for his belt where a nasty-looking night-stick hung in a holster.

"You can't do that," he said.

"I just did," I said, and putting the Mercedes in reverse, backed up into a three-point turn and drove off in the opposite direction. A moment later he was behind me again flashing all his lights, but this time I didn't let him get ahead of me. Using Gwyneth's map, I took a few turns and found my way back to the gatehouse. By then another little blue and white car had joined the parade. I assumed they'd turn off when I left the club, but they kept at it. So I drove another hundred feet, slowed and pulled off to the side of the road.

The young guy jumped out of his car, yelled fuck and slammed the door. As he came toward me he pulled the nightstick out of its holster. I left the Mercedes and moved toward him at the same pace, so when he raised the stick we had some combined momentum. I grabbed his wrist with one hand and midway up the stick with the other. Then I snapped it into his face, cracking him on the forehead. He stayed on his feet, but lost his grip on the nightstick. I pulled it free and continued on to the next car, out of which came a much bigger guy, meaty around the shoulders and bloated at the waist. He was older, with a Pancho Villa moustache and a greasy, florid face.

He also had a nightstick on his belt. And a gun.

Before he had a chance to figure out which one to draw, I got my foot behind his heels and bashed him on the chest with my elbow. The air woofed out of his lungs when he slammed to the ground. As he tried to catch his breath, I dropped down and stuck a knee in his sternum, giving him something else to grapple with while I dug his gun out of the holster. It was an old-fashioned police revolver, I guessed a thirty-eight caliber Smith & Wesson. I stuck it in the rear waistband of my pants. Then I stood up and looked behind me for the other guy, but he was flat on his ass, holding his head with both hands.

I walked back to the Mercedes, tossing the nightstick on the ground in front of him as I passed by.

"Try to be more patient with people," I told him. "It'll serve you better."

In my rear view, I could see the flashing lights reflected in the trees, dwindling with each curve of the road, eagerness for further pursuit apparently spent.

CHAPTER 14

Jackie Swaitkowski called my cell as I was pulling back into the Swan's parking lot. This time I answered.

"Did you get my email?" I asked.

"I did. I can't believe it."

"You don't have to believe anything if you understand the instructions."

"I'll need help on the legalities, assuming I can't talk you out of it," she said.

"Burton will help."

"Help you come to your senses, I hope."

"Just see what you can do," I said. "We can discuss my senses another day."

When I walked into the foyer of the Swan, Christian Fey was on a ladder holding a wall sconce with one hand and using a pair of needle-nose pliers to dig around its internal regions with the other.

"Hope you turned off the circuit breaker," I said.

He looked down at me, expectantly.

"No sign of Axel," I said. "You haven't heard from him?"

He frowned and shook his head.

"Nothing. Very frustrating." He went back to the sconce. "The wiring in this place is an electrical fire waiting to happen."

"What made you decide to buy the place?" I asked. "Not much of an investment when you consider the costs."

He looked down at me.

"With all due respect, Mr. Acquillo," he said. "I've had a far smoother transition from the corporate world than yourself."

"You can say that again. Though you might not know all the facts."

"I'm sure I don't," he said. "And neither do you."

"Where're your other guests?"

"Out doing what you were doing. Looking for Axel."

"You sure that's a good idea?" I asked. "What if they find him?"

He gently let go of the sconce, letting it hang from the wall by its wiring. He climbed down the ladder and went into the bar. He took out two bottles of water and handed me one.

"What did you mean by that?" he asked, in a low voice.

"You don't know what made him run off. Maybe it was them."

"And why would that be?" he asked, whether he really wanted to know, or knew already and wanted confirmation, was a hard call. I couldn't help him either way.

"Beats me, but you can't ignore a simple correlation."

"There's nothing simple about Axel."

"Or you," I said. There was a lot I wanted him to tell me, but I didn't know how hard to push. He was still ostensibly in charge of the place, and without Anika's contrivances, I knew I wouldn't get too far. "None of this is any of my business, and you can tell me to shut up and go away anytime you want, but I gotta ask you one question."

He neither agreed nor disagreed, so I kept going.

"Why do you want to help those jamokes with N-Spock 5.0 when they treated you like such crap?"

"You seem to think you know something about my business affairs."

"Two can play the Google game," I said. "There's a lot out there, and I can guess what isn't."

This amused him.

"I wouldn't be so sure about that," he said. "And you're right, it isn't any of your business," he added, though not as harshly as the words would suggest.

Anika came into the room. She examined our faces, as if to glean from there the topic of our conversation.

"No luck?" she asked me.

I shook my head.

"But I did meet Desi Arness. And Sacco and Vanzetti, the best trained anarchists on record."

She arched her eyebrows.

"Oh? And what did they have to offer?" she asked.

"Nothing useful. I hear you outbid Desi for the Swan."

"That was easy," said Fey, "his heart wasn't in it. He already owns most of the island, anyway. They're better off with at least one landmark out of his hands."

"But it was all friendly," I said.

"Oh, sure," said Anika, before her father could answer. "We want to get along with everybody."

I didn't think I'd learn more from Fey at that point, and Anika wouldn't speak freely in front of him, so I had to settle for small talk before excusing myself and going back outside. The storm had caused the trees to lose some of their color, but it still looked like autumn—the red, yellow and orange tones deepening as the sun headed toward the horizon. And felt like autumn, with erratic bursts of the northwesterly slipping the chill air under my windbreaker and burning my cheeks.

I'd returned the key to the station wagon, so I decided to walk to the western end of the island to check on the arrival of the replacement Fishers Island State Police force.

I went directly to the ferry office, which was back in operation. A piece of plywood covered the broken window-pane. Behind the ticket counter sat a woman with a thick head of frizzy red hair, parted in the middle and brushed down to her shoulders. Her face, too old for the hair, was high-cheekboned with an angular nose and pointed chin.

"So you're back in business," I said.

"Never should've been out, but yes. We are. With reduced runs. Here."

She slid a computer print-out of the temporary schedule across the counter.

"Do you know if there's a state cop back on duty?"

She turned around and looked toward the barracks, as if she could see through the walls.

"There should be, Lord knows. We could call."

She picked up a phone and dialed a number read off a piece of paper taped to the counter.

"I just wanted to see if someone was here," she said into the phone. "I'm calling from the ferry office."

She nodded a few times, then looked about to get off when I asked if I could talk to the person on the other end of the phone. She gave up the receiver with some reluctance.

"Not too long," she said. "That's our only line."

"Officer, this is Sam Acquillo," I said into the phone.

"Stay where you are," said a deep male voice. "I'll pick you up."

I didn't know what being picked up implied, but I was committed. I thanked the red-haired woman and went out-side to wait. In a few minutes Poole's cruiser pulled up, driven by a young guy in a New York State trooper's uni-form. He had very clear brown skin and a close-cropped mat of black hair. When he got out of the car I saw he was about my height, but had a few inches on me at the shoulders. His handshake telegraphed plenty of reserve power. A pair of round, thin black-framed glasses perched on the end of his nose.

He introduced himself as Ashton Kinuei.

"Glad you finally got here," I said.

"Just an hour ago. We launched as soon as the marine bureau got the okay. Still a bit bumpy. Trooper Poole sends her regards."

He told me she was going into surgery to repair the damage inside her mouth, but was otherwise in recovery mode. He asked me if I knew who did it.

"No idea," I said. "But I can tell you what I do know."

We sat in the cruiser while I briefed him on everything I could remember, leaving out the altercation with the two security meatballs. I had no idea how that one would go, but I was hoping professional embarrassment over getting their asses kicked and the fact that they'd attacked me outside the club would keep it under wraps. Though the one guy's missing sidearm might take some explaining.

Kinuei typed steadily on a small laptop while I talked, interrupting with apologies to clarify a point or to spell a name. I felt the repressed grip of anxiety loosen from around my heart as I listened to his calm, deliberate manner. I thought at that moment, all will be well.

"You have a series of events and impressions here," he said, "but no beliefs or conclusions. Anything you're not sharing?"

He looked up from his tiny computer over the top of his glasses.

"I'm an engineer. We're congenitally committed to empirical reasoning. Sure, I have some guesses. But I can't support them with anything more than a hunch. And my experience with police investigations is to keep my hunches to myself until there's at least a shred of corroboration."

"I'm told you've had more than your share of that type of experience. From both sides of the equation."

"Yes, sir. Which I hope only supports my approach."

He went back to his laptop and tapped out a few more lines. He wasn't a small guy, but his fingers were long and lean, and he typed like a jazz pianist. I waited.

"You have friends in interesting places," he said, then looked over at me again, his expression both amused and filled with admonition. "I don't care."

"Me, neither," I told him. "I just wanted to get somebody out here. The whole situation's got me a little nerved out."

"So about the barracks' ordnance . . ."

I reached in the pocket of my windbreaker.

"Here's Glock one," I said, tossing it on the seat. "I hid the other. The Remington's out of reach for a little while. I'll get 'em back to you as soon as I can. No worries on that. I hate guns."

"I'm sure you will," he said, expressing both warning and conviction.

He drove me back to the Swan where I introduced him to Anika and Christian Fey, who had mixed reactions. Fey nearly beamed with relief, Anika stood back, her jagged smile at half-mast. I felt sorry that they had to go through another grilling, this time with added content, but they couldn't expect the cop to be a mind-reader. As I listened to them, it became clear that Ashton Kinuei was more than a grade above the already well-trained New York State trooper. Erudition sweated off his carefully articulated sentences.

When the interview drifted into technical esoterica, he didn't blink. After a half-hour survey of contemporary software development processes and protocols, including a brief diversion into the pros and cons of fifth generation programming language, from both technological and sociological perspectives, Kinuei said, "I will need to speak to Mr. Hammon and Mr. 't Hooft. Are they available?"

"They're out sightseeing," said Fey. "I expect them back for dinner."

"You'd be amazed at how much you can see in four square miles," I said.

"They're also looking for my son," said Fey.

"Any intellectual property disputes relating to your company's software is out of my jurisdiction," said Kinuei. "Unless it connects to the death of Mr. Sanderfreud. Should I be pursuing that avenue of inquiry?" he asked Fey, his face a wall of professional remove.

Both Feys took longer than they should have to respond. Finally Anika said, "We don't know what happened to Myron. I thought that's what the police were supposed to figure out."

Kinuei was pleased by that.

"We are, ma'am. I appreciate the reminder."

We waited around together for Hammon and 't Hooft to show, but eventually Kinuei cashed it in. He asked the Feys to have them call or stop by the barracks when they had a chance. He said to remind them they couldn't leave by ferry without him knowing it, so to save any fuss, to just make contact.

I walked him out to his car.

"Who are you really," I asked.

He looked over at me as we walked across the parking lot.

"Assistant District Attorney, Eastern Suffolk County. On loan to the state police, where I did five years while putting myself through law school, so no disrespecting the qualifications."

"Not me. I'm all respect. So what do you think?" I added after a pause.

"Never heard so much bullshit in my whole life. Correct that. I've heard worse bullshit, just from stupider people."

"I'm sorry to hear that. I so much wanted to believe," I said.

"This is no longer your problem," he said. "No sense hanging around."

"Everybody's so concerned about my senses."

"Though if you want to hang around, I can't stop you."

"We need to find that kid," I said.

"Since he's eighteen, he's not a kid and we don't have to find him until he becomes a missing person, which presents a far higher standard as to what constitutes missing."

"But we're still going to look for him," I said, using the royal 'we' to imply that included him.

"We are," he said.

When we reached the cruiser, I asked him one more question.

"What's your gut say? What do you think is going on?"

He thought about it.

"Whenever there's stupid big money involved, it distorts things. Can't jump to conclusions like you would in a routine case, where all the players are either poor or ignorant or both."

My regard for Ashton Kinuei went up another notch. It compelled me to say, "Don't let the sleepy little backwater thing fool you. This island's got some teeth."

He dropped into the cruiser, fiddled with the electronics on the dashboard, then rolled down the window and slammed the door.

"Gettin' me back that shotgun would be a comfort," he said, before turning on to the road and disappearing into the freshly failing light.

◆

I went up to my room, but instead of going to bed, I packed up my backpack and left the hotel. I dug our dinghy out from under the dock and rowed out to the middle of Inner Harbor, where I figured it was safe to start the motor, then followed my nose through the breakwater, past a pair of private buoys, then using the little flashlight I always kept in my back pocket, found the entrance to my secret anchorage. A few minutes later I lit up the long white hull of the *Carpe Mañana*.

As I killed the motor and drifted up to the stern I could hear a familiar bark. Lights flashed on over the cockpit and the forepeak.

When I cut the motor and drifted into the transom, I yelled, "Don't shoot. It's me. Sam."

"How do you know I won't shoot anyway?" Amanda yelled from somewhere below.

As I grabbed a stanchion in an effort to steady myself, Eddie appeared above, hopping on his front legs, his face in full grin, tongue out.

"Hey man," I said, reaching up to scrunch around a designated spot behind his ears.

I secured the dinghy and scrambled up the swim ladder. I was unsteady climbing into the cockpit, so Eddie nearly bowled me over trying to say hello. I told him to knock it off, which only encouraged him.

Amanda came up the companionway.

"I'd wag my tail, too, if I could," she said.

"Don't sell yourself short."

She fell into me and wrapped her long wiry arms around my neck.

"Goddamn you, Sam Acquillo," she said.

"Nice to see you, too."

We dispensed with further discussion for the rest of the night, heading directly to the quarter berth, deferring all that unresolved dross to yet another day.

CHAPTER 15

"We have a decision to make," I said, my first words of the morning.

Those words had been churning around my mind for at least two hours, having woken up with a head full of conflicting impulses, fears, internal arguments, cautions, and a few spectral images caused by slipping unawares into real sleep.

"I should be flattered when you say 'we'—but it always annoys me," said Amanda.

"It does?"

"Because you don't really mean 'we'—you mean 'I.' I have no say in the decisions you make. You might even believe that you take my interests into consideration, but you never do. We're still together because I usually defer to whatever you want to do, in order to keep conflict out of the relationship, but that doesn't mean I always endorse what is about to happen."

"Oh."

With that as a starting point, it didn't seem like we were entering into a seamless decision-making process. I lay there in silence wondering if there were a half-dozen or a few hundred occasions upon which Amanda had seemed to agree with a proposed course of action when in fact she would have approached it in a completely different way. I knew, at the same time, that one of my abiding failings as a human being was to be riddled with self-doubt, yet never appear as if I was. This led to the mistaken belief on the part of people close to me that I was driven by pure, unalterable conviction, when the opposite was usually the case.

"Okay," I said, braced. "Then you decide. I'll just give you the alternatives, and you say yea or nay."

"Does it matter if I know what you want to do anyway?"

"You won't. I'll present the options in a purely unbiased fashion that will be impossible for you to divine beforehand."

"Okay," she said, squirming more deeply into the tangled mess of sheets and unzipped sleeping bags that constituted the quarter berth's bed linens. "I'll play."

I told her about the arrival of Ashton Kinuei and my spontaneous belief in his ability to master all the complicated elements of the case, physically and intellectually. With none of the biases that I had likely acquired as a result of my natural sympathies toward the Feys.

"It's human nature to pick a side," I said. "No matter the doubts that might arise along the way."

"I picked you. So there's your proof."

"So now there's really no reason for us to stick around. It's now rightly out of our hands."

"Okay, so what's the counter argument?" she asked.

"I don't want to go yet."

"So that's it? No reason?"

"I'm worried about the Feys. I'm on their side."

She laughed.

"So your unbiased alternatives are the obvious, prudent and reasonable option versus what you actually want to do, for no good reason whatsoever. And I'm supposed to arbitrate that?"

"Yeah. Go ahead. Your call. We'll do what *you* want to do."

"You told me you've only had two intimate relationships in your life. With your divorced wife and me. And you're in your late fifties. Now I know why."

I'd heard similar opinions expressed by my daughter on those few failed occasions when I tried to talk her out of her idiot boyfriends.

"What's that got to do with this?"

"I rest my case," she said.

"So what're we going to do?" I asked.

"I'm going to stay here as long as I can stand it. Then we're either going to sail this thing together to Southampton, or I'm going to motor over to New London with Eddie like we told everyone I've already done and take the ferry home."

She squeezed me hard, then pulled herself out of the quarter berth and went to take a shower. I lay there for a while looking up through the forward hatch, then yelled out to her, "See, now we get to do what you want to do."

Maybe sustaining successful relationships wasn't as hard as I thought it was.

◆

The next trick was to get the dinghy back unnoticed, a step in the process I hadn't considered until that morning. Had I done so, the obvious thing would have been to leave the boat while it was still dark and come in the last hundred feet or so the way I left, by oar. It was now about 7:30, and the sun was well up, so that option was off the table.

Before leaving, I swam to shore with Eddie and hung out while he did all the stuff he liked to do, including a close inspection of the man-made and naturally occurring crud on the beach. Then I went back and took a shower off the transom, changed into fresh clothes, re-packed my backpack with additional essentials, and after a review of communications protocols with Amanda, took to the water.

I went straight across from the lagoon, staying well north of the breakwater that protected the yacht club, the Black Swan and the marinas further down the channel. I hoped to find a place on shore to hide the dinghy that didn't mean cutting through private property to reach the coast road. What I found was a good hiding place in a wooded area clearly belonging to someone's summer home, but since the odds of them being there in October were pretty low, that was good enough.

I clawed my way through the underbrush up to the road, then walked to the Swan where Anika was out in the yard, as usual fussing with the landscape.

"Maybe if you just left everything alone it would do better," I said, crouching down next to where she was snipping twigs off an exhausted perennial.

"That's the kind of thinking I associate with my father," she said, without looking up. "Maybe if your generation thought differently the world would be a more beautiful place."

"So, no word from Axel."

"No word. Where'd you sleep last night?"

"You're not the only one who gets to have secrets."

"I don't have any secrets," she said.

"That's all you have."

She stopped pruning for a moment, then went back at it.

"I took a calculated risk with you," she said. "I'm still deciding if it was worth it."

"That depends on what you were trying to achieve. What do you do with that computer in your room?"

"Write emails to my friends, go on Facebook, Google stuff I want to know about. Same as anyone else."

"Same as Axel?"

"All he does is virtual warfare with a bunch of pathetic digital shut-ins. What else would he do?"

"Access the development servers at Subversive Technologies?"

She stopped pruning again, sighed, then dropped from an awkward squat onto her butt.

"There's an interesting accusation," she said.

"No accusation, just supposition."

I joined her on the ground.

"You don't know much about computer security," she said.

"I don't know much about bank vaults, but I can break into any one I want if I have the combination."

She used her pruning shears to poke at the ground.

"Servers aren't bank vaults. You might leave fingerprints in a vault. In the development servers at Subversive, you leave your name, address, the time you came to visit, how long you stayed and what you did while you were there."

"Not if you know how to be invisible."

She smiled indulgently.

"Things in computerland have progressed a little since the late nineties. Kids no longer get to hack into the grown-ups' playground."

"Unless the kids helped build the swing sets."

She liked that, but tried not to let it show.

"Even if he could hack Subversive, why would he?" she asked.

"If he could, why wouldn't he?"

"I like you better as a boat bum."

"I'm trying to find your brother. Are you?"

Before I was booted out of the corporate world, I'd occasionally be afflicted by management's desire to assess my assets and liabilities. They often did this to people in the middle ranks, the part of the company that did the most work in return for the least recognition, so I didn't take it personally. One of these projects involved a psychological profiling that was supposed to help us better form and manage interpersonal relationships. You weren't supposed to be able to flunk this test, since the idea was to place you on an unbiased, non-judgmental personality spectrum. I think I managed to flunk it anyway, because they made me take the same test two or three more times, after which a woman from human resources asked to see me in her office.

"I just wanted to put a face to the data," she said. "We've never seen such unusual scoring. My boss thinks you're doing it on purpose."

"How would I do that?"

"Theoretically, you couldn't, unless you were intimate with the test methodology," she said.

She had that pale, exhausted and slightly shiny complexion that formed on people who worked in the company's over-worked, insecure professional sectors—like personnel and marketing—where it was generally understood that you were always a CFO's passing whim away from getting canned, no matter what the firm's financial prospects. Her mannish white blouse was too tight to button completely over her ample chest, and her blue skirt struggled to contain her lower half. I wanted to suggest a little more time in the gym, but even I knew that wasn't the kind of thing you said to women in human resources.

"Your people like working for you and your supervisor calls you his best trouble-shooter. Everyone else is afraid of you, or just thinks you're an asshole. After looking at the results of your profile, I can see why."

"I can't help that. If I do something I'm not supposed to do, you can call me back in here. Until then, you can tell the guy who came up with all this psycho mumbo-jumbo to cram it in a place I'm not allowed to specify."

"The gal's psycho mumbo-jumbo. It's my test."

"So let's make a deal. You stop pestering me and I'll stop screwing up your bell curve."

If the HR lady was one of those patsies who said they were afraid of me, she didn't act like it. She smirked instead, a soft glow welling up from those weary eyes.

"You don't always have to say what's on your mind," she said.

◆

Decades later, Anika said to me, "You don't always have to say what's on your mind."

"Yes I do. All I have is what's on my mind. If you don't want to hear it, don't talk to me," repeating what I'd told the HR lady.

"You're a lot better at stuff like finding my brother than I am." she said. "I know because I've studied you."

"Did he take a laptop with him?"

She took a few beats to answer.

"Yes."

"Has he emailed you?"

She waited even longer this time.

"Yes. And no, he didn't tell me where he is. Just that he's safe."

"From what?" I asked.

"I don't know. The elements. Wild beasts. Muggers."

"Why won't he tell you where he is?"

"He doesn't want to be found," she said.

"Do you want to find him?"

"Yes. He can't be alone. It'll kill him."

"When are you going to tell me what's really going on?"

"When I can trust you with my life. Your girlfriend is very pretty. I don't blame you for being faithful to her. In fact, it makes me like you more. Even though you don't pay proper attention to me and you've killed people."

"I told you, I was acquitted," I said.

"You killed two Venezuelans who were trying to kill you. So it was legal, and you got off. But you still did it. I have your whole police file on my hard drive. I think God brought you to me. Even though I don't believe in God."

"Forward Axel's email to Amanda. I'll take it from there."

Even with the age difference I could translate her expression into the words, "Oh, please."

"No offence, Sam, but if Axel doesn't want to be tracked, he's not going to be tracked."

"You're probably right. But what can it hurt?" I asked. "Unless you don't want me to find him, in which case, we need to change this conversation."

The disdain on her face shifted toward frustration.

"Fine. I'll send it to you. Without the text. That's private."

"Don't need the text," I said, and was about to say more when a clap of thunder filled the air. We both looked up at the blackening sky.

"Not again," she said.

"It's October. The weather's very unstable."

The sky wasn't just turning dark, it was the brownish grey dark that felt so foreboding, with good reason. I'd seen it before. I realized that with all the terrestrial commotion of the last few days, I'd completely neglected checking the skies above, a dangerous lapse at that time of year, in that place. I asked Anika what she knew.

"With all the hub-bub lately, I haven't checked," she said.

With no further discussion, we went into the Swan and up the three flights of stairs to her artist's garret where she kept her computer. She logged on and in a few minutes we had the official NOAA forecast.

A named hurricane, Jillanne, was moving north about eighty miles off the coast, but close enough for the East End of Long Island and Southern Connecticut to feel some major effects. Today would see increasing winds. The next day a steady degeneration in conditions, with some rain, but mostly building wind and seas. The day after that, full-out gale force winds, small boats get to port, double-up dock and mooring lines, batten down the hatches, put in water, batteries and canned food, fuel up the generators, tape up the windows, and pay insurance bills and debts to God in full.

"Not again," said Anika.

"Another reminder who's in charge here."

Without taking her eyes off the screen, she reached up and gripped my shoulder.

"If we lose power again, Axel will be offline and helpless. That won't work," she said.

I shook her hand off.

"Help me bring him in or let him fend for himself. You can't have it both ways," I said, and then left the loft, finding my way downstairs to the breezy world outside, where I went out onto the docks to watch for signs of whatever was coming. The air felt uneasy, heavy and wind-whipped at the same time. I'd felt this before, years ago as I waited for a cyclone to smash into the oil rig I was optimizing in the tepid waters off Malaysia.

I realized with a start that what we'd experienced a few days before was just a prelude, a sneak preview of the main event. A tease. A feint. A cruel diversion.

I plucked my cell phone out of its holster and called Amanda.

"Keep your eye on your mailbox," I said. "You should be getting a forwarded email that Axel wrote to Anika. As soon as it arrives I'd like you to forward it on to Randall Dodge."

"Okay, sure. Is that all?"

"No. We have a decision to make," I said.

"Not another one."

"There's a big storm on the way. Maybe a lot bigger than the last one."

She didn't answer right away.

"Maybe I'm not up for that," she said, finally.

"You should head for New London now. Tie her up as well as you can and get back to Oak Point. I'll meet you when I can."

Another pregnant pause.

"Most of me wants to do that, but a stupid little part of me wants to stay here to be near to you. One for all and all of that."

"I want to know you're safe," I said.

"You can't always get what you want. I think we agreed on that."

When I was married, I never got what I wanted, which was mostly my fault. I didn't know what I wanted, and even if I had, I lacked the stomach to assert my will. Instead, over the years my heart simply slipped away, a few degrees at a time, until what remained was a corporeal form representing Abby's husband Sam, but not much else.

"Okay, stay put for now if you want," I said. "I'll figure something out."

"Are you going to tell me what that is?"

"When I figure it out."

I turned around and looked overhead at the ruffled tree limbs, then back down at the Swan. I had a lot more to figure out than what to do with Amanda. Something I'd never do with a mind so evenly divided against itself. Since Hammon and company drove into the hotel's parking lot, my instincts for trouble had been on high alert. I'd seen a lot of trouble, so those instincts I could trust. But I had a deeper desire to be done with trouble altogether, to leave it for someone else to grapple with. Somebody younger and not yet burnished over with wrenching experience. That was the argument of my conscious mind, the part that was desperate to be back home, to see the opening of the harbor inside of which was a small private marina, with young dockhands cast by Ralph

Lauren and a jolly red-faced harbormaster awaiting his new charge, Burton Lewis's *Carpe Mañana*.

This should have been enough to motivate the obvious behavior, to set forth with the necessary action. To drive me off that island while there was still time to beat the next storm and elude other tempests not born of natural forces.

But for some idiotic reason, it wasn't.

CHAPTER 16

This time, when I saw the Town Car pull into the parking lot, it was followed by a Ford Excursion SUV, out of which stepped two guys in polo shirts and sport jackets carrying duffle bags and briefcases. No golf clubs.

They spoke with 't Hooft and Hammon for a moment, then all four went into the Swan. I saw this from across the street, where I was headed up the short hill toward the interior of the island. I wanted to go back down and meet the new guests, but that would have looked too eager. So I kept walking.

I made it to Gwyneth Jones' place in brisk time and was happy to see her tending her store.

"How's business this time of year?" I asked her as I walked through the door.

"It sucks. Though other times of the year aren't much better."

"Not even the high season?"

"Funny, no. I'm wondering if it's the inventory. Maybe I should get in some new lines."

"Just keep the computers."

"Have at it," she said, pointing in their direction.

I wrote Amanda and asked if she'd received the forwarded email from Anika. She wrote back that she had, and immediately after, forwarded it to Randall Dodge. As promised, Anika had deleted the text, but as far as my technical knowledge allowed, it looked like she'd left what Randall needed to dig around for clues to its origins. I wrote her back with thanks, and asked her to stay tuned for further emails and phone calls. And to keep monitoring channel sixteen.

She wrote that she and Eddie missed me and signed off, "Central Communications."

I called Randall.

"I assumed an explanation was on the way," he said when I told him who was on the line.

"What are the chances of tracing where this email came from?" I asked.

There was a long silence while Randall perused the technical information that lay behind the email.

"Connecticut," he said.

"Not Fishers Island?"

"Could be. The island's a lot closer to New London than Southold. Have to keep digging. I might be able to get to a neighborhood, but maybe not the exact house. Though there's a lot of data here. Might be easier than it looks."

"Do what you can. We're getting another storm, so I'm not sure how long the power and cell service will hold up."

"You're wanting this ASAP," he said.

"I am. I'm in your debt."

"I'm in Jackie's debt, so I think that makes us even."

"If you can't get through any other way, give the info to Joe Sullivan and ask him to relay it here over VHF to the state police barracks. He'll do it after giving you a hard time. Pretend you can't hear him."

After we signed off I looked around for Gwyneth, who'd disappeared. I found the door behind the counter from whence she'd once emerged, and knocked.

"I need to pay you," I called through the door.

It whipped open, startling me.

"I like the pay part," she said. "Not everybody does it."

"Makes it hard to stay in business."

"Who cares about that?" she said. "I only charge so people won't disrespect me."

"I like a little philanthropy myself sometimes," I said.

"My father owned most of the copper deposits in Montana," she said. "What's your excuse?"

❖

The walk back to the Swan took the customary fifteen minutes. I went in through the front door, checked the bar and the restaurant, then went through the French doors in the back and found Hammon and his crew seated around a circular table, feeding off a wheeled cart loaded down with pastries and bowls of sodden, colorful fruit. Anika was leaning against the service bar at the edge of the patio, and Del Rey was out on the docks, on a chaise longue, either resting her eyes or sound asleep.

I approached the table.

"Reinforcements?" I asked Hammon.

His gaze would have been reptilian if not slightly warmed by annoyance. 't Hooft's face was blank. He cupped his right fist in his left hand, rotating it like a ball and socket joint.

Both the new guys were big and muscled. The older, maybe forty, had a mashed in nose, not unlike mine, and high cheekbones that had seen a lot of sun. His curly grey hair was neatly combed, offering a nearly feminine contrast to his hammered-out face. The other guy was probably late twenties, with a cleaner, paler complexion and a coat of black stubble on his scalp. His face was fleshier, almost fatty around the eyes, which were set in his cheeks like black marbles.

Surrounded by all that human mass, Hammon looked almost delicate, like a finely crafted doll.

"Gentlemen," he said, "this is Sam Acquillo. Sam, meet Jock and Pierre," he said, pointing first to the younger guy, then the older.

"Allo," said Pierre, offering his hand. Not surprisingly, we got into a brief contest of mash-the-other-guy's knuckles. It was his idea, though he made a quick retreat when I squeezed back. I was unsure about my overall physical abilities, but the last few years swinging a hammer had done wonders for my grip.

Jock just nodded, so I did the same.

"I just thought we could use some assistance," said Hammon.

"Finding the boy?" I asked.

"That's right. Jock and Pierre are old associates of my good friend 't Hooft. Nigeria, Colombia, Iraq. You know."

"I don't, but I'll take your word for it," I said.

"We were wondering when you were heading back to Long Island," said 't Hooft. "It seems like now would be a good time."

"Really?" I said. "I was just starting to get settled in. I like it here. Friendly place. Nice weather. Affordable real estate."

Hammon smiled at me, though I'm not sure which part of the conversation sparked the response. Jock and Pierre were quiet, studying me, their eyes fixed and unblinking. Assessing. Pierre's shoulders were slumped, but his head was thrust forward, alert. His eyes were wide in their sockets. His right hand rested on his thigh. I wondered where the gun was stowed; his pockets looked flat and the sport coat showed no obvious bulges.

"We hear the weather's going to get nasty," said Hammon. "What does that really mean?"

"Who knows. Happens this time of year. Nothing's per-fect. Don't let it scare you. The Swan made it through '38 and everything after that. Built like a tank. There might be some thunder and lightning and a little wind. You guys worried about that?" I asked, looking from face to face.

"Oui," said Pierre. "Shaking in our undershorts."

They laughed at this, so I laughed with them

I got the general sense that the conversation they wanted to have would be difficult with me sitting there. So I decided to hang around for a while. I brought us all fresh coffee, commented on the fall in barometric pressure, which I could feel, but doubted any of them could, surveyed the group on loyalty to the New York Yankees, asked if anyone knew how to balance a stock portfolio, and otherwise kept them happily engaged until Jock, the silent one, said, "Listen, pal, love to talk all night, but we have some private things to discuss."

"I didn't know we were pals," I said. "So what're we talking about?"

"I said it was private."

"About finding Axel Fey? Your plan of attack? I thought we were working on this together. One for all and all that."

"If I thought you could help I wouldn't have invited Jock and Pierre," said Hammon, agreeably.

"Pretty impressive people."

Nobody wanted to comment on that, so it lay where it fell.

"Okay," I said, getting up to leave. "Suit yourself."

"Oh, Sam," said Hammon before I had a chance to move away. "I seriously recommend that you let us handle every-thing going forward. It would be better for everybody."

"I bet it would," I said, heading back over to the bar.

Anika was wearing a sleeveless white shirt over a short denim skirt. I noticed for the first time a tattoo on her left shoulder. It was the number twenty-five in a deep burgundy.

"I didn't know tats came in that color," I said.

"Got it for my twenty-fifth birthday. Special order. Though now it's more like eighty-six. They warn you about how the stupid things evolve."

"I think the stupid part is getting one in the first place," I said.

"That's the kind of thing a father would say."

"Not surprising. I am one."

"No daughters, I hope."

"One daughter. My only kid. About your age, and even more aggravating. So who're the new boys in town?" I asked, jerking my head in that direction.

She took a pull from a bottle of water on the bar, then wiped her hands on her denim skirt. Then she left the bar area, waving me to follow, which I did through the lobby, around the reception desk and into a small office. It had the sour, faded feel of a room still to be updated and restored. The only evidence of the Feys was a small white board screwed into one wall covered with a checklist, most of the items unchecked, and a computer on a side table against the other wall. The screensaver was a crude animation of Albert Einstein and Socrates playing chess.

She shut the door behind us.

"Did I tell you that Derrick Hammon is a crypto-fascist, sociopathic fucking sick creep survivalist nut bag? Adventure man—climbing mountains, deep diving wrecks, high altitude parachuting. His ideal vacation is stripping down to his boxers, painting his body and living in the woods for a week, killing little bunnies and shit with his bare hands and eating them raw. Don't believe me? It's worse than that. His best friends are ex-Special Forces, the kind who go freelance after discharge. Nowadays we call them private contractors, like they're the same people who lay tile in your bathroom. He pays them to train him in counterinsurgency tactics, which really comes in handy in suburban Boston. What do you think 't Hooft is, a database manager? Jesus Christ, for a so-called sophisticated person, you don't know shit."

She said all this in a forced whisper, only a few inches from my ear. As she spoke, I could feel an atomized mist of saliva spray against my cheek. Her breath smelled of toothpaste and wine. When I turned to look at her, her face was slightly flushed, her eyes narrow, but glistening with stress and intelligence. Her broad mouth made more so by her lips, redder and more swollen than I'd remembered them.

"No, you didn't tell me. Would've been good to know. So he's brought his A-team here to track down Axel. And you don't want them to," I said.

"Duh."

"So why do you let them stay here? Where's your father in all this?"

She drew in a deep breath, held it, then let it out noisily. With all the intimate whispering, she'd moved close enough for me to feel the outside curves of her clothed body. I held my ground.

"There's a pretty serious cop on the island now," I said. "I doubt he'll want paramilitary ops taking over his jurisdiction."

"People can get themselves into really, really difficult situations, even when they think all they're doing is living their lives," said Anika, in the same full-throated whisper. "Especially when you're a wing nut family with far more curiosity than common sense. It just happens, one stupid step at a time, and before you know it, it's like an ultra cosmic nightmare to the nth power. Do you have any idea how powerful technology is becoming, and how few people actually know how to turn the knobs and pull the levers? We've got a society of teenagers out cruising in daddy's Maserati."

"Okay, so what does that have to do with our situation?"

She shook her head violently enough to toss her hair into her face.

"No cops."

All my cop friends were devoted to Occam's Razor—that the explanation for any phenomenon was nearly always the most obvious. And its variant: if you think something's true, it probably is.

"What did he do?" I asked.

"Who?"

"Your father. What do they have on him? What drove him out of the company? What's causing him to sit by passively while Hammon and his goons invade your family's home? He doesn't strike me as the kind of character who'd just roll over for nothing. What did he do?" I repeated.

She pulled the chair out from under the computer station and sat down. She put her hands together and gripped them between her bare knees, as if to clench her secrets more tightly to her body.

"I'm going to pretend you didn't ask that," she said.

"You better answer if you want my help. You don't know how close I am to ditching you and this whole sorry mess. If you're as good a researcher as you say you are, you'll know I've been through some cosmic nightmares of my own in recent years. I don't need to play around in someone else's. It's one thing to go out on a limb for people you didn't know a week ago, it's another to be lied to, jerked around and kept in the dark. You're not the first person to think manipulation was a good strategy with me. It isn't."

With her hands still held between her knees, she bowed her head, with only her nose showing between falling waves of hair.

"It's not why I wanted to sleep with you," she said, softly.

"And it's not why I didn't. What do they have on your father?"

She shook her head.

"They have something on him," she said. "I can't tell you what it is. It's not my place. If that's a deal-breaker, then just go."

The door to the office opened and a man walked in. He peered at me, then at his daughter, who looked up at him and smiled a weak smile.

"Hi, Dad."

CHAPTER 17

"Sorry," said Fey. "I didn't know you were in here. Is something wrong?"

"Besides the obvious?" said Anika.

He squeezed his lips together and stood silently, a vivid testament to my charge and Anika's partial admission. I wanted to put it to Fey right there, but that would have meant exposing Anika, the consequences of which I had no way of knowing. I didn't have to care, but something stopped me. Maybe she was a better manipulator than I gave her credit for.

"We were just talking about finding Axel," I said. "You haven't heard anything, I take it."

He shook his head.

"Nothing. Are you leaving us?" he asked, nodding at my backpack, which I'd slipped off my back and dropped on the floor.

"Yeah," I said. "I gotta get back. Looks like you got plenty of support here."

"Indeed," he said. "The forces are assembled."

I picked up the backpack and put it on my back.

"Thanks again for letting us lay over. With all you got going on, it was a good deed."

"You may thank my daughter," he said. "Good deeds are more her specialty."

I did thank her and left, glancing into the bar as I went through the lobby. The gang was still in there, huddled around a round table. I walked out into the bright autumn day, went out to the street and looked both ways.

One of the things I learned from twenty years of trouble-shooting large, complex hydrocarbon processing systems was that in the absence of any logical, coherent, reasonably promising angle of attack, action was better than contemplation.

I turned right, toward the ferry dock. I passed the yacht club and stopped in at the gas station. Track was at his post behind the grimy desk. He wasn't happy to see me, but I made him happier when I told him I was leaving.

"It's sort of painful to leave after everyone's been so kind and welcoming," I said.

"Then you'll have to hurry on back," he said. "We'll be waiting with the same greeting."

"I had a nice chat with Desi," I said. "Turns out we have a lot of friends in common. Maybe I'll stay with him."

He didn't look like he believed me, though a breath of doubt drifted across his face. I left him with that and headed up the road. In about twenty minutes I was at the general store. I stopped in and asked for directions to the ferry dock. The clerk and the lone shopper were all too happy to oblige, briefly contesting the best route, with the shopper sketching her preference on a napkin. I thanked them both and left.

Not long after, I reached the ferry dock. The red-haired woman behind the ticket counter was at the ready.

"When's the next ferry?" I asked.

"Gettin' out of Dodge?"

"I hear there's another storm coming."

"That is correct. A real hurricane this time," she said. "Headin' up the coast, and kissing Long Island on the way by. They're talking up to sixty knots steady. That's gale force at least."

"When?"

"Day after tomorrow. You've got plenty of time. Unless you want to take the two," she turned around and looked at the big clock behind her, "which is in about a half-hour."

"Give me a walk-on," I said. "I've got to look after my boat. She's anchored in New London."

I bought the ticket and went back outside. I walked around the back of the ferry office, then cut through a parking lot of an adjacent building and took a narrow street, nearly an alley, out to the road that curved around the southern coast and headed back east. I took out Gwyneth's map and followed it to an old naval outpost on the southeast corner of the island. I went down the battered driveway, around an abandoned brick building, pulled off my backpack and sat on a rock facing out to sea. I took out my cell phone and called Randall Dodge.

He answered the phone by saying, "Your theory's holding up."

"How close can you get?"

"A section of road in the hoity-toity part of town. Humboldt's Crossing, between Meadowland and Page."

I studied the map.

"I see it. Near the middle of the country club, close to the airport. Any chance of getting the exact house?"

"Not without directly hacking the service provider," he said. "They could easily catch my ass."

"I thought Indian hackers moved through cyberspace like ghosts on the wind."

"It's been a while. I'm a little rusty on security protocols."

"I truly appreciate what you've done."

"Happy to do it, Sam. You can tell Attorney Swaitkowski that you've cashed in the last of the favors I owe her."

"Not a problem. I finally got her a paying gig."

I hung up with Randall, and feeling like my luck with Native Americans was running strong, called Two Trees. When he answered, I told him where I was and asked if he could possibly come pick me up. When he said he could, I asked him to keep it to himself, that I'd explain when he got there.

"You're trying to get somewhere undetected," he said.

"Like a ghost on the wind."

While I waited, I saw the ferry enter the mouth of the channel. There was no way to know if the lady in the ticket office would look to see if I got on, but the odds were she wouldn't. She had no reason to, and with no one else there to man the counter, had little wherewithal.

I heard the sound of a car heading down the drive, so I got up and went around to meet Two Trees. He leaned across the passenger seat and opened the door for me. I sat down with my backpack in my lap.

"Where you headed, Cap'?" he asked. I pointed to a spot on the map. He nodded. "I know what you got in mind."

"How much more would you like to know?" I asked.

"The more you tell me, the more I'd have to give up if the new cop puts it to me. What's your druthers?"

"Here's what I'd like, and you tell me what's okay for you," I said.

I told him that the Fey boy had gone missing soon after one of Fey's former business partners was found hanging in the shower. His other former partner was not only looking for the kid, he'd brought in two serious hard cases to help with the search. Anika Fey made it clear this assistance was unwelcome, but there was nothing she could do about it for reasons that were hers alone. Nobody wanted the cop involved, including Anika, so for the time being, I was going to honor that. I had a bead on where the kid might be, through sources I preferred to keep to myself.

"You can tell Kinuei any or all of that if he asks," I said. "Or even if he doesn't, though I'd like it if you held off. None of this constitutes a crime that I'm aware of, so there's no compelling obligation."

"Other than potentially pissing off our local fuzz," said Two Trees.

"Other than that."

We drove silently for a few minutes, then I said, "Since you're already part way in, how about aiding and abetting a bit."

He looked over at me.

"That depends."

I pointed to another section of the map.

"Which of these houses do you know for sure are empty?"

He leaned over for a quick look.

"All of 'em," he said. "And they'll be that way till Memorial Day. I know because I drive 'em to and from the airport every year."

"If you were a precocious kid with a laptop, which one would you pick to hide out in?"

I'd yet to see him smile, but the equivalent brightened his face.

"Ah," he said.

He waited until we arrived at the spot I'd showed him on the map. I thanked him and was about to get out of the car when he said, "I was a precocious kid myself, in some ways. For my money, I'd pick the Hillman place. They've got signs posted all over that warn of surveillance cameras and electronic alarm systems. Only the alarm company, to the best of my knowledge, doesn't exist. I've checked. Since I know what a cheapskate Gene Hillman is, wouldn't surprise me if he just bought the signs. They still have Sound Security checking up on the place, though that's a club thing. They check on everybody."

"Blue and white cars?" I asked.

"That's them. Nasty bastards from off island. They have their own little house in the club and everything's brought in for them, so they don't have to fraternize with the rest of us."

I pulled out the map again. He pointed to the Hillman's.

"If Kinuei asks me if I told you this, I'm saying no way. Just so you know," he said.

When the car was out of sight, I crossed the road and started down a path under a canopy of neon leaves, lit by the sun blasting in from the western sky. According to Gwyneth's map, the path crossed into the club, continued on under tree cover, and then opened up on a field. Although several estates backed up on the field, there was a right of way up to the road. To reach the Hillman's from there meant about a mile of exposure if I stuck to the road. I decided to figure that out when I got there.

It took about fifteen minutes to breach the border of the country club. The gate was a white metal bar, a symbolic gesture at best, since there was no fence on either side. A sign proclaimed the seriousness of violating the line, unless you were a member of the club, in which case, welcome! I ducked under the bar and proceeded for another half-hour, until I reached the field.

By now it was about four in the afternoon with plenty of light left in the day. I walked back up the path, then moved into the woods, eventually finding a clear spot invisible to passers by. I sat down, opened my backpack and took out a small handheld compass. I'd taken it from the boat's ditch bag, a pre-packaged, watertight sack you were supposed to toss in a lifeboat as you abandoned your sinking ship. I used the compass to get my bearings in relation to Gwyneth's map. I marked the key compass points on the map, along with approximate distances calculated by the time it had taken me to reach my present position. I realized most twelve-year-olds could pull up a GPS on their cell phones, but I wasn't that lucky, and anyway, what did they know about dead reckoning?

I restowed the map and the compass and lay down on the ground, using my backpack as a pillow. It was unlikely that I'd sleep, but I could at least husband my strength while waiting for the sun to go down.

This lasted until I became too twitchy to lie still, so I just sat cross-legged on the ground and busied myself with a pen and pad of paper, writing notes and jotting down observations about the Feys and their associates. Then I started making boxes and connecting them with arrows along which I noted certain actions taken by the different players. I'd always found making schematics very soothing. One of my greatest assets as an engineer was the willingness to veer from orthodoxy and speculate on the unheard-of. Like a lab rat who jumps the wall of a maze, this often yielded unexpected results. But then again, I never lost touch with what lay at the heart of engineering: logic and order, efficient interconnections and optimized process flow. Boxes and arrows not only reminded me of that, they revealed the beauty and elegance of the machine world itself.

After drawing a schematic titled "Black Swan," I went to a fresh sheet and made two columns, with the headings, "knowns" and "unknowns." Next to the knowns, I put question marks if I didn't trust the source, which meant a lot of question marks. The unknowns stretched to another page. Some of these I decided were irrelevant, and crossed them out. But it was still a long list.

I repeated the process, this time attempting to put each column in order of priority, which helped. At the top of the knowns was, "Axel ran away." At the top of the unknowns was, "What does Hammon have over Fey?" I drew a two-ended arrow between the two, and wrote over it, "Connection?"

I continued on down the columns, drawing more horizontal and diagonal lines. It provided no answers, but did give clarity to the questions. It wasn't until I could no longer read by the fading sun that I put away the pad, reluctantly.

◆

The weather report had called for a clear night, but the moon was scheduled to stay below the horizon past midnight, then rise as little more than a sliver. I stood at the edge of the field and looked into darkness. Across the field, several hundred yards away, was another stand of trees, interrupted at irregular intervals by the ridge lines of tall houses. Working off memory and the map, briefly lit by the pocket flashlight held in my mouth, I strode confidently into the field. It was mostly tall grass, but a lot lumpier than it looked that afternoon. I was glad to be wearing light hiking boots and blue jeans, but I kept an easy pace, afraid of twisting an ankle, or worse. Thus engaged, I reached the other side and saw no sign of the right-of-way, which, according to the map was an unpaved tractor path.

I checked the compass, flicking the flashlight on and off as quickly as I could. I was a few fractional degrees off where I was supposed to be, so I course-corrected and in a few minutes almost tripped on to the right-of-way. It was the width of a regular road and paved with gravel. I followed it to the street.

I checked the compass again to get my bearings and was happy to see the waypoint I'd marked on the map line up with reality. I'd waited for this moment to formulate the next part of the plan, but all I could come up with was to walk along the road, keep my eye out for vehicles, and scramble for a place to hide should one come along.

None did, saving my nerves and dignity, until I reached the intersection of Page Lane and Humboldt's Crossing, when the trees above lit up and both nerves and dignity took their losses.

From an uneasy vantage point under some sort of bristling shrub, I saw the car slow down and turn onto Humboldt's Crossing. It was one of Sound Security's blue and white tin cans. I couldn't make out the driver as the car passed by, but I could track the taillights as it moved down the road, beyond where Two Trees had fingered the Hillman place.

Assuming a reasonable amount of time would pass before the area had another drive-through by security, I felt less exposed during the ten minutes it took me to reach the Hillman's house. As promised, a sign next to the mailbox freely disclosed the presence of an elaborate and deadly accurate electronic alarm and closed-circuit TV system. Below the headline was some small print that likely went into the types of punishment intruders would assuredly receive, but I didn't risk the flashlight just to find out for sure.

As I walked down the driveway, I took note of trees and clusters of shrubbery visible in the dim light, any place I might hide if the security car came back this way. The house in front of me was tall, but narrow, with two clear stories and a third formed by large dormers set in the roof. The three-car garage was joined to the east side, the bays facing the street. I walked around and leaned against the garage wall as I forced my hands into a pair of surgical gloves, also filched from the boat's safety supplies. I looked in the garage window. There were two cars covered by what looked like fitted canvas—one big, one little. I continued around to the back of the house, with only starlight to see the condition of the windows and doors.

I'd been moving silently over grass and brick paths, and was jarred by an ugly sound when I opened the basement hatch, the rusted flap hinges complaining the way they often do. I froze with the door partly open and waited, holding my breath and straining my ears.

Nothing. I waited another few minutes, then as slowly as my arms would allow, eased the hatch door the rest of the way open. There was another door at the bottom of the stairwell. As lightly as I could, I descended the stairs and tried the knob. It opened.

Now it was really dark. I saw nothing, and Gwyneth's map wasn't going to help. It wasn't the first time I'd been in a jet black basement I wasn't supposed to be in, unsure of security measures and mindful of the way a little sound can get very big in a silent house. The key was finding the electrical panel, which would confirm or deny the existence of electronic surveillance, and tell you other things if you knew what you were looking for.

Panels are usually on exterior walls, so I turned right and started feeling my way along, using one hand to search for the box, the other for obstacles in my path. It was slow going, and after a painful, albeit silent bang to my knee, got slower still.

No darkness is absolute once your pupils reach maximum dilation. And even through the gloves, my hands were teaching me a lot about the space. It was furnished, with pictures on the walls, stuffed chairs and sofas, and coffee tables, like the one I'd encountered with my knee. So when I hit a perpendicular wall, sooner than I should have, I guessed that the utilities for the house were on the other side.

I turned the corner and continued to follow the wall, until I touched what should have been proof of the theory— an inside door. I felt for the knob, which was round and smooth. No lock. The knob turned soundlessly and I opened the door.

Sparkling red and yellow lights told me the electric panel was likely to the left of where I stood. I shut the door behind me and thought, at this point—entirely enclosed in the working part of the basement—I could afford to use the flashlight. So I slipped it out of its holster on my belt and shot it in the general direction of the panel, lighting up the face of Axel Fey, who was standing less than ten feet away.

CHAPTER 18

So much for silence. His scream was probably louder than my grunt, and certainly higher pitched. I leaped forward and grabbed him by the top of his shirt.

"Don't kill me," he cried.

"Shut up," I whispered as loudly as I could, Anika-style. "It's Sam Acquillo. The boat guy who's been staying at the Swan."

"I'm going to fucking die of sheer terror," said Axel, slumping slightly in my grip. "My heart's rupturing in my chest, I can feel it."

"You're not dying. Here, sit down," I said, dragging him down with me.

From where we sat on the floor I scanned the area with my flashlight. There was a mattress near the panel, with a pile of cans and plastic water jugs nearby. Axel's laptop was on an old wooden milk crate pulled up to the mattress. A power cord and Ethernet cable swooped up to the panel. Candles in candle holders circled the bed.

"I got to hand it to you, Axel. You worked it out."

"Not good enough. You can't take me back there," he said, almost as one sentence.

"How come?"

"Not as long as the Gestapo are there."

"What's the big deal with them?" I asked.

It was hard to read his face even in perfect light, but I tried anyway with the flashlight.

"Could you stick that thing somewhere else? I'm going blind."

"Sorry. So what's with Hammon and company?"

"I'm not at liberty to say, okay? They can't be there forever. I can stay here till next spring. You wouldn't believe how much shit there is in this house. Cheap brands, but who cares."

"You could still get caught," I said.

"I did get caught, but you're smarter than the goon squad who stops by at the exact same time every day and spends the exact same minutes walking around the house in the exact same direction. Morons."

"No argument there. So they've been here already?"

"Yeah," he said, turning the word into two syllables the way kids do when you've insulted their tender sensibilities.

"So I wonder why I saw one of their cars head down the street about a half-hour ago."

I couldn't see if that worried him or not.

"I don't know," he said. "I only know they come here once a day. Max."

"Good," I said. "So pack up your stuff. We're getting out of here."

Even with the light turned away, I could see the force of his reaction.

"Don't you listen? I said no way. You can't make me."

I told him about the additions to Hammon's posse, including their alleged background and capabilities. He wavered.

"If I could find you, they can, too," I said. "They could be on their way here now. I don't know what happens after that, but I bet you do."

"Shit."

"I'm the best thing you got right now, Axel. Better than hiding in a cave waiting for the end to come."

I watched while he jammed stuff into his backpack. It was smaller than mine, but neatly fit his laptop, some clothes, an iPod, a variety of cords and a toothbrush. I pointed the flashlight at his worn-out high-top sneakers.

"Are those your only pair of shoes?"

"What's wrong with them?"

"Nothing. Follow me."

I led the way to the basement hatch and out to the backyard. The little orange slice of a moon was struggling to get above the horizon, but it was still mostly a world of black and slightly blacker shapes and shadows, especially now that my night vision had been compromised by the flashlight. Axel lurched along behind me, literally clinging to my coattails.

We were about to turn the corner around the garage when the trees lit up with a pale brilliance animated by windblown branches. Headlights coming down the driveway. Two sets, moving fast.

"You still want to argue?" I said to Axel, grabbing his hand and pulling him into the backyard. "Do what I say and keep your mouth shut."

I pulled him headlong across a patch of lawn and into the woods beyond, doing the best I could to ward off lowhanging brambles that scraped my face and tore at my forearms. Little involuntary sounds crept from Axel's lips as we entangled and disentangled with grasping bushes and spidery vines. When I saw the movement of the light above slow, I took his shoulder and pulled him to the ground, using my own weight to power our descent. We both woofed out air on impact. I put my arm around his shoulders and shushed in his ear. He nodded his head.

I had a decent view of the back of the house from where we lay, though the headlights backlit the scene, turning everything into black cutouts. I heard car doors slam and voices calling to each other. Human shapes came into view, turning the corner of the garage, large shapes, moving quickly, crouched, holding handguns with both hands. Bright lights sprang out of nowhere, filling the backyard and revealing Hammon's mercenaries still in their sport coats and casual slacks, scanning the house with their own powerful flashlights, guns now held in one hand. Axel started to whimper, and I tightened my grip on the back of his neck until he stopped.

One of the men flung open the basement hatch and yelled something to the others. 't Hooft and the two dopes from Sound Security came running. They studied the hatch for a few moments, then Jock and Pierre went down the hole. A few moments later, the others followed. I yanked at Axel's collar.

"Time to go."

We bounded up and thrashed our way deeper into the woods. At that point, all decorum was lost. My only objective was to get clear of those guys and find a calm place to plan my next move. Which happened five minutes later when we burst out onto the backyard of another stately Fishers Island home, this one with a light over the rear patio.

I forced Axel back to the ground while I assessed the situation. A light didn't mean the folks were home, it just meant they had a light on, likely controlled by a timer. I dug out the map and compass, and my little flashlight, and tried to figure out where we were.

"You don't have a phone with a GPS by any chance," I asked him.

"No, but I know where we are. Almost at the airport," said Axel, a little louder than I wanted.

"How do you know that?" I whispered, hoping he'd get the hint.

"I walked around here sometimes at night," he whispered back. "It gets boring cooped up inside all day."

"Which way?"

He pointed toward the left of the house in front of us.

"I'd go that way."

I went back to the compass and map and found no reason to challenge the strategy. I said let's go, and took off, Axel right behind me, with no physical provocation.

We slipped by the big house and found the road that I imagined led to the airport. I started down that way and Axel took my arm and pulled.

"It's the other way," he whined, in full voice, which under the circumstances I had to let pass.

"Okay," I said. "Lead on."

We switched positions and I followed him over the hilly little street to a path that led to a wide, flat and open area that I correctly identified this time as the airport. The little shack and windsock nailed it.

I sat on the ground and Axel followed without prompting.

I pulled out my cell phone and called Two Trees.

"Now would be a good time to check up on the airport," I said when he answered.

"Has cargo arrived?"

"It has. Call it a distressed shipment," I said.

"Maybe better to bring the old truck. Has a lid over the back."

"It would," I said.

"If it starts."

"When you get to the shack, flash your lights three times. Then look to the south, southwest. You'll see a flashlight. Head that way. Keep your lights off on the way over if you can."

"Keeping them on is more the problem."

Now all I had to do was wait, something I was ill-suited to do. Though not as bad as Axel. Almost immediately he started to twitch and wriggle while humming a discordant little melody. He clutched his backpack to his chest as if expecting someone to come along and snatch it away. All I could think about was lighting a cigarette and pouring a finger of Absolut, so who was the sorrier case?

"Why'd you run, Axel?" I whispered.

"We discussed that already. None of your business."

"Keep your voice down."

"You're the one who's talking."

"I'm whispering. You don't know how to whisper?"

"I know how to whisper," he said, demonstrating poorly.

"What made you pick that house? You can tell me that."

"All the phony security signs. Who'd be fooled by that?"

"Not Two Trees," I said.

"The airport guy? What's he got to do with it?"

"He's coming to get us."

"Oh, the wisecrack about distressed shipment," he said. "You'd be distressed, too."

"I would. It took some guts to do what you did."

"Not really. I didn't have a choice. How'd you find me?" he asked.

"The Hillman's IP address. A wireless card would have been smarter."

"I don't have a wireless card. You were on N-Spock? I started working the help desk when I was eight years old. After school. We might have overlapped."

"If so, not by much."

"Anika gave you my emails?" he asked.

"Just the back end. Not the messages."

"I don't know why she did that."

"She was worried about you," I said.

"That's not what I mean."

I was going to ask him what he did mean, but I caught sight of headlights coming down the long driveway toward the airport shack. I told Axel to hug the ground, and I did so myself. A pickup truck with rounded fenders and roof rolled up to the shack and the headlights went out. Then they flashed three times. I rolled over on my back, held up my flashlight, switched it on and waved it at the truck for a few moments. Then I rolled back and saw the antique pickup lumber over the grass toward our position. When he was twenty feet away I stood up and flashed my light again. He turned toward us and stopped.

"You'll have to move some crap out of the way, but there's plenty of room back there for both of you," said Two Trees when I reached the driver's side window of the mid-fifties Chevy pickup. I could smell the moldy upholstery, causing an eruption of lost memories of my father's 1957 Belvedere.

"Take us down the road to the Swan, but don't stop till you get a hundred yards past the gas station. I'll slap the fender when we're clear. I'm in your debt."

"Yeah, yeah, climb in the back."

True to his word, there was some stuff in the way, but we managed to cram ourselves in under the hard cover, and with a great deal of effort, pull the hatch closed behind us.

"We're going to suffocate in here," said Axel. "There's not enough oxygen. I can already feel it."

"No, we're in luck. These old trucks were built to haul hunting dogs. So they had a special ventilation system back here. Lots of air."

What those old trucks also had was a type of suspension designed to maximize concussive forces when traveling over rough terrain. So the next few minutes were devoted to finding handholds, bracing ourselves and avoiding crushing each other as the bed of the truck lurched like an amusement park ride gone haywire.

When we hit hard asphalt and things settled down, Axel said, "That thing about the dogs? Pure bullshit."

"You're not suffocating, are you?"

Even on smooth road, it wasn't the most comfortable ride. The vibrations were nearly as bad as the noise, which was barely endurable. I tried at first to divine the route Two Trees was traveling by general movement, but the roll, pitch and yaw made that impossible. Miraculously, I could hear snippets of music coming from the cab. Mothers of Invention.

This wasn't the ideal moment to reflect on the spasmodic turns my life seemed to take, despite my best efforts to maintain an even keel, to simulate the order of a well-configured flow scheme, but that's the way my mind worked. There wasn't time to trace and make sense of the path that had led me from agreeing to pick up Burton Lewis's new custom sloop from the builder in Maine, to being tossed about the bed of a superannuated pickup truck with a terrified, autistic Swiss, barely a step ahead of pursuing mercenaries in the employ of one of the country's leading software developers. But that was the long and short of it.

It made me angry, but at whom it was hard to tell. I'm not so simple as to think the universe cares enough about one mangled, benighted engineer to orchestrate such an elaborate muddle, but it makes you think.

The exact direction of our flight was hard to make out, though the velocity was clear. I could hear it in the roar of the engine and the metallic whir of the old gear box. I'd worked on 50's and 60's Chevies at a repair shop when I was in high school, when those cars weren't that old and I was too young to think the mechanic's vocation was anything less than noble and essential. So, as I lay there beside the whimpering Axel Fey, all I could think about were carburetors and linkages, tappets, spark plugs and distributor caps, pressure plates and sloppy universal joints. I could hear them all, and feel their plaintive irregularities in the primitive reaches of my consciousness.

And then it all shuddered to a stop. It was too soon to be at the drop-off point, so I stayed still, encouraging Axel to do the same by a firm grip on his forearm.

"Howdy, Two Trees. Wazup?" I heard someone say from somewhere outside the truck.

"I'm driving home," said Two Trees. "Wazup with you?"

"Driving home from what? I didn't see any plane come in."

"It was a stealth bomber. They're invisible. Don't you read the papers?"

"Some people think you're a witty guy. Not me."

"There's help for that," said Two Trees. "Get a sense of humor surgically implanted. Think how much more fun you'll have."

"What's in the bed?" asked the voice.

"Tools. What's in yours? The next-door neighbor?"

"That's not funny."

"Yes it is. If you had a sense of humor you'd know that. Now if you don't mind, I got a wife waiting impatiently. Oh, I guess that's redundant."

I heard the engine rev and the shift lever drop into first gear.

"Open the lid," said another voice from further away.

"Who the hell is that?" said Two Trees. "A new boss?"

"Do what he said. Open the lid."

"With all due respect to Sound Security, fuck you. I'm paid by the same people you are, so if you want to look in my trunk, talk to them."

I felt the truck move forward, then lurch to a stop.

"You're blocking my way," said Two Trees.

"We can't let you out of here without checking under the lid," said the original voice from outside, now slightly out of breath.

"What's this 'we' shit? Who're those guys?"

"Just open the lid."

I heard the familiar chunk of the transmission sliding into reverse, the whine of the gears as the truck flung backwards, then another bang followed by forward momentum. Outside, yells sprang from all directions, but the truck continued on, rpms at the limit through all three gears.

What had been an uncomfortable ride became lunatic. I wrapped an arm around Axel and tried to keep him from getting pulverized by the hard metal surrounding us. A few moments into this leg of the ride, I heard the sound of branches scraping the side and underbody of the truck. We were in the woods. I clutched Axel even tighter and tried not to yelp from each passing impact with flying objects sprung from the detritus scattered about the truck bed.

As I began to wonder how much more of this we could take, the truck abruptly stopped. The front door slammed and the tailgate flew open.

"Come on, come on," said Two Trees, pulling at our pant legs, dragging us out of the truck. "Stay flat and pretend you're invisible."

We did as he said and watched the bulky little truck pull away. Nearby, headlights were dancing through the trees, heading in the opposite direction. I pulled my backpack in front of me, opened the zipper and felt around for the hard muzzle of Poole's Glock. It came out inside its holster. I strung my belt through the holster and took out the gun. Axel watched the whole maneuver with an expression it was too dark to decipher.

"I'm not seeing this," he said.

"Good. Don't look. Just do exactly what I tell you to do when I tell you."

"You're bossier than Anika, which is hard to do."

When the headlights had nearly disappeared, I dragged Axel to his feet and pulled him with me deeper into the woods. I wasn't ready to risk the flashlight, so collisions with saplings and entanglements with underbrush were ongoing impediments, but we kept a hard pace. Axel complied as well as he could with my demands, but no one, including Axel himself, considered him much of a physical specimen. After manhandling his frail physique, I knew this performance far exceeded his capabilities. So when he pitched forward to the ground with a little cry of desperate exhaustion, I let him lie.

I sat down next to him and felt his forehead, then his pulse, which beat like a trip hammer. I lit the flashlight, stuck it in my mouth, then pulled out the map and compass and tried to get my bearings. The airport was more or less equidistant between the north and south coasts. I guessed, based on the angle of the airport entrance, and the predominance of tree cover, that we were closer to the north coast, but there was no way to be certain. Using the compass, I could at least move in that direction and try to find a landmark that would reestablish our position. Though not until Axel took a breath without it sounding like it was his last.

"Good work, kid," I told him. "You showed a lot of heart."

"Run, run, run," he gasped out.

"We're going to have to move again in a little while, so don't get too comfortable."

"I can't move again."

"You can. You just don't know it yet. Take deeper, slower breaths and try to compose yourself. Tell your heart to slow down."

"How do you do that?"

"Calm your mind," I said. "Your body will follow."

"Oh, great. A fucking guru."

"No. A fucking boxer. Different religion, same advice."

"I know why Anika likes you. You're even weirder than she is."

We lay there staring up at the sky for a lot longer than I wanted to, but I really didn't know how much the kid could take.

Then I thought about the boys in the Ford Excursion. I told Axel that we would have to go soon, but we'd be walking instead of running, and I'd carry his backpack for him. I told him we were heading for the north coast, but I had to find a landmark to get oriented.

"You can't take me back to the Swan," he said.

"I'm not."

"Then where?"

"You'll know when we get there."

"In other words, you don't know where the hell we're going," he said.

I took his backpack and rigged it to hang from mine. Then I stood up, squirmed into the load and reached my hand down to Axel. He let me drag him to his feet and followed me as I picked my way through the woods. He was quiet and his breathing less labored. I looked back occasionally and saw him studying his feet as he moved over the darkly treacherous ground. I wanted to say to him, "Balance, one of the benefits of a calm mind," but it would've probably made him trip.

After about twenty minutes of this we fell out onto another road. It ran east-west, so according to the map it was one of three possibilities, though a left hand turn was called for in all cases. Axel followed silently.

I was happy for the smoother terrain, but concerned about the exposure. The darkness made it difficult to spot places to hide, but also made it easier to detect oncoming vehicles. I debated the trade-offs in my mind as a way to pass the anxious time.

The debate was somewhat decided when I heard an approaching vehicle before I saw the headlights. I yanked Axel with me directly into the woods, where he dropped before I had a chance to force him. It was a black SUV, though not conclusively the one in pursuit. I gave it plenty of time to disappear down the road before heading back to the street. We walked on, further slowed by unease. Axel was at my side, looking behind us every few feet. I was afraid he'd fall, but glad for the vigilance. We passed a mailbox on which was painted a street number and the name of the street. I looked at the map and pinpointed our position.

Several minutes later the tree cover lifted and we walked out into an open area, with fields on either side. The crescent moon was up by now, and even its faint light was enough to allow us to see a crossroads up ahead. I knew where I was, less than ten minutes from either the Swan or Gwyneth's shop. Neither were good options, but I decided to head for the intersection and make up my mind when I got there.

We were nearly there when a dark shape rose up out of the field. Axel made an animal sound as the shape came toward us with long, resolute strides. I shoved Axel behind me.

"Well, well," said Derrick Hammon. "I suppose you didn't need our help after all."

CHAPTER 19

At the vaporous emergence of Derrick Hammon, Axel started hopping and making groaning, mewling sounds. I reached behind me and grabbed him at the belt line, calming him. With the same hand, I pulled the Glock out of its holster and aimed it at Hammon's chest.

"Cell phone," I said, using my other hand to beckon him closer.

"You're not going to shoot me," he said, though he did as I asked.

"Pull your pants down to your ankles," I said. "Leave the underwear on. The kid's had enough terror for one night."

"Pretty kinky," said Hammon.

He undid his belt and let his loose khakis fall to the ground.

"Axel, do you want to go with this man?" I asked.

"Shit, no way," he said. "What are you crazy?"

"So there's my legal justification for shooting you if you try to stop us."

"You can't escape Jock and Pierre," said Hammon. "But you'll wish you had."

"Good. Then I can shoot them, too."

"What did the boy tell you?"

"Everything," I said.

"No I didn't," Axel yelled. "I didn't tell him a fucking thing!"

In the dim, moonlit night, I saw Hammon smile, or maybe it was a sneer. Either way, it was a good target. I put the gun back in its holster, took a step forward and smashed him in the face with my good left hand.

Knocking someone out with a single punch is a lot harder than people think. Hammon was small, but fit, and with my right fist out of commission, I had to rely on my weaker left. I gave it everything I had, throwing all my weight behind a power jab, snapping my fist the way I was taught by my addled old trainers. It took. Hammon's head whipped back and he crumpled to the ground like an imploding building.

It's not the blow to the face that does the work, it's the brain smacking into the inside of the skull. So I hoped I'd only given him a concussion and not an early death.

Axel squealed and started hopping again. I grabbed him by the shoulder and once again pulled him along, this time across the field to the north and into another formless mass of murky undergrowth.

Ten minutes into another thrashing dash through ill-cared for woods, Axel gave out. I kept him from falling by holding him around the waist. He didn't weigh much for an eighteen-year-old, but was plenty heavy enough under the circumstances. I tried to take my own advice and calm the mind, but it was having none of it as I felt the creeping approach of exhaustion. So instead of calm, I switched to rage, growling profanities with my rapidly weakening breath.

Branches raked my face and vines yanked at my feet. The ground began to pitch downward, which improved our velocity, but made it harder to stay upright. Axel's staggering attempts to help the effort tipped the balance, and we both fell headlong, with my face and chest taking most of the blow. My right cheek caught something sharp, and I felt a rivulet of blood run down the top of my shirt. I wiped it off with my sleeve as I got us back on our feet, and more carefully this time, continued down the steep incline.

Then suddenly we were out of the woods again, now in the backyard of a small house. There were lights on inside and a dog started to bark. I made for the driveway at the end of which was parked a panel truck. Along with another car parked farther down, it provided brief cover on the way out to the street.

Security lights lit the ensuing scene. We were across the street from Buchanan's Marina, one of several small out-fitting and repair operations at the rear of a channel that began at the Swan. We crossed the street and I stowed Axel and the backpacks under some foliage and told him to be quiet and stay put. He was breathing too heavily to answer, but he gave his head a feeble nod.

I dug a set of Vise-Grips and a pair of wire cutters out of my pack, part of the collection of tools I'd brought on the expedition. I felt around my cheek before moving off. It was slick with blood, but the cut was more long than deep. It could wait.

The marina had two docks running perpendicular to the shore. I walked down the first, assessing what was avail-able. A small, white, hard-shell tender, the type of auxiliary boat preferred by traditional sailors, popped out of the low light. I rejected it for that reason, but pulled out the oars and laid them on the dock. Farther down were two matching aluminum-hulled open boats with squared-off corners, raised helm and big four-cycle motors. Cushioning around the gunwales confirmed that they were the marina's working boats, used to both push and tow customers' boats in and out of the slips.

Even better, they had oarlocks.

I retrieved the oars off the dock and brought them with me onto the aluminum boat, where I first sat at the helm and checked out the controls. Then I moved to the rear and examined the motor, with poor results in the limited light. I set the oars in the oarlocks, which were a little oversized, preferable to the other way around, then went forward and untied the line. I used one of the oars to paddle backwards into the channel, then both to push the boat forward over to the waterline.

I had to step up to my knees in the water to make a quiet landing, pulling the bow of the boat up on a tuft of grass. I retrieved Axel, who was lying on his back with his knees drawn up, staring up into the leafy bush.

"It's Sam," I whispered, hoping to avoid startling him. "Stand up and hand me the backpacks. You only have to walk a few feet."

"I can't."

"Come on."

He rose as if testing for broken bones in his arms and legs, then dragged the backpacks over to my feet. I picked them up and got them reinstalled on my back. I walked him to the boat and held the bow.

"Get in," I said.

"You bought a boat?"

"No, I'm stealing it. Get in."

"You can't steal a boat."

"I'll give it back. Call it a loan. Get the hell in."

"I'm afraid of boats."

"Get in the boat or I'll drown you myself."

He picked up his right foot, hesitated, then put it back on the ground. He gripped the edge of the boat and lifted his left leg, waved it over the side for a few moments, then dropped it back again.

"I don't know how," he said.

"Just step in. I'll support you," I said, gripping a familiar handhold at his shoulder.

This time he made it, though I thought he'd fall over when the boat tipped slightly in the water. I had him sit in the bow facing the helm while I pushed the boat off the patch of grass and into the water. Before clambering aboard, I turned it around and gave it a little shove. The noise from all this sounded impossibly loud, but I was committed. The boat drifted into the channel as I found a place to kneel with a minimum of pain and wield the oars, which were short for the purpose, but workable.

I braced myself for angry yells, floodlights, gunfire over the bow, but none were forthcoming. Instead, all we heard was the bump of the oars inside the oarlocks, the soft slap as the blades entered the water, chirping bugs in the trees and the occasional flip of a fish breaking the surface.

I held close to the far side of the channel, which was undeveloped marshland and clear of lights. The boat had a minimum draft, though I managed to hang us up a few times as I hugged the waterline. We passed a few more modest houses built directly on the water, some with boat docks and moorings, and cars and trucks parked in the driveways. Local people, likely the third or fourth generation living there.

The channel widened as we turned a corner and moved past the Swan. I didn't know if Axel knew where we were, and if so, if he saw the hotel go by. Few lights were on, inside or out. The parking lot was on the other side of the building, so I couldn't see who was there. I knew from living at the end of the dock that this side of the quickly widening channel was hard to see at night. Though in a few minutes it was open all the way and we were in the Inner Harbor, heading for the opening in the breakwater.

I began to row harder, less concerned with the sound of the oars bumping around the oarlocks, motivated as much by the agony in my knees as by fear of apprehension.

When I made it all the way into the Inner Harbor, I whispered, "Axel, you still alive?"

"No, I'm dead. Where are we?"

I told him, explaining that we'd recently rowed past the Black Swan. Without being noticed. He moaned and said something that I couldn't make out. I shipped the oars, struggled into a squat, then stood up at the helm, which I lit with my flashlight. All the essentials were there: start button, throttle and gear lever. The motor started on the first crank and ran smoothly and almost silently. A marina mechanic's baby.

It was a quick trip along the south side of West Harbor to where I'd secreted my dinghy.

"You ever telling me where we're going?" asked Axel.

"No, I'm going to show you," I said, looking down at where he huddled inside the bow. "First, we have to switch boats. Keep your head down," I added as I killed the motor and drifted through the branches that spread out from the trees growing on the shore. I flicked on the flashlight and saw the dinghy where I'd left it, seemingly untouched and ready for boarding. I normally hated dinghies, the definition of a necessary evil, but seeing the little inflatable caused a surge of affection in my breast.

"Good dinghy. Good, good dinghy," I said.

"Great. He's talking to boats."

"Did you know a sense of humor can be surgically implanted?" I asked as I came alongside the dinghy and slipped my hand under the nylon rope strung along the top of the pontoon. I pulled it tight against the marina boat and told Axel to climb aboard. He strained to get to his feet, his legs likely as firm and controllable as a pair of rubber bands. I reached down and helped him up.

His hands were soft and slippery. After he made it to his feet I checked my palm and it was slick with blood. I took his hand back and looked.

"You're cut," I said.

"You think? You should see you. Where's David Cronenberg?"

He learned the dynamics of boarding an inflatable tender the moment his foot hit the sole and the little boat zinged out from under him. Before he fell backward, I put my hand between his shoulder blades and shoved him the rest of the way in. He fell against the opposite pontoon, then bounced back into the bow, his favorite place.

I transferred the backpacks, tied the aluminum boat to a branch overhead, then came aboard. In less than a minute I had the motor started, the line pulled and the dinghy underway.

"What's next?" said Axel, his eyes closed and his head laid back against the curved rubber bow. "Is there a helicopter waiting?"

"See, that's what a sense of humor feels like."

"I'm not trying to be funny."

"I believe you."

"Don't believe anything," he said.

"That's a pretty cynical thing for an eighteen-year-old to say."

"Who said I was eighteen?"

"Anika."

"I'm twenty-three," he said. "There's your proof."

"Why would she lie about that?" I asked.

"Why does the sun come up every day? Goddamn color head. Christ, I'm beat to holy shit."

"How old is Anika?"

"Thirty. I know that for sure because my mother told me."

"I thought your mother died bearing you."

He huffed.

"Not exactly. Unless you think playing mahjong on the beach in Miami every day is like being dead."

I looked at my compass as we sped across the harbor, using the little button that turned on the backlight, which wasn't adequate, so I had to use my flashlight. During all this maneuvering, the finicky dinghy took a few unexpected zigs and zags.

"Whoa, who's driving this thing?" asked Axel.

"Remote control guidance system developed by the NSA, though some think the Illuminati are catching up with the technology."

"Funny, hah, hah. Just please don't flip the boat over."

"I know. You can't swim."

"Who said I can't swim?" he asked.

"Your family's from Switzerland, right?"

"Yeah. So what?"

"Just checking."

I slowed the dinghy and panned across the harbor with my little flashlight until I saw the glimmer of reflective material on the private red buoy at the head of my secret channel. I eased up on the throttle and felt my way along.

"Would you've really shot Hammon?" Axel asked.

"I don't know. Depends."

"On what?"

"I don't know," I said.

He was quiet for a bit, then said, "You really walloped him."

"He responded well, we'll give him that."

"Anika said you were a professional boxer."

"Short career, but you learn things."

"I learned how to get beat up without getting killed," he said.

"Comes in handy later in life."

I backed off the outboard until we were at a slow crawl through the narrow inlet. The sky was now completely overcast, but strangely lighter. I could see both banks of the inlet and beyond into the tiny harbor, and then after another turn, the glow from the portholes of the *Carpe Mañana*. A dog barked. My heart leapt.

"Quiet, fur ball," I called.

I opened the throttle for a short burst, then pulled out the lanyard that held the kill switch open, and glided silently into the sloop's graceful transom. Eddie stared down from above and made ecstatic noises.

I heard Amanda running up the companionway. I climbed over Axel as we bumped into the back of the boat, making a successful grab at the swim ladder. Amanda looked over Eddie's head into the dinghy.

"Permission to come aboard," I said.

"I should kill you," she said.

"Not until I get a drink."

As the dinghy whipped around from the shift in load, I handed up the two backpacks, then helped Axel grip the swim ladder, and with Amanda's help, hoisted him up and into the cockpit. I tied off the dinghy, then made it up over the transom under my own power.

Eddie seemed to have lost what little reserve he possessed.

"Okay, okay," I said, digging my hands into his thick fur and letting him knock his long nose into my face. "Hasn't that woman fed you?"

We turned our attention to Axel, who was collapsed on the cockpit floor, embracing himself, his eyes closed and his face clenched in a silent grimace. With some coaxing we got him below and laid him out on one of the settees in the center salon. Amanda sat on the edge of the settee and used her long fingers to comb back his hair, revealing his face, streaked with angry red scratches.

"What happened to you," she said, then looked back at me. "Oh, my God, what happened to *you*?"

I dug two bottles of water out of the refrigerator and handed one to Axel.

"It's been a long night."

Amanda took my water bottle and poured some on a paper towel, which she used to dab the blood off my cheek.

"Look at you," she said, "you're a mess."

I found the first aid kit and dumped the contents out on the navigation table. Using hydrogen peroxide and an antiseptic cream, we did our best to attend to Axel's hands and face, then mine. While this was going on I briefed Amanda on the events of the evening, just the facts, leaving speculation for a time when Axel was out of earshot.

Then I called Two Trees.

"That was jolly," he said, answering the phone.

"You alright?"

"I would be if I wasn't married. For some reason she doesn't like hiding in a barn."

"You're in a barn?"

"Those guys are gonna be pretty mad at me. I thought it was better to keep my head down till that damn cop answers his phone."

"How long have you been trying?" I asked.

"Since I got here. What is that, coupla hours?"

I apologized for putting him in that spot. He ignored me and asked where I was. I told him what happened after he dropped us off, up to swiping the marina boat. He didn't press me to go further.

"If you get a hold of that cop, tell him to call me," he said. "If this goes on much longer I'll be safer out there."

Amanda remained silent through the call, then said, "We need to contact that policeman."

"No cops," said Axel from where he lay on the settee.

"That's not up to you," she said.

I poured a tall vodka on the rocks and sat on the opposite settee.

"She's right," I told him. "Your family secrets aren't as important to me as our safety. Your choices now are to come clean or convince me you can't. Either way, I'm calling Kinuei."

He sat up on his elbows.

"Anika really won't like that."

Amanda huffed.

"It's not up to her, either," she said.

Axel lay back down and stared up at the ceiling.

"My father got caught doing something at the company that was really bad. Something he could go to jail for. Hammon and Sanderfreud used it to kick him out."

"Blackmail," I said.

"Yeah. They kicked him out and made him turn over the keys to all the code."

"What do you mean?"

"Father headed up development. He was the only one who had complete documentation on all the applications. He had to give it up to these consultants they brought in. Only the dummies still couldn't figure everything out. Ha, ha."

"Anika told me there's a piece missing. They don't really have everything they need."

"She told you that? What a blabbermouth."

"It's true?"

"Oh, yeah. N-Spock is supposed to be the ultimate problem-solving software, and fourth- and fifth-generation programming languages are built on the premise of problem solving. Only the kinks haven't all been worked out, especially when you're talking 5GL. Nobody really knows how to do that crap. There's a ghost in the machine—let's you get halfway through the data transfer and then makes the application start eating itself. Awesome shit, in my opinion, but not for Subversive, as if I care, the lousy pricks."

"Your father told me you worked on 5.0."

"You're kidding. Another Chatty Kathy in the family. What am I, the only one who can keep his mouth shut?"

"Fey said you just worked around the edges," I said. "But you did a lot more than that, didn't you? That's why Hammon wants you. To force you to de-bug the program. That's why you ran."

Axel glowered at me.

"My father wrote the backbone of 5.0 at night in our basement," said Axel. "It's in a 4GL that essentially recon-figured the entire application. Leapfrogged all that boring incremental development. After that, it was just a matter of hanging the functionality and user interface off the core like ornaments on a Christmas tree. And they couldn't even get that right."

I looked over at Amanda to see how she might be reading the conversation. She shrugged.

"We need to call the policeman," she said.

Axel looked like he was about to say something sar-castic to her, but when I shook my head he thought better of it. I got out my cell phone and called the Fishers Island barracks. I got an answering machine. When Axel heard me leaving a message he chuckled.

"If you want to report a murder, press one. Armed rob-bery, press two," he said.

"It is odd," said Amanda.

I kicked myself for not getting Kinuei's cell phone number when I had the chance.

A breeze blew down the companionway and the boat tilted slightly. We both looked up at the ceiling as if you could see through to the sky. There were more decisions to be made, only now they seemed a lot more difficult. I had Axel, and I had Amanda and Eddie and the boat. Also two handguns and a shotgun. I could have talked myself into believing we were permanently secure, but cold reason argued otherwise. As much as I thought Hammon a self-revering jerk, his boys seemed like the real deal. I'd handled plenty of goons and street thugs, but this was different.

People like Jock and Pierre, probably not their real names, had training and technology and resources at their disposal that regular criminals couldn't dream of. I wouldn't stand a chance and there was no percentage in believing otherwise.

As of that moment, however, they hadn't found us. New London could be one or two hours away, depending on wind and currents. It was late at night, and the wind was beginning to pick up, not to abate until the outside edge of a hurricane blew by. It was now or never.

"Has Eddie peed tonight?" I asked Amanda.

She looked over at him.

"Have you? No. We were about to go when you showed up."

I took him to shore while Amanda prepared the boat for cast-off. Most of this involved securing moveable objects that could turn into missiles if things got rough, and closing the boat off to flying saltwater. It's not often Amanda got to literally batten down the hatches, a thought she found endlessly charming.

Soon after, I started the motor and went forward to raise the anchor. Amanda had the helm, and turned toward the channel as soon as we were free. I went back to the cockpit and gently whispered instructions to her as we threaded the narrow opening and motored into the Inner Harbor.

When we cleared the channel, Amanda relinquished the helm and I got to stand there feeling the glorious sensation of a good-sized sailboat moving under power over an open body of water. The chrome wheel cool in my hand, the breeze now officially wind, with the anemometer reading ten knots. The bow gently rose and dipped over the little waves building in the modest fetch of West Harbor. The sky at the eastern horizon was getting lighter. I checked the clock on my cell phone. Six in the morning.

Amanda sat on the helmsman's seat behind me, put both arms around my waist and hugged. I reached down with one hand to grip her forearm.

"I worried," she said.

"So did I."

"You take too many chances."

"You're probably right."

"Why this time?" she asked.

"Curiosity."

"About the girl? It's okay, you just have to tell me."

"It's not like that."

"It isn't? She's young and available. Worse for you, she's smart and in some kind of trouble. And she has curves in all the places I don't."

"I like your curves fine."

"You like me all around, otherwise you wouldn't keep knocking on my door and inviting me to sit next to you on your Adirondack chairs and look at the bay. But you never tell me you love me."

Before heading for the open water, I steered the boat across the harbor, then pulled back on the throttle as we approached the shoreline. I put the gearbox in neutral and gently disentangled from Amanda's embrace.

"I'm lousy at the conventions of intimate relationships," I told her.

"So am I. Maybe that's the bond."

"Maybe. I'm going to pick up the utility boat I swiped from the marina and bring it with us to New London. Then I'm going to use it to come back here for Anika. I have my reasons, but if you think it's because I want her instead of you, saying you're wrong won't change that. I'd rather you just trust me because you do."

She looked at me as if trying to read text off my face. Unspoken words of her own buzzed like a swarm of insects around her eyes.

"Can I know those reasons?" she asked.

"It's a hypothesis. I'd rather it cook a bit before setting it on the table."

"You're risking your life for a hypothesis?"

"Can you think of a better reason?"

"You're evading. I've seen this before. It's what you do when you're not sure you should be doing what you're doing," she said.

"If I knew what I was doing it wouldn't be a hypothesis. I'm one of *your* hypotheses, since you don't know what you're doing with me."

"I don't, but I'd rather keep doing it for now, though God knows why," she said. "Probably because I love your dog."

"He loves you back. Of course, he loves anyone who feeds him brie on tiny pieces of toast."

I gave her the helm and asked her to keep the boat more or less in the same position. Then I climbed down into the dinghy and motored over to where I'd left the marina boat. It was still there. I tied the dinghy's towline to the stern of the other boat, clambered aboard and started it up. Moments later I was towing the dinghy out to the *Carpe Mañana,* waiting where I'd left her, Amanda having decided not to ditch me quite yet.

The mounting winds and shifting currents, however, had made holding her position somewhat of a challenge. She threw me a line when I came alongside, which I used to rig the marina boat to a cleat at the stern of the *Carpe Mañana.*

We motored out into Fishers Island Sound where the true nature of the weather revealed itself. The wind out of the east was pushing twenty knots and the waves were a messy combination of wind-blown chop, swells blown in from the Atlantic and the riptides that frequently formed in an area west of Fishers called the Race. The net effect of all this was a rough ride and a very seasick Axel Fey.

"What should I do for him?" Amanda asked from below.

"Give him a bucket."

With the wind more to the east than north, and blowing adamantly, I knew we'd make better time under sail than with the engine. So I put the boat on auto helm and ran around the deck, getting things ready to raise the sails. I tumbled back into the cockpit and did just that. As soon as the reefed mainsail caught that angry easterly, we took off, and I killed the engine. A few minutes later, I had the big Genoa headsail out and we were skimming up, down and over the heightening seas, but moving at least two knots faster than we could manage under power, and without the noise and diesel smell of the engine.

The sun by now was up there somewhere behind the cloud cover, painting the seas a bloodless grey. There were few other boats in sight, and thus far, no giant ferries coming in or out of the port of New London. The other thing to watch for were submarines, a hazard unique to that particular harbor.

I let Amanda in on this when she brought out coffee and toast.

"That's what Mr. Berman, the retired radio guy, told me," she said. "I still find it hard to believe."

"Yup. They build 'em and fix 'em right here in Groton, across the river from New London."

"Maybe they'll lend us one. Make your return trip a little more discreet."

"Good idea. Why don't you call ahead."

The wind continued to build, edging up into the low twenties. I knew this without looking at the wind gauge, based on the whitecaps and herringbone pattern on the surface of the agitated water. The boat hardly seemed to notice as she cut through the swells and gracefully danced over the erratic chop. The repair to the steering cables held. I had no rational reason to think it wouldn't, but time would have to pass before echoes of that trauma would be purged.

I checked on the two little boats in tow, bobbing and weaving in the sailboat's wake. In looking back, the receding contours of Fishers Island gave my heart an involuntary lift. To be gone for good. Another thing to long for.

"I want to go to France," said Amanda, reading my mind. "Or Italy. Live in a hotel and read books for a few months. I'd go alone, but I'd rather you come with me. I'm embarrassed to say I like your company."

"Okay."

"Just like that?"

"I've optimized petrochemical plants in both those places. I'll give you a tour."

I switched on the auto helm, let go of the wheel and relaxed back into Amanda. She wrapped her arms around my chest. "For that to happen, you have to come back from Fishers, with or without the curvaceous Anika."

"Okay."

"Splendid."

My plan was to grab a mooring in the field just inside the mouth of the Thames River. Instead, I grabbed two, doubling the chances Burton's sailboat would survive the coming blow. It took a while to rig the lines in a way I hoped would evenly spread the loads on both cleats and moorings. I brought the marina boat up to the transom and tied it off hard against the swim ladder, then separated it from the dinghy, which I tied to an aft cleat. I had to wake up Axel, who took the news with some shock and alarm.

"I can't move my arms or legs," he said. "My face stings. I can't go anywhere. Let me stay here. I'll keep it clean."

Not too long after, I had Amanda, Axel and Eddie in the marina boat with some luggage, a few bottles of water and a bag of dog biscuits. Eddie ran to the bow and sniffed the complicated air blowing down the river from New London and Groton. Axel clutched his backpack to his chest and radiated fragility. On the way into the harbor I made a few phone calls.

I brought them to a dock just south of the ferry landing. After some awkward pitching about, we were off the boat with all the travel gear. Amanda took Eddie's leash and Axel lay down on the dock, using his backpack as a pillow.

"Joe Sullivan will pick you up at Orient Point and take you to Burton's. Burton will provide the usual protections," I told Amanda. "Please don't argue with me about that. I'll be safer if I know you and Eddie are safe."

"Is it too much to ask that this be the last time you stow me at Burton's as a safety precaution?" she asked.

"No. It's not too much."

"What about Axel?"

"Stow him there, too, if he's willing. If not, the hell with him."

"I'm willing," said Axel from his supine spot on the dock.

Amanda picked up her bag and cinched her grip on Eddie's leash. I kissed her and was about to tell her that I loved her when she walked away, down the dock on her way to the ferry, towed along by the eager mutt.

Axel reluctantly followed, his battered sneakers barely clearing the wooden slats.

CHAPTER 20

The sun was still climbing in the sky, but it was getting darker, the cloud cover turning a blacker shade of grey. The wind blew in noisy bursts, the air unnaturally warm and heavy with the promise of rain. I got back in the marina boat and headed for the mooring field.

On the sailboat, I took a shower, then replaced my backpack with the waterproof ditch bag, which could also be configured to wear on my back, adding and replacing several items, including a selection of tools and gear from the amply stocked tool kit and spare parts bins supplied with the boat. I wrapped the shotgun in a towel covered by a large garbage bag, and used duct tape to make a tight cylinder. Before leaving, I secured the *Carpe Mañana* against the impending storm, stripping off the sails and dodger, and tying down anything that might blow away. It wasn't easy work, especially as the effects of the night before started catching up to me.

My last act aboard was to radio the New London harbormaster to let him know an unattended boat was going to ride out the weather in his waters.

The marina boat was designed and rigged in a fashion opposite to the one I most needed at that moment. Its shallow keel, squared-off bow, low freeboard, open helm and large motor were all intended to aid in pushing and pulling much bigger boats, and for easy on-and-off around a busy dock. Not for striking out across windswept seas, where I needed a deep keel, sharp bow, lots of room between the deck and waves, and a cozy watertight cabin. But that was the way it was.

Recognizing the real possibility that the boat could flip over, I brought along a safety harness with a life jacket built in, and a quick-release tether I could use to clip myself to the helm. I tied the ditch bag to the front of the helm, clipped the handheld radio to my belt and put my cell, now in a Ziploc bag, in the inside, zippered pocket of the jacket.

As I cruised down and out the mouth of the Thames, I was fooled into thinking I'd over-prepared. But as soon as I met open water, all such illusions were washed away as I plunged into a set of real waves. They were steep and poorly organized, foamy at the top and stacked up on each other, so I barely hit the trough before I was climbing the other side.

The first important task was to find the right amount of throttle. I needed enough power to make steady headway, but not so much that I'd fly off the crest of a wave, lose steerage and consequently all control at a critical moment. The *Carpe Mañana*, with her deep V of a hull and heavy displacement, would slice through the waves like a cleaver, where the marina boat skimmed across the surface, sliding up the slope, then slapping down the other side, only to be flung suddenly to the left, and then to the right, before scaling the next watery cliff.

I'd never ridden a mechanical bull, but I couldn't help thinking, this has to be a lot like that.

The safety harness and tether turned out to be more essential than precautionary. On a dozen occasions, I felt my feet rise off the sole of the boat, my grip on the wheel both savior and hazard as the jerks and jolts threatened to broach the valiant little craft.

I almost convinced myself that I had control of the helm when water off the blunt forward edge started to spray into my face, blinding me and filling the bottom of the boat to an alarming degree, until I realized the water weight provided some much needed ballast, reducing bounce and the jittery swings that had thus far dominated the trip. I just reminded myself not to allow too much of a good thing to come in over the bow.

Rather than head back into West Harbor, I struck a course toward the ferry channel that penetrated the far end of the island. This meant a greater exposure to the uniquely treacherous vagaries of the Race, but that was unavoidable. There was no percentage in hugging the shore, especially now that it was in the lee of the storm, and as always cluttered with rocky shoals and other hidden menace.

The marina boat was no happier with her worsening circumstances, forcing me to slow down another few knots, both to ward off capsizing and reduce the amount of seawater slopping around my feet. Though not soon enough. It wasn't unusual in the Race to have a pair of swells temporarily pile up on each other, amplifying the effects. One of these unholy joinings must have formed right as my attention was on the helm, tossing the starboard corner of the bow up in the air and throwing me backwards into the boat, my hands ripped from the wheel.

There wasn't much point in calling a wave a motherfucker, but I did anyway, the last words I got out before getting the wind knocked out of me, the tether fully extended and just long enough to allow me to land flat on my back. The boat pitched forward and I rolled into the port side and watched the foamy green water stream by, inches from my face, and for a few intriguing moments, I was sure we were going over. I gripped the lanyard that freed the tether from my harness, and was about to pull when the boat ripped off in the other direction. The wheel spun at the command of the boiling seas.

Instead of pulling the lanyard, I grabbed the tether and used it to yank myself back on my feet, took hold of the wheel and tried to regain my bearings. A bleak grey image of Race Rock Light, the old lighthouse that stood a mile off the Fishers' western coast, was on my port side, so I spun the wheel to the left and stole a glance at the landmass before giving the churning waves my respectful attention.

I knew the seas were more than the wind should warrant, running ahead of the storm as they did with a hurricane moving up the Atlantic. But that would soon change, as the wind caught up and the waves, inhaling the enraged force, fulfilled their gorged potential.

A hurricane isn't weather, it's a thing. A monster that invades, ravishes, then moves along. It doesn't care what it does to you, nor to itself, as it dies in soggy exhaustion deep in the mainland, or frozen to death in the North Atlantic. All it knows how to do is feast on warm water, curl into itself like a cobra, gather speed and strength to better lay waste all within its swirl. It's a hungry thing, an indiscriminate beast, blind and relentless and ultimately doomed, but impossible to ignore, foolish to deny.

I had to get to that channel.

Among the many illusions that afflict sailors is the idea that somewhere nearby the water is much calmer than the unfettered snot you're currently embroiled in. This is borne of both a trick in visual perspective and profound wishful thinking. Knowing both these things well, I still angled in closer to shore, thinking this was a cagey way to outsmart the elements.

What I got instead was a greater battering, the wave action predictably stronger the closer you got to the shallower water along the coast. I cursed at myself this time and angled back out. I dug my feet into the soggy bottom of the boat, took a better grip on the wheel and drove on through the muck.

If you stay alive, all torture ends eventually, and such was the case with that race across Fishers Island Sound. Seemingly out of nowhere the opening of the ferry channel appeared, signaled by the red and green markers. As the breakwaters to either side quelled the waves, I torqued up the throttle and shot through the hole.

I cursed aloud again, though this time less a complaint than a celebration.

Though calmer than the seas, the channel was far from placid. The trick now was to make it all the way inside without bashing into the breakwaters, or farther down the channel, the tall dock walls. The water ballast, unintentional though it was, worked to great advantage in keeping the boat low in the water, allowing me to keep the throttle up without losing steerage.

Inside the channel, the water opened up into a harbor just big enough to allow the ferry to turn around and dock. On the other bank were a few houses, with their own docks. I pulled up to the first one and tied off the boat. Finally at rest, I could feel the true wind, blowing in from the northeast, auguring no good.

I stowed my iridescent yellow foulie in the ditch bag and replaced it with a dark blue, semi-waterproof rain jacket. I used a set of bungee cords to fix the shotgun to the ditch bag, which I put on my back, and walked around the harbor to the ferry office. It was closed, according to the sign on the wall, not to reopen until after the storm.

I walked up the small hill to the Fishers Island state police barracks and went inside. No one was there. I went around the desk for a quick check of the holding cell. Ashton Kinuie was lying down on the cot inside the cell, apparently asleep.

"Don't you ever answer your phone?" I asked.

He shot upright.

"Acquillo. Get me some water."

I looked around the room.

"Where?"

"There's a little 'fridge behind the desk."

I went and got him a bottle of water.

"What're you doing in there?" I asked, shoving the bottle through the bars.

"Fuming. When I'm not dying of dehydration."

I looked down at the keypad mounted on the front of the cell.

"How do I get you out?"

"You don't. They reset the combination. HQ will have to send someone over who can override the electronics. Not happening now."

"Who's they?" I asked.

He looked up at me with baleful eyes.

"Two white guys wearing black ski masks. Only one of them spoke. They got the drop on me. To be honest, I thought they were going to kill me. Instead, they put me in the cell and reprogrammed the keypad like it was something they did every day."

"How long you been in here?"

"Two days. I've been trying to sleep to conserve energy, but I was getting very thirsty. They only left me one bottle of water. You can live a long time without food, but not without water."

I went back to the little refrigerator and took out all the water that was in there, about eight bottles. I shoved them all in his cell.

"They can at least get some more cops out here," I said.

"Maybe. You got a cell phone? This is going to be embarrassing."

I went outside to spare him the audience and looked around. The wind was up another half-notch, and multi-colored leaves were filling the air. No one was on the street, no cars, no people. The old buildings and the too-cute cottages within eyeshot were dark and hunkered down, wary beneath the standing hardwoods that had all grown up since 1938.

I went back inside.

"Eight to ten hours," he said. "The weather's got everyone in a panic. As always, this island's just an annoying pimple on the ass of the East End."

"So now what?"

"A burger would be a good idea. With a big salad on the side."

Another dilemma. The closest place to buy food, the only place you could buy food if you didn't count the Swan, was the general store. It was halfway between the barracks and where I'd originally stashed the dinghy, way too exposed a route. I didn't want to endanger Two Trees anymore than I had already, and I couldn't contact the Swan, so that left a single option.

I called Gwyneth Jones.

"How're you with conspiracies?" I asked her when she answered the phone.

"JFK was killed by a lone gunman, crazy as that sounds."

I asked her if she could go to the general store, buy a bunch of canned goods, and a can opener, plastic dinnerware, paper cups and plates, fresh fruit and bottles of water, plus a toothbrush and toothpaste, liquid soap, a washcloth if they had one, and to secretly bring them to the ferry dock.

"With another storm on the way, nobody'll think twice about the purchases. When you get here, park behind the ferry office." Which I could see from the barracks. "I'll walk down and meet you."

"I thought you were long gone."

"That's what I want everyone to think," I said.

"That sounds conspiratorial."

When she got off the phone I conferred with Kinuei about what else he'd need. He told me where to find a big Maglite flashlight, a handheld VHF and a box of batteries. Then the matter of the shotgun came up. I reached in my pack and pulled out the Glock, and two boxes of ammo.

"Unless you order me to give it up, I'd like to hold on to the shotgun for now," I said.

"What're you up to, anyway? Level with me and I'll see what my answer is."

So I did, mostly. I gave him the basics—that I'd managed to locate Axel's approximate whereabouts, gone there and extracted him, just ahead of Hammon and his hired guns— and then Axel and I made our way through a variety of means across the island to where I had secured my dinghy, then on to the sailboat, on which we escaped to New London. Leaving out all the illegalities made for a much sketchier story than I'd have wanted. He noticed.

"On what basis can you assert that these men were attempting to kidnap the young man rather than simply trying to locate him on behalf of the family?"

"Axel was hiding. When I found him, the last thing he wanted to do was go back to them."

"Why?"

I took a deep breath.

"I don't know for sure," I said, truthfully. "But clearly there's extortion of some type involved. Oh, and by the way, you think it's a silly coincidence that a pair of highly skilled operatives got you locked up in your own jail? That you're only here because Trooper Poole got beat up?"

He frowned at that, for obvious reasons.

I'd been checking for Gwyneth every few minutes, and was happy to see her pull into the parking lot right at that moment. I told Kinuei not to go anywhere until I got back.

"Don't enjoy this too much," he said.

I jogged down the hill to the parking lot and knocked on the window of her old Citroën. She rolled down the window through which she handed two heavy bags of provisions.

"Here's the receipt," she said.

I doubled the amount she'd paid out, folding the bills in such a way that it wouldn't be apparent until she paid closer attention. I didn't know whether she'd accept the commission or not, but I didn't want to spend the time debating it.

"Are you going to become the Robin Hood of Fishers Island?" she asked. "Robbing from the über-rich and giving to the merely well-off?"

I told her she might not be that far off.

"Good," she said. "Make sure I'm on the receiving end."

I waited for her to scoot away in the improbable little car, then hiked back up the hill to the barracks. I transferred the goods through a little door meant for the purpose. He opened two of the larger cans and dumped the contents on a paper plate. I let him eat until he was ready to talk again.

"So why'd you come back here?" he asked through a mouthful of cold beef stew.

"They're still out there searching for me and Axel. I think they'll assume we're still on the island, especially as the weather gets worse. When they discover he's gone, it'll be bad for the remaining Feys. But I have some time. If my hypothesis is correct."

"You have a hypothesis? What is this, physics lab?"

"Sort of," I said.

"Are you going to tell me?"

I shook my head.

"It's just a guess. I need to play it out."

"Then give me the shotgun," he said, putting his hand through the little door. "For my sake and yours."

There wasn't much to do at that point but comply. And part of me took his words to heart. There's a reason why I hate guns. They've been known to go off in ways that no one would have predicted, or preferred.

I stuck it through the hole along with several boxes of shells.

"You can keep the towel," I said. "Help with cleanup."

He didn't know about the security guard's S&W .38, and didn't need to. I wasn't keen on completely disarming, dislike of guns or not.

I asked him if there was anything else I could give him before I left. He shrugged.

"My self-respect? Probably not."

"Don't be too tough on yourself," I said. "Those two are world-class hard cases."

"And you can handle them? What do you have that they don't?"

"A sense of humor?"

◆

By now it was midafternoon, but still several hours before nightfall. I retraced the path to the abandoned military installation where Two Trees had picked me up the day before. This being the most densely built-up part of the island, I could travel most of the way down narrow alleys and through parking lots and backyards, providing a sense of security that was entirely false, but even that I was glad for. I made it all the way to the brick building without seeing another human being, though I had no idea if any had seen me. I walked around to the bluff above the water and sat down.

The seas were now in full ferocity. From that height, you could see the general wave pattern blown along by the increasing northeasterly. But I knew from experience that below the peaks and troughs a contest was underway between the surface movement and the mighty advance of the shifting currents, millions of gallons of seawater disgorging from the Sound, or flowing back in from the Atlantic Ocean. The result would be a species of turbulence that most would find difficult not to attribute to purposeful malevolence.

Visibility was barely two miles out, but no boats were to be seen. The island was once again a lawless, encapsulated place, as unreachable as one of the moons of Jupiter.

I lay down on the mist-dampened grass and closed my eyes. In addition to all the straining effort, battering and fearful blows to my nervous system aside, I'd lost a whole night's sleep. As I pondered all this, my limbs succumbed to an internally administered narcotic, and mid-thought, I was knocked out.

◆

I woke in utter blackness, blacker than the images that paraded behind my closed eyes. The wind was now a steady presence, a pulsating whoosh heard mostly in the tall trees above and behind me. No stars, no moon, no lights from the cluster of buildings around the ferry dock. Power out again. I checked my cell phone. No service. Deaf, dumb and blind.

My brain and body were clogged with fuzzy cotton, but I perceived the intimations of renewal, a recharging after a deep sleep. I splashed some of my bottled water on my face. I stood up, slipped the ditch bag on my back, shook out my head and moved off into the dense, perfidious night.

CHAPTER **21**

My blue rain jacket had a hood. This served to both cover my face and keep the wind-driven rain, still more sporadic than pervasive, from soaking my head. I put my hands in the pockets of the jacket and did my best to walk a straight line against the teasing gusts of wind.

What I still didn't have was much of a plan. Actually, I had no plan at all, beyond heading toward the Swan and hoping something would come to me along the way. As a young engineer, I'd rarely move an inch without thoroughly thought out and neatly drawn schematics. I'd labor over these, as much to assure the soundness of my thinking as the beauty of the visual product, the ruled precision of the boxes and arrows, engineering symbols and hand-drawn typography.

Somewhere along the way I gave that up. Probably about the time I moved into management and no longer had the luxury to linger over a single project, to lovingly handcraft or polish a solution. By then, I knew too much, and needed to do so much in a very condensed amount of time. But I learned that sometimes the perfection of the plan was a trap, a seduction of aesthetics, where an ugly act of brutal intuition would have forced a better outcome.

The air on Fishers Island was all motion, the wind noise joined by the sound of generators, distant and close by, their engines at different rpms, nearly harmonized.

The trip around the northern end of the island to the hotel followed a generally downward incline, past the general store, now blacked out like most of the houses and minor estates that fronted on the West Harbor. You didn't see the Inner Harbor complex, including the gas station, fuel dock, yacht club and the Black Swan until you turned a sharp corner at the bottom of the hill.

What I saw first was a flashlight out on the fuel dock. I paused and watched. I assumed it was Track checking the water conditions and securing whatever equipment he had out there. It was dark inside both the gas station and the little shack out on the dock. I walked on by, well protected by the wind noise and murky night.

The yacht club and the Swan next door were also completely dark, though I knew from experience that the light inside the bar area was invisible from the outside.

I found the big rhododendron at the base of Featherstone's driveway and crawled underneath. Then I waited, studying the front of the hotel. It was about nine o'clock when I first checked my watch. Two hours later, the Ford SUV lumbered into the parking lot. It parked next to the Town Car and four men got out. If they spoke to each other, I couldn't hear it above the wind. They went inside and I went back to watching.

I watched until one in the morning, as long as I could take watching utter nothingness, then went across the street and followed the hedge around to the side of the parking lot where the front ends of the three vehicles were lined up. I squatted down and took out my ancient, folding Buck knife and a pair of heavy-duty wire cutters. I left the ditch bag on the ground and wriggled under the hedge on my back, and then under the Excursion.

The first task was relatively easy. I opened the Buck knife and stabbed through the sidewalls of the two front tires, an operation the knife was uniquely suited to perform. The next bit was more of a challenge. Rolling up on my left shoulder, I felt up into the engine compartment with my right hand. The engine was still warm, but not hot to the touch. At first, all I felt was the side of the engine block and some heavy, bolted-down components. Then I came across the oil filter, a formidable test of my hand strength, but eventually moveable. I unscrewed it and dropped it to the ground.

Then I turned my attention to the front brakes, finding and tracing the line that carried the brake back to the master cylinder, which was mounted up behind the engine near the transmission well. The line that brought the fluid down from the reservoir was made of a strong steel mesh surrounding a flexible synthetic tube. It took both the Buck knife and the wire cutters to get through it, but eventually I succeeded.

Since the Town Car was also a Ford product, I was able to apply some of the technical learning from the Excursion. This time, however, I left the tire slashing till I was out from under the car, fearing the much lower ground clearance would mean I'd be crushed by the sinking chassis. The lower height was an advantage with the other activities, since I could reach further up into the engine compartment, allowing a richer yield of sensitive wiring.

Sandwiched as the Town Car was between the SUV and the Mercedes, I was hidden from view as I took care of the Lincoln's tires. Finished with that, I crawled back under the hedge and lay on the grass, catching my breath.

I had a different concept for the Mercedes.

Among the tools and spare parts on the *Carpe Mañana* were stocky cables with alligator clips at either end used to help reconfigure the battery banks in the event of some failure or emergency. I put the one I brought in my teeth and crawled under the Mercedes.

As with the Fords, I located the starter and the cable that ran from the battery to the solenoid. I cut out a foot long section and used the Buck knife to strip an inch of insulation off the remaining ends. I coiled up the cable and secured the loops with heavy plastic zip ties. I snapped one alligator clip to the line from the battery, then the other to the stub hanging off the starter motor. I unhooked the alligator clips at both ends and squirmed back out from under the car.

I grabbed the ditch bag, ran across the road and dove back under the rhododendron. I rolled over on my back and listened to my heart thump in my ears. My limbs and the back of my neck ached from the stress of working in tight, pitch black spaces, as soundlessly as I could manage it. Expecting discovery at any moment, my nerves were no better. As my internal systems settled down, I allowed myself a few seconds of satisfaction. One less advantage for the opposing team.

I rolled back over and studied the Swan. The ridgeline of the building ran perpendicular to the road, so the gable window closest to Anika's bed was to the right if you were looking at the front of the building. This side had a narrow strip of land that provided a heavily landscaped buffer between the hotel and the property next door. A brick path took you back to the dock area, passing the outdoor shower along the way. Myron Sanderfreud's favorite place to hang out.

I actually considered standing on the path and tossing pebbles up to Anika's window, but as numerous hopeful suitors through the ages have learned, this strategy is likely to yield unwelcome consequences.

So I just lay there and deliberated on foolish and quix-
otic enterprises, hoping that as a counter-influence it would
produce an entirely undeserved revelation.

And then I fell asleep.

◆

I woke to a shout. A sooty grey light filled the air, now fully
engaged by a steady wind strong enough to topple the
unaware. I was uncomfortably on my side with my head on
the ditch bag at a painful angle. I rolled onto my stomach
and propped myself up on my elbows.

Jock was in the parking lot. I could see his head rise
above the hedge, then disappear again as he examined the
destroyed tires. I heard him yell again, then saw Pierre run
out the front door. They spoke to each other, then the two of
them looked around the neighborhood, as if the tire slasher
was standing nearby, knife in hand.

I checked my watch. It was 7:00 AM.

't Hooft came out of the hotel and joined the huddle.
Even from a hundred yards away, I could see it was an animated conversation, complete with waving hands and jutting jaw lines.

Nothing much happened until about 7:15, when Pierre
went to retrieve Anderson Track. Track walked around both
vehicles, popping up and down to look at the tires, and
finally just shaking his head. The body language was clear:
he couldn't replace that many tires, not that time of year and
certainly not during a major storm.

The big mercenaries weren't happy about it, and it
showed, but to Track's credit, he didn't flinch or falter, but
rather had his chest out and his hands on his hips as he
shook his head and undoubtedly said things like, "I can't
make tires appear out of thin air. You'll have to wait till they
start running the ferry again."

Jock gave him a little shot to the sternum, knocking him back a few steps. 't Hooft took Jock by the jacket and pulled him back. Jock seemed apologetic toward 't Hooft. Track took that opportunity to make a retreat, waving them off as he stalked back to his gas station.

Soon the hoods on all three vehicles were open and everyone but Del Rey was out in the parking lot. I couldn't know how well they assessed the damage, but it didn't matter. They weren't going anywhere in the SUV or the Town Car, and if they discovered how to fix the problem with the Mercedes, so be it. It was worth the chance.

Anika stood watching the men mill around the vehicles. She wore a floor-length kimono, and stood with her arms folded over her chest. Occasionally, she'd look away and scan the area, her eyes drifting past where I lay under the bush. I tried to send telepathic messages, the exact content of which I was undecided on, so that's probably why they didn't reach their destination.

I heard the hoods slam shut and watched the whole crowd disappear back into the hotel. An hour later Hammon, 't Hooft, Jock and Pierre emerged wearing non-uniform paramilitary outfits, their shoulders bent into the wind. At the road, they split into pairs and went in opposite directions, 't Hooft and Jock up the hill toward the general store and Hammon and Pierre east-bound toward the country club.

Of all the activities at which I'm grievously inadequate, waiting tops the list. Many times I've acted entirely contrary to my best interests just to end the tedium of a forced wait. Yet waiting was what the current situation demanded, and all I could do was endure it in grim silence.

Fifteen minutes was all I could bear. I dragged the ditch bag with me out from under the bush and put it on my back. Then I walked across the road and up to the hotel, through the front door and up to the reception desk where Anika, still in her kimono, was shuffling things around, in the distracted way you do when activity is its own justification.

"Got a room for the night?" I asked.

Her eyes opened wide enough to show white around the pupils, and a sharp little intake of breath seemed to catch in her throat.

"Oh, my God, are you crazy?"

"Where's your father?"

She turned around to look at the office door behind the counter just as Fey walked out. He wasn't an easy guy to read, so I couldn't tell if he was glad to see me or not.

"Any word on my son?" was the first thing he said, to his credit.

"He's safe and out of their reach. Now it's your turn."

They stood staring at me.

"We can do this if you move right now," I said. "Wear something warm and waterproof."

Fey tried to interrogate me, but I took him by the arm and gently pushed him toward the stairway.

"Bring the keys to the Mercedes," I said. "I don't know how much time we have."

While they were upstairs, I stood at a window next to the front door and kept a lookout. It was another form of stressful waiting, worse for not being totally in my control. So I was happy to see Anika appear in a bright yellow poncho.

She handed me the car keys.

"Where's Fey?" I asked.

She shook her head.

"He won't leave. He says he can't," she said. "That's okay. He can take care of Eloise." She took my arm and pulled me toward the front door. I acquiesced, afraid to wait for more explanation. I handed Anika my backpack and she sat in the passenger seat while I shimmied under the car and hooked up the alligator clips, using another zip tie to hold the whole bundle to the chassis.

I sat behind the wheel and started the car, feeling another involuntary wave of satisfaction passing through my mind. I backed up, looked down at the shifter to put it into drive, looked up again and saw 't Hooft several yards in front of the car with a rifle aimed at our windshield. Before I could calculate the odds of running him down before he got off a round, I heard a tap on the passenger side window. Jock had another gun, a vicious long-barreled semi-automatic with a folding stock nestled in his armpit. The muzzle was pointed at Anika's head.

I put the transmission in neutral and watched 't Hooft come toward us. Jock opened Anika's door and told her to get out. I got out myself, so I was standing when 't Hooft dropped his weapon to the ground and threw a right jab at my face. I blocked it with my forearm, which immediately went numb from the power of the blow. I shook it out and danced to the left, away from the car. He tried the same punch again, but this one I just dodged, planting a left on the back of his head as he moved through the swing.

Now my other hand was numb. I clenched and un-clenched my fist and stayed up on my toes. 't Hooft glared at me and turned in place, flat-footed, his fists in a parody of a boxing pose. I moved in and gave him a combination to the gut, and a jab to the face as I backed out of range again. My broken right hand lit up in pain, but I could still move my fingers. 't Hooft held his stomach and squinted as if in vague discomfort, though still standing securely on his feet. Now I could tell where this was going. I was way out of my weight class. I'd just beat on him till I was exhausted, then he'd deliver one clear shot and put me away.

I dropped my hands and called him a few rude names. He responded by charging. I ducked under a wild swing and punched him hard in the right kidney. He bellowed as I leaped for his rifle where it lay on the gravel.

Jock got there first, stepping on the barrel and hitting me with what must have been a punch, though I had no idea where it came from. Tears filled my eyes and a fuzzy roar went off inside my head. I backed off and watched him hand his gun to 't Hooft and then come at me with limbs twirling like a dervish. Seconds later I was on my back, an array of hurts springing up all over my body. Nearly blind, I still had no trouble seeing the barrel of a gun pointing down at my forehead.

I remembered when Rene Ruiz broke my nose and effectively ended my boxing career. That night I also lay flat on my back, looking up at people standing over me—Rene, and the ref running through the count. All I had to do at that point was lie still while consciousness drained away, and feel the blood pour across my face and into my mouth, the acid taste of certain defeat.

CHAPTER 22

It took my ex-wife Abby's family about a dozen generations to breed all generosity and good will out of their world view. The brute selfishness of the prior iterations had at least been rewarded by the kind of wealth unbridled avarice could often produce. But by the time Abby's father was at the family helm, a precious gentility and effortless entitlement had taken hold. So assured were they in their rightful pre-dominance, that the steady decline of their family fortunes had proceeded unnoticed.

I saw my father-in-law at the head of the table, asking me when I thought my salary would break through to six-figures. The question made me nauseous and dizzy. His son, glassy-eyed and grinning through a fugue of amphetamines and endless folly, said anyone who didn't modify the exhaust systems on their Beamers should have their cars confiscated and re-distributed to the more worthy.

Abby, though outwardly disdainful of the tenor of the conversation, nestled comfortably into her eighteenth-century Hepplewhite chair and lit a cigarette, blowing the smoke in my face, taunting me.

"I know you want one," she said. "And I don't even smoke."

This made me even sicker, so sick the pain radiated out through my arms and into my hands. I looked down and saw my knuckles on fire.

Abby's family members were speaking all at once, male and female voices intertwining or cancelling each other out, a mini-babble gathered around the dining room table.

"His hands are cold. You've given him a concussion," said Abby's sister, a sexless scold in short-cropped hair and sensible shoes. "Nine out of ten people with concussions are schizophrenic within the year. And that's a fact, buster."

"Schizo, cool," said her brother.

The scene began to fade away, but the voices continued.

"Good," said Derrick Hammon. "Makes us even."

"My pleasure, boss," said Jock.

"It's pleasant to hurt people?" asked Anika.

"I don't know," said 't Hooft. "Ask diehard there. If he ever wakes up."

"Men are idiots," she said.

"Here, here," said Del Rey.

I was lying on the floor, but it didn't prevent me from feeling I was about to topple over. Another concern was my digestive tract, which was nearly in open rebellion, the ache both inside and out. I focused what little mental power I had on talking things down, quieting the internal storm.

I heard the last neurologist who examined me say, "No more concussions. The next one could have you drooling in your Wheaties."

"Not yet," I told him.

"Not yet, what?" said 't Hooft.

I opened my eyes.

Anika was rubbing my right hand. I was in the bar, lying in the middle of the room. Del Rey stood above Anika. I lifted my head to look around, and after another wave of vertigo cleared away, saw the rest of the jolly hotel denizens sitting around under the bloodless blue light of about a dozen fluorescent lanterns distributed around the bar. Christian Fey leaned against the wall, his arms folded.

"You win," I said to Jock.

"Usually do," he said.

"He likes to think," said Pierre.

"So it's official, Hammon," I said to the ceiling, unwilling to bend my neck back far enough to look at him. "You're in a criminal enterprise. Big risk."

"Calculated risk. And well worth it. What did you do with the boy?"

"Don't tell him," said Fey.

I gripped Anika's busy hand.

"You think I could get into a chair?" I asked her.

"That's up to you."

She pulled me to a sitting position. Some of the floor came with me, and for a moment it was in slow rotation. I held both sides of my head.

"Fuck me," I said.

"I've been try-ing," she whispered in my ear.

I let another few moments go by, then with Anika's help, got to my feet and then literally fell into one of the low upholstered barroom chairs. Del Rey handed me a glass of water.

"Here, drink. Cures all ills."

I did as she asked, though the only ill cured was a dry mouth. I thanked her anyway. Hammon brought another chair over and the others followed suit. Anika knelt at my feet and held my hand. I didn't like it, but was too wobbly to resist. Del Rey went behind the bar and busied herself. Both 't Hooft and Hammon watched her without comment, the silence in the room drawing everyone's attention to the wind noise outside. A shutter clattered somewhere, as if to give the moment a theatrical effect.

Hammon turned his gaze back to me. I was pleased to see black shadows beneath his eyes and a bright red line running perpendicular to his upper lip.

"Where's the boy?"

"Fuck you," I said.

"Very well," said Hammon. "The negotiating positions are established."

"You're right. Here's the deal. Let everybody go and I'll forget the whole thing happened," I said.

"Hah," said Pierre. "Funny guy."

I said something to him in French that roughly described an unnatural joining between himself and a particular family member. He lurched up, but once again, 't Hooft was the moderating influence, pulling him back into his chair.

"You trying to die, Acquillo?" he asked in his Dutch-inflected English.

"I'm already dead," I said. "But who's counting?"

"I can't believe you're talking about killing people," said Anika. "You're sick, Derrick. Greed has driven you insane. You can't spend all the money you already have. What difference does it make if N-Spock 5.0 releases on time or not?"

Hammon's swollen eyes spat red.

"The difference, my dark little angel, is your brother deliberately put me in this position," he said. "Clever, clever techie, he poisoned N-Spock in order to poison me. I want that antidote and I shall have it," he added with a grandiose toss of his head.

"What a dick," said Anika.

Hammon sat back in his chair and smiled indulgently.

"Let me lay out the situation," he said, "just so everyone's on the same page. We have a simple transaction on the table. All your side needs to do is deliver Axel Fey, and all he has to do is deliver the patch. And that will be the end of it. N-Spock 5.0 will release as planned, it will regain dominance in the marketplace, and the Fey family will begin receiving its five percent royalties as per the buyout and stock transfer agreement."

"You're a fucking gangster, Hammon," I said. "Don't try papering over that miserable fact with a bunch of corporate bullshit. I've heard it all and more from smarter and more evil people than you."

The room was quiet for a moment.

"Permission to kill this old bastard," said Pierre.

Hammon looked like permission would soon be on the table.

"For a guy in your position, you display a remarkably feeble sense of self-preservation," he said to me.

A sudden brilliant flash of light burst in through the door to the lobby, and a millisecond later a clap of thunder shuddered the building.

"Mercy," said Del Rey.

"It's just a storm," said Hammon.

"Not yet it isn't," I said.

"What you suggest is preposterous," said Fey to Hammon. "I keep telling you. Axel has never even seen the core of 5.0. This is lunatic fantasy."

Hammon whipped his head around to look at Fey.

"We have the analytics, Christian. His signature's all over it."

Fey threw up his hands. Pierre leaned forward in his chair.

"You think you have proof," I said.

"Analytics don't lie," Hammon said to me. "Once you know what you're looking for. It took security months, but they established profiles of every developer on the 5.0 team. Their coding styles, or signatures. Then they aligned signatures with known users and traced their paths in and out of the application, isolating the interloper and determining how he was getting in. When we found the back door, we waited for him to log in, then followed him home. To the Black Swan as it turned out."

"Ridiculous," said Fey.

"I'd think it was you, Christian, but then I'd have to believe that you're pretending to be your son."

"If you know where the hacker's been, why can't you fix what he's done?" I asked.

Hammon looked unhappily familiar with that question.

"If we could do that maybe we would have done that by now," he said, stringing out the words.

"Well, better get back on it, Hammon," I said, "because Axel's off the island and out of your reach."

He sat silently, looking at me.

"Get Fey and the women out of here," he said to no one in particular. "Bring them upstairs."

Anika didn't move.

Jock walked over to her.

"Don't touch me," she said, but left the room behind Del Rey and her father, followed by 't Hooft.

Hammon continued to stare at me, trying to either read my mind or torture me to death with his devastating gaze.

"The question isn't whether Jock and Pierre can extract the information we need from you. It's when, and how much unpleasantness will be involved," he said.

"Who're you, Sidney Greenstreet? Where's your fez? You've got the facts. Axel's off the island in a place you can't get to. So that's that. Right now you're still ahead. Except for a little dustup, which you can blame on me, you haven't done anything illegal. That's provable, anyway. You can walk away from this clean. Go back and put a case together against Axel, if he's really the hacker, and see if the courts can compel him to give you the patch. Delay release and get a little egg on your face. So what?"

Hammon didn't seem to be listening, or if he was, unable to fully process what I was saying. He put his fingers up to his forehead as if calling on a higher power to instruct him on what next to do. It must have been forthcoming, because his change in tactic was nearly visible on his face. He sat forward with his elbows on his knees, took a deep breath and said, "There's a covenant. We have to release Q1 or we'll be in default. Revenue from 4.0 is the collateral. They'll take the company."

As Anika made clear, people could go on the Internet and find old business articles that analyzed my fall from the heights. A favorite theme portrayed me as a technocrat with little head for business. They were right. I never cared at all about the numbers, and only dealt with financial stuff when I was trying to save my divisional budgets from the hyenas in other parts of the company. But even I found it hard to imagine Subversive would have bet the whole company on a risky venture like 5.0.

He read that on my face.

"It wasn't just the development costs," he said. "Other investments were made. There's an issue of liquidity."

I chewed on that for a while. Then I thought to myself, aha. Then I laughed.

"You bet the company's equity and it all went off a cliff. And nobody knows," I said. "It would kill the stock. You wouldn't be able to get credit from a loan shark. You're dead man walking."

"No, *mon ami,* you are," said Pierre.

"Would you mind muzzling that poodle?" I said to Hammon.

Pierre shot a hand at my face, but this one I managed to dodge, which threw him off balance, causing him to fall against the wall. Jock was on his way over when Hammon stood up in front of me.

"Cut the shit, boys. They'll be plenty of time for that," he said.

For what? I thought.

Pierre tried to look like it was a trifling matter, but you could see embarrassment shadowing his face. I grinned, happy it was him and not Jock who'd thrown the punch. Now I knew who in the room was invincible and who wasn't.

Hammon sat down again, pulling his chair closer to mine.

"I'm telling you these things because I need you to understand how serious I am. I need the boy's patch. We've already been through the computer in his room. There's nothing there, so it's all on his laptop. He can send it to Subversive from anywhere. You need to tell him to do that. He needs to know that if he doesn't, when we're done with you, we'll move on to Anika."

It was my turn to stare at him in silence. He didn't look too good. The shot to the face had added color here and there, but also taken it away. His eyes were red and watery, and dancing with zealous intensity. Anika was right. The man had been driven a little crazy, but not for the reason she thought. Greed can feel like a jolt of cocaine to the brain. Fear more like the insertion of a long, cold knife.

"Was everyone in on the bad deals?" I asked.

He licked his lips, lingering for a moment on the red split beneath his nose. He shook his head.

"No," he said. "I've told you enough."

"Come on, Hammon," I said. "You want me to cooperate, I need to know the whole story."

"Wait outside," he said to his boys, without taking his eyes off me. They went out to the lobby, closing the heavy glass door to the bar behind them.

"Removing the boy from the island was a very foolish thing to do," he said to me.

"I don't know about that. If you had your hands on him I'd probably be dead by now. You've got a way to keep the Feys quiet, but not me."

"Maybe not if you care about the girl. She'd certainly rather her father not end up in jail."

I saw the rough flow scheme I'd drawn that night in the woods on the way to snatch Axel Fey. The columns of knowns, and unknowns. I drew another box in my head, and connected it to the others with an imaginary arrow.

"Fey made the bets," I said. "On his own, secretly, without approval. He had access to the funds through the corporate data systems, which he controlled. The money's tied up in investments that have lost all their value, but are still on the books, because neither the investment house nor the investors can afford the write down. The money's gone, but no one knows it, not yet, anyway."

It took Hammon a while to respond, so accustomed was he to never uttering the fearsome truth.

"Sanderfreud discovered the scheme. Fey would sweep all our available cash and working capital out of their normal accounts and put the money into auctions and overnights. Then he'd sweep it all back again, taking the earnings and covering the movement by altering the account records. One night, for some insane reason, he put everything in a fund that was already in free fall, though apparently he didn't know that. The next day it froze up completely and hasn't thawed since. Such a thing had never happened before, but we now know such things are more than possible, they're inevitable."

The dominoes were all in place. If N-Spock didn't release when it was supposed to, the bank would call their loan, which they couldn't cover because all their assets were tied up in a worthless, illiquid fund.

Then another thought occurred to me.

"How did you buy out Fey? With what?" I asked.

Hammon finally had something to feel happy about.

"We didn't. We just said we did. Besides getting him to cough up the returns he made on our money, we have his name on a piece of paper releasing all his holdings back to the company, and a non-compete that banishes him from all software development for ten years. He won't starve, but any current or future equity he might have had in Subversive has gone poof. And rightly so, you'll have to agree."

I did, on the face of it.

"Okay, you've got Fey, though on the other hand, he's got you. He'll go to jail, but with the truth out, Subversive could still go down the tubes, release or no release."

"No," he said, before my words were hardly out of my mouth. "5.0 is a game changer. The banks will line up to cover our capital needs. The stock will soar, easily replenishing our cash reserves."

He may or may not have been right about that, but what mattered was he believed he was. Like all entrepreneurs, his focus was on the goal, and his powers of self-delusion were all-consuming. Like Fey, he wasn't afraid to place his bets and pretend there could never be a negative outcome.

"You think I'll go along with all this to save Fey because of his daughter," I said.

"That's your play, Acquillo. Any idiot can see you're banging her. There's no other reason for you to still be here. So here's your chance. Axel will do anything she tells him to, and she doesn't want her daddy to go down. That's the deal. Make it happen, or I'll stop trying to make this easy and just turn everything over to Jock and Pierre."

I let that sit for a moment, deliberating. Then I said, "I can't contact him until we're back online. I need a phone or at least Internet access."

Immediately his face lightened, a hint of triumph passing through those hungry eyes.

"Wise decision," he said, moving his chair back out of my immediate space. I took the opportunity to attempt standing, which went far better than I thought it would. Even the floor seemed inclined to stay put.

"Mind if I get a drink?" I asked. "They say it's the best thing for a concussion."

"Knock yourself out," said Hammon, enjoying what he thought might have been a joke.

I hobbled over to the bar while Hammon asked Jock and Pierre to come back into the room. Pierre glowered at me, my efforts to build on our common Gallic heritage apparently gone for naught. Jock, on the other hand, looked loose and at ease, almost bored. I asked if I could pour a drink for anyone and Jock said a beer would be great.

"While it's still halfway cold."

It was early even for me, but I had to start moving around to assess the damage and test my own faculties. I poured a long vodka on a handful of ice from the rapidly melting ice bins.

I cracked Jock's beer and he came over to retrieve it. We clinked glasses.

"Jesus Christ," said Pierre.

I downed some of the vodka, which had a salubrious effect on my nerves, but did little for my shaky insides. I asked Hammon if I could go lie down. He said why not, and told Jock to bring me upstairs and put me with Anika in her attic room.

He followed me to the second floor, then let me climb the narrow staircase to the attic on my own, closing the door behind me with an easy warning not to try anything stupid. When I reached the attic, Anika rushed over to me and grabbed my head, using her thumb to pull open my eyelid. She stared into my pupil.

"Do you know what you're looking for?" I asked.

"I want to see if you're still in there." I clinked the ice in my glass of vodka. "I guess you are," she said, looking down at the glass.

I pulled free from her grasp and sat down on the bed next to Eloise. The cat got up and moved a few feet away, looking at me with unguarded apprehension.

"I'm okay," I said to Anika. "Just a little wobbly. That kid can hit."

"Derrick has really lost his mind," she said. "I'm getting frightened. I don't know what to do."

She wore her Carnegie Mellon sweatshirt, shorts and bare feet. With only two windows at opposite ends of the room to let in natural light, supplemented by a pair of electric lanterns, the attic felt cheerless and exhausted. She scooped up Eloise and sat down next to me on the bed, her legs straight out in front so her heels dangled over the edge. The cat looked wary, but eventually succumbed to Anika's gentle stroking and curled up in her lap.

"You could start by telling me the truth once in a while. Just for a change of pace. See how it feels."

"What a terrible thing for you to say to me," she said, less forcefully than her words would indicate.

"If a man acts as if everything a woman tells him is true, even though he knows it isn't, mostly, does that still make him a chump?" I asked.

"I don't like the word chump. Sounds passive, but it's really aggressive."

"Hammon told me Subversive lost a lot of money on bad investments. The only way to get working capital was to put N-Spock 4.0 up for collateral, with the loan callable if 5.0 doesn't release when it's supposed to next year. Did you know that?"

She looked into my eyes again, in a clinical way.

"I guess your brain is still working all right," she said. "You must have a very hard head."

"In a manner of speaking. So tell me."

She leaned forward, gripping her legs at the knees, and spoke at the floor.

"Do you believe everyone has a secret life?" she asked.

"No. Most people don't."

"Right. The ones who do are always the least likely. 'I can't believe it, he was such a quiet unassuming guy,' they say. Like, duh. When is conventional wisdom going to catch up with reality? It's always the quiet unassuming guys who go on shooting rampages. Or steal millions of dollars from their companies."

"Your father. I know all about it. Hammon told me."

She smiled an intense, manufactured smile. A dark frown would have been less disturbing.

"So you know 5.0 wasn't the only thing he was working on in our basement."

I almost felt a faint twinge of feeling for Derrick Hammon. He wakes up one morning to discover his billion-dollar company is broke, and though it's still a going concern, revealing its fragile condition could easily cause the whole thing to unravel. His only way out is a project controlled by the very guy responsible for the financial disaster, a project that should have successfully ridden to completion, but is now very much in doubt.

"But why would your brother want to sabotage 5.0? Why bring on the wrath of Derrick Hammon? What's in it for him and why did he think he'd get away with it?"

She leaned back against the wall again and started raking her fingers through her jet black hair, pausing occasionally to check the ends, as I'd seen her do several times before.

"He's weird. I don't know why he does what he does."

"He told me your mother is still alive."

She dropped the strand of hair and turned toward me.

"He did? The dork. Okay, she's alive, but not to us. She left right after Axel was born and never looked back. I don't think my father noticed right away. 'Oh Daddy, Mommy's gone.' 'Don't you see Daddy's busy? Be a good little girl and bring me a sandwich.' It was easier to pretend she actually died. What difference does it make to you?"

I'd been trying to ignore it, but the sound of the wind outside was gradually increasing along with its velocity. I got up and went over to the window. The trees were swirling in bursts of furious movement, steadily giving up the last of their autumn leaves. It was barely midday, but the cloud cover enshrouded the island in a dank and blood-less gloom.

Instead of sitting back on the bed, I rolled the office chair over from the workstation.

"What did you do with my backpack?" I asked.

She looked puzzled.

"It must still be in the car," she said. I probably looked disappointed. "It isn't?"

"I saw you open the passenger side door while I was getting my ass kicked. Jock was doing the kicking and 't Hooft was enjoying the show. You had plenty of cover."

She looked away with what might have been a pout, it was hard to see in the dim light and through that veil of black hair.

"It's in the bushes along the front of the house. Near the corner," she said. "You should be thanking me."

"I should be doing something. I'm not sure what."

"I know what you should be doing, but you keep turning me down."

I finished off my drink and discovered what I most wanted to do was lie down on the floor and go to sleep. Though a murmur of fear still cycled through a remote region of my nervous system, it wasn't enough to counter an aching exhaustion that pulled on my limbs and jammed up my brain. I slid off the chair and sprawled out across the Persian rug that covered the attic floor. I asked Anika if I could borrow a pillow.

"Kick me in about two hours," I said.

"What happens then?" she asked.

Eloise jumped down off the bed and walked up to my face, brushed my cheek with her whiskered muzzle, then strolled away. I wondered what she thought of my odds. I knew what the neurologist would say. Not good. He'd shown me an fMRI of my brain, which was a beautifully colorful thing, though not to him. He'd point out all sorts of blotches and patterns in shades he didn't like. I'd barely try to follow what he was saying. It wasn't worth it, since there wasn't anything I could do about it. Instead, I'd just looked at how pretty my brain looked all lit up like a psychedelic Rorschach test, or one of my daughter's art projects.

What did Axel call Anika, the artist? Color head.

I pushed off the bottom of my consciousness and swam back to the surface. I propped myself up on my elbows and looked at Anika, still sitting on the bed, playing with her hair and bouncing her feet on the edge of the mattress. I willed my recalcitrant limbs to put me back on my feet and walk me into the center of the room where I could get a good look at her painting.

"What happens if the roof blows off?" I asked her.

"It'll be ruined."

"That'd be a pity."

"I took photos," she said, pulling a flash drive strung on a slim cord around her neck out from under her sweatshirt. "The re-creation would take a while, but nothing would be lost."

"Color corrected?" I asked.

"Perfectly," she said. "Why wouldn't I? It's a painting."

"Of course it is."

CHAPTER 23

I got my two hours of sleep, and an hour after that, since Anika failed to wake me when I asked her to. Since I'd not suffered a brain hemorrhage while sleeping, and did actually wake up, it was easy to forgive the lapse.

Waking up was one thing. Getting up was another. There might have been a part of me not tender to the touch, or not stiff as the tin man after a night in the rain, but it would have been lonely. I knew from those years in the ring that if you could move any body part without passing out from pain, it wasn't broken, and if it wasn't broken, then moving was simply a matter of will and existential resolve.

I swore a little on the way to my feet, but I got there. Anika steadied me and rubbed my shoulders. She had strong hands, stronger than Amanda's, though geared more toward function than caress. I thanked her anyway.

By this time it was dark outside and the wind was howling like a medieval chorus on a tour from hell. The frame of the Swan was tensioned under the load and I could hear the vertical members and sheathing creak and groan with lateral stresses, and feel the structural tie-ins straining to fulfill their purpose.

I told Anika it was time to leave the attic with anything whose survival she hoped to ensure.

"Like your cat," I said. "Too late for the painting. How about the hard drive on your computer?"

She got Eloise into the cat carrier, gathered up a handful of clothes, and after employing a few deft maneuvers with my Swiss Army knife, removed the hard drive from the CPU. Thus burdened, we descended the stairs and opened the attic door, nearly bashing into Jock, who was standing in the hallway talking to Christian Fey and Del Rey. He told us he was ordered to keep us in the attic, but was moved by the argument that the order should be contingent on the roof staying put. He went downstairs to check with Hammon.

Anika told her father we were taking over one of the rooms, then left to drop off her stuff. I asked Fey about his insurance.

"Adequate, but you don't honestly think it will come to that, do you?" he asked.

"Maybe. Probably not. Do you have any plywood? It's a little late to board up windows, but we might need some in case of a breach."

"A breach? I have ply in the shed. Maybe two four-by-eight sheets. And a battery-powered drill and some screws."

"By the way, you two, you're scaring me," said Del Rey, holding a cocktail with a healthy charge of ice, something I took note of.

"Do you have a handheld VHF radio?" I asked him. Mine was in my backpack, safely stowed under the bushes in front of the house. I hoped.

"I do."

He went down to the first floor to retrieve it. I was left alone in the dark hallway with Del Rey, who looked unsettled by the sudden intimacy.

"What happened with Sanderfreud and the Fey kids?" I asked. "You tried to tell me before, but I wasn't listening. I am now."

"I don't know. They had a falling out. Nobody would talk about it."

"We only have a couple minutes."

"It doesn't matter," she said, her tongue thickened by drink. "I looked after them when they needed me. Not that anybody cares."

"Hammon's headed over a cliff. Don't let him take you with him."

"What do you know about it?" she asked, her chin up and her eyelids at half-mast. "You don't get to pick the people you end up with. Fate picks them for you. I could have done more at the company if they'd let me," she added, in a neck-wrenching right turn. "I was one of the original N-Spock developers, I'll have you know. Smartest damn chicky in the building. Only it's hard to join the boy's club when you're not a boy. I was good, though. You'd be a-*mazed*."

She fell into me, stopping herself with a thin hand that clutched at my shirtsleeve. I supported her while she re-established equilibrium.

"Sorry," she said. "Tee many martoonies."

Fey arrived with a handheld VHF, a modern, lightweight, waterproof model, fresh out of the catalog. I took it and went into the bathroom and tuned in the clearest NOAA weather channel I could get.

The news wasn't good. The storm, defying all predictions, had made a sudden eastward jog, putting all of the New England coast and parts of Long Island in the path of sixty to eighty knot winds. Up to a hundred, if you counted the gusts. They predicted with confidence both the velocity and wind direction based on the highly organized nature of the storm.

I checked my watch and took note.

When I got back to the hall, Anika was there with Jock, Fey and Del Rey.

"I think we should keep heading toward the lower levels," I told them. "Just to be on the safe side."

"I don't believe anything's safe," said Del Rey. "But lead on, MacDuff."

The storm did me a favor by picking that moment to slam a gust into the side of the hotel, causing a tremor everyone felt from the feet up. Without comment, Jock herded us down the stairs.

't Hooft was there to greet us. He helped Del Rey negotiate the final steps, then led us all to the restaurant area at the back of the hotel. The French doors that comprised the outside wall facing the docks shuddered in the wind, though precautions had been taken: the doors were latched and tied off at the doorknobs with clothesline and wedged shut with the dining room chairs. There was still plenty of seating for everyone, some of which was occupied by Hammon and his crew. They were drinking and eating cheese and sliced meats off a large tray. Pierre held a lit cigarette between the thumb and index finger of his right hand. As the smoke found my nostrils, envy caught at my heart.

I went behind the service bar and found the fixings for a vodka on the rocks, netting a handful of ice from the slosh at the bottom of the ice chest. Then I sat down, staying a healthy distance from Jock and Pierre, just outside earshot and the swing of an ambitious fist.

Anika joined me, banging a chair up to mine into which she dropped like a sack of sand. A tiny splash of wine from the glass she held dropped on my thigh, creating a cool spot as it rapidly evaporated. She put her lips conspicuously and uncomfortably close to my ear.

"What's your plan with the backpack?" she asked.

"Lean back and act like we're talking about the World Series," I whispered, hoping my irritation showed.

She did as I asked.

"Okay, Mr. Paranoid, what do you have in mind?"

I made her clink glasses.

"You'll know when something happens," I said.

"When what happens?"

"You'll know."

"You don't trust me," she said.

"Not entirely."

"I don't deserve that."

"Yes you do," I said. "That and more. You're a very bright woman, but not aware of your own behavior. I'm not completely wise to your game, but I know you have a game, which is almost as good."

She gave my knee an affectionate slap, a gesture favored by Jackie Swaitkowski.

"But you like me anyway, don't you?" said Anika.

"I do," I said, in a moment weakened by the unexpected association with Jackie, never more than a friend, but a friend that had bred in me an unqualified devotion. Whether she knew it or not.

"You came back for me, even after you were safe and sound," she said.

"I did. Not very successfully as it turns out."

"I'm wearing you down."

"I can't say that I know you," I said, "but I think I know enough."

She writhed in her chair in a fluid, preening way, as if channeling her cat. It was part pleasure with my words, part preamble to what she was about to say.

"I know you," she said. "You're afraid of death. You finally have a life you hope is worth living, but you're unsure, afraid to repeat all the same mistakes. You love your girlfriend, but you don't trust her enough to go in whole hog. So you pretend it's a great relationship even while you fret over what could be fatal shortcomings. You're exhausted by your own ambivalence and are secretly longing for an alternative to present itself. That alternative is staring right at you, and you *like* it."

Her words were punctuated by a slight lift of the floor, timed with the sound of the wind battering the west wall of the hotel, and a little involuntary yelp from Del Rey, who grabbed at a nearby curtain to keep from falling. Both Fey and Hammon looked over at me with questions on their faces, but I ignored them.

"What's under this floor?" I asked Anika.

"Not the basement. A crawl space? This part was added on by the former owners so they could have a restaurant. My father keeps ladders and big planks under there."

"The wind's getting underneath," I said.

"Is that bad?"

"Depends on your definition."

Another gust blew the Persian carpet in front of us a few inches off the floor. I looked over at Hammon who was buried in a conversation with Jock and Pierre. 't Hooft sat with them, but was distracted, apparently more engaged by the furor going on outside. He got Hammon's attention by gripping the other man's arm.

"Somebody should go out there and check on conditions," 't Hooft said to Hammon.

Jock stood up without hesitation and gave Hammon a casual salute. Hammon nodded to him and I watched while he put on a windbreaker and zipped it up. Hammon looked over at me.

"You've been through these storms before?" he asked.

"Some storms like this, yeah," I said.

He looked at Jock.

"Take Acquillo with you," he said. "I want his opinion."

Jock shrugged and grinned at me, which I read not so much as a warning but a wished-for expectation that I'd try something stupid. I gave him the same sort of salute he'd given Hammon and stood up. I was still wearing my rain jacket, torn at the elbow from one of the various maneuvers I'd put myself through, but otherwise functional.

We walked to the front of the hotel and opened the door. A giant punched me in the chest and tried to yank the doorknob out of my hand. Jock grabbed the edge of the door and held it while we both fought our way outside. When we were clear, he let go and the door slammed shut.

"Shit," he said, "it's really blowing."

We were peppered by light debris spun up from the ground, and while the air was mostly dry, it felt pregnant with the promise of rain. The wind was blowing in from the west, so I led us around the east side of the hotel, down the brick path past the outdoor shower and out to the docks. Everything that could be cleared off the dock before the last storm was gone, so the only motion was an erratic sway of tall aluminum poles that supported the dock lights. I pushed myself to the end of the center walkway to where we'd docked the *Carpe Mañana*, put my arm around a pier and shot my little flashlight into the Inner Harbor.

It was as if the wind and water had decided to merge into one. I felt the saltwater on my tongue, pelting my cheeks and burning my eyes. The only definition you could see in the waves was in their frenzied, frothy rush across the harbor. On the other side of the channel clumps of tall grass and wild rose were flattened out and slathered with sea foam, which skittered across the surface of the water and sprayed up into the air. A small motor boat, once a foolish straggler out in the mooring field, was half-buried in the foliage, upside down, its white and blue hull bared to the sky like the belly of a big fish.

I wet a finger and stuck it in the air. Then I took the hand-held compass out of my jacket pocket, and took a reading.

I had what I needed, so I signaled to Jock that I was going back, and the two of us lurched and staggered our way to the hotel, retracing our steps down the brick path and around the side.

"Look at the drowned rats," said Del Rey, when she saw us coming into the restaurant, stripping off our jackets and wiping off our faces with table linen. "So I guess it's finally raining."

"That's not rain," I said. "It's the Inner Harbor."

They were still trying to figure out what I meant when Fey asked, "So what's the prognosis?"

I shrugged in a broad theatrical way, playing to the dispersed nature of my audience.

"No big deal. It's just a little wind. I say we drink the Swan dry and pretend we get along."

Del Rey liked that.

"Hip-hip, hooray," she yelled, holding her glass above her head.

Hammon jumped up from his chair, stalked over to her and grabbed her wrist, gradually lowering her hand to avoid spilling some sort of clear concoction out of the glass. He whispered something in her ear that made her freeze, everything but her eyes, which shifted from side to side, expressing more of what she felt than what she saw.

"You're no fun," she said to the room, an all-in-one statement of defiance, contrition and disappointment. She shook her hand free and walked an irregular line over to the bar, head high and back straight. Hammon shook his head as he watched her, and then catching himself, slumped back in his chair. 't Hooft whispered something that caused Hammon to nod brusquely and flick his hand in the air, as if swatting away a noxious thought.

The weather noise outside suddenly died down, so abruptly that all conversation in the room stopped and all eyes flashed toward the walls and ceiling. Having been in a hurricane before, I knew what was coming next.

The roar started low, but built up fast, from the bottom up. You felt it in your feet, then up through your body, and eventually, when it reached your ears, you were already distracted by the concussive force of the blow.

The Swan took it broadside, a mighty gust that sent convulsions down the walls and into the foundation, which my engineer's instincts said was straining to hold the building in place, stressed but defiant against the kinetic forces arrayed against it.

Del Rey screamed and 't Hooft dashed across the room and took hold of her. Anika just stared at me, as if I was in collusion with the storm. Jock looked amused, but Pierre was impressed.

"So that was a pretty big piece of wind, eh?" he said.

"Not at all," I said. "It's just warming up."

Nobody seemed to like that.

"I thought you said the wind was no big deal," said 't Hooft.

"For a place like this?" I said. "Not that I've actually examined the structure," I added, looking up at the ceiling as if I could see straight through to the rafters.

"You say you're a carpenter?" Hammon asked me.

"I am."

"And an engineer?"

"More on the mechanical side, but I know what holds buildings together," I said.

The wind swept from west to east across the back end of the restaurant, as if a ghostly calvary had just rushed by. Hammon's self-control, never fully in place, loosened another notch or two.

"Maybe you should take a look around," he said, pointing at Jock to go along with me. "Assuming you know what the hell you're looking at."

"That'll have to be your call," I said.

Hammon wearily gave his final assent, so my new buddy and I headed out for another exploration. I told him we should start in the basement.

We swam down into the cool, wet and moldy air, guided by my intrepid little flashlight. Fey had given me the basic lay of the land, but we still had to move cautiously to avoid colliding with old furniture, crates filled with drinking glasses, rotting canopies, lawn games, folding tables and all the other detritus accumulated by a resort hotel over the decades. My objective was the sill, where the foundation of the building was joined to the frame, a juncture important enough for modern building codes to require substantial reinforcement. For a reason.

We reached the foundation wall at the back of the hotel where the restaurant had been attached as an addition years before. I used a crate to get up high enough to stick my head between the floor joists where I could examine the sill and crawl space under the restaurant. The storm noises were dampened somewhat by the structure overhead, but plenty loud enough, and when another big gust hit, I had the flash-light trained directly on the sill plate, a single two-by-eight plank of wood that served as the interface between the stone foundation and the floor members.

I saw what I needed to see.

"Looks okay so far," I said to Jock. "Let's head up to the attic."

He followed me up the three flights of stairs and hung close to me as I crawled out over the joists to the inside of the eave, the tight V formed where the roof, the exterior wall and ceiling for the second floor all came together. I watched as the wind massaged the hotel and I lightly ran my hand over the old framing material like a faith healer working the county fair.

"Christ, it's noisy," Jock yelled, demonstrating his point.

"We're pretty close to the action up here," I yelled back. "Let's go back down."

He waited until we were on the second floor to ask my professional opinion.

"We're fine," I said. "The place is built like a bunker."

"I been in bunkers," he said. "This is no bunker."

"Okay, pick a better metaphor. I'm not going to fight you over it."

He snorted.

Nothing much had changed when we got back to the dim and shadowy restaurant. Del Rey sat with Hammon and 't Hooft, though apart, her eyelids half-closed, but her chin held high, her cocktail loose in a limp right hand. A thick strand of hair had escaped from the pile on top of her head and lay like a yellow comma against her nose. The way 't Hooft looked at her, I imagined him wanting to reach over and flick the strand off her face. I almost did it myself.

"What's the verdict, Doc?" she asked when she saw me approach.

"The Swan's good for another hundred years," I said. "Don't worry about the noise. It sounds a lot worse than it is. How come I'm not drinking?"

Anika went to replenish my glass. I was left with Christian Fey, who looked unsure of what to do with himself, whether he should be sitting uneasily or leaping up from the table to run off on some more productive pursuit. I sat down next to him.

He leaned back and looked at me, as if slightly affronted by my presence. But then he said, "I haven't adequately thanked you for securing the safety of my wayward son."

"You don't have to thank me," I said. "I do things for my own reasons."

"Thank you anyway."

I realized it was one of the few times I'd been alone with Fey without Anika there as a buffer.

"You don't think Axel sabotaged 5.0," I said to him.

He shook his head.

"The thought is absurd. Axel has done his share of destructive hacking, I know to my eternal sorrow, but it's all child's play compared to what afflicts 5.0. You can't imagine the diabolical wizardry of such a thing. I'm desperate for them to let me examine it."

"Then why does everyone else think he did?" I asked. "Isn't that why Hammon's here?"

"Hammon's a fool."

"But he knows your son," I said.

Fey leaned forward in his chair and put his hand on my knee, about the last thing I'd expect him to do. I fought the urge to pull away. His look was hard and cold.

"No one knows my children," he said in a voice I could barely hear over the battering wind.

Anika brought my drink and two glasses of wine on a small tray over to the table. After she'd handed out the drinks and sat down, I asked Fey, "Why didn't you leave the Swan with me and Anika? Did you know they were waiting for us?"

"I couldn't decide what to bring and what to leave," he said. "You were right to go on without me."

"Best laid plans," said Anika with a little shrug.

There was another lull outside. Everyone in the room looked toward the walls of the restaurant. I shifted my chair away from the table, took Anika by the hand, and pulled her toward the door into the hotel. A moment later a savage gust exploded against the back of the hotel, blasting through the big windows and glass doors that overlooked the docks. Wind, rain, tree limbs and table settings suddenly filled the air. The table where Hammon and company sat next to the windows launched toward the ceiling, propelled by the

wind and the bucking floor. Del Rey, standing behind the
service bar, screamed and covered her face. I saw most of
this through a blizzard of water and debris as I pulled Anika
by the wrist toward the back wall.

Before we reached the door, a deafening screech came
from above as the roof of the restaurant lifted off the walls
and blew up into the back of the hotel. I shoved Anika
through the door and followed her, banging hard against
the jamb as the floor fell out from under me. I looked back
into the chaos and saw Hammon and Pierre pinned against
the east wall. 't Hooft had a grip on the sleeve of Hammon's
light jacket. The wall waved like a sail in the wind. Del Rey
screamed again, and everyone looked across to the opposite
wall where she clung to the top of the service bar. 't Hooft
let go of Hammon and started to work his way over the dis-
integrating floor. Hammon reached out and yelled at him to
stop, but without looking back, 't Hooft shot him a middle
finger and pressed ahead. I saw no sign of Jock, and had no
more time to look, busy as I was trying to get Christian Fey
up out of the hole that was once the crawl space under the
restaurant.

I knelt down, gripped the door jamb and extended my
hand. Anika wrapped her arms around me and pulled backwards as Fey reached up and grabbed my forearm, allowing
me to grab his. He wedged his foot into a chink in the old
stone foundation and stepped up as I pulled his arm, and
aided by Anika's weight, yanked him through the door and
into the hotel, where we all landed in a heap.

I shoved him off me and stood up, helping Anika, and
then Fey do the same. We were in a room that served as
a broad hallway, leading to the front lobby, or into the bar
area. I shut the door to the lobby, then herded the Feys into
the bar, shutting that door as well.

"What about the others?" shouted Fey.

"We have to keep the wind pressure out of the hotel. If they can make it to the hallway, they can make it here," I shouted back.

To help prove my point, the building was shaken by another big gust, following which came the sound of the restaurant roof tearing apart and scattering to either side of the hotel and through shattering glass upstairs.

"You said it was good for another hundred years," said Fey.

"Can't be right all the time," I said, pushing them ahead of me through the bar and toward the front door. When we got there, I told them to stay at the rear of the lobby away from the windows. I opened the front door, which the wind nearly wrenched off its hinges, and jumped down behind the bushes that lined the front of the hotel. I kept my back to the shingled siding and inched along, searching the ground for my backpack, which I found at the corner, just where Anika said it would be.

The Mercedes was also where I'd left it. A big tree limb lay in front of the car, but there was room to drive around to reach the street. I squirmed under the chassis and saw that the clip-on cable was still in place. But not surprisingly, the keys weren't in the ignition. I popped the hood and dropped my pack on the seat so I could dig out two more cables, these lighter and more flexible. It had been a long time since I'd looked in the engine compartment of a Mercedes, and longer still since I'd hotwired one. There were surely modern safeguards against such a thing that would be tough to ferret out even under the best of circumstances.

I snapped off the cover of what I thought was the engine control unit, a device that electronically managed both ignition and fuel supply. I found what I hoped was the line that fed power to the unit, and traced it back to a fuse block under the dashboard. There I switched the line to a feed that saw current without needing the key turned in the ignition and prayed for an appropriate amperage. Then I went back to the engine and ran another cable directly from the battery to the starter and turned over the engine.

It caught.

My astonishment was quickly interrupted by a blast of wind that tried to wrench the raised hood off the car. I slammed it shut, grabbed my backpack and went back to get Anika and Fey.

They both wore rain jackets, and Fey handed me one of my own. Anika had a fanny pack around her waist and held a soft cat carrier. Eloise looked through the web mesh with unrestrained terror. I put Fey in the front passenger seat, telling him to keep his head down, and had Anika lie down in the back. I sat in the driver's seat and shifted into reverse so I could back up and make room to maneuver around the limb. I was spinning the wheel and about to throw it into drive when a fist came through the window and snapped across my cheek, the pulverized glass raining into the car and biting into my cheek.

Before I could make sense of what just happened, the fist turned into a vice that grabbed me by the throat. It wasn't lack of air, it was the imminent possibility that my larynx would be crushed that motivated me.

I shoved the floor shifter into drive, then pulled the .38 out of my backpack and shot the guy in the elbow. The hand released its grip and I stuck the accelerator to the floor, glancing out the smashed window just in time to catch the sight of Jock, bent over, his arm held close to his body, his face still the impassive mask it had always been. His good hand was pulling a big, black gun out of a holster on his belt.

I drove around the big limb, crunching over several smaller branches, and turned right onto the street. I heard the pop-pop of a semi-automatic and saw little holes open up in the windshield. I yelled at the Feys to keep their heads down and tried to steer the station wagon with my eyes barely clearing the dashboard.

After passing the yacht club and gas station, I followed the road around a corner and down into a slight dip. When I got there, the dip was full of seawater blown in from a breach in the shore line of the West Harbor.

My cursing alerted the Feys, who sat up and looked at the whitecaps racing before the northerly wind.

"Can we make it?" asked Fey.

"I don't think so. The car will stall and we'll be stuck in the churn. The current is probably a lot worse than it looks."

"What're we going to do?" said Anika.

I didn't know, but before I could admit it, a pickup truck came around the corner and stopped behind the Mercedes, essentially pinning us in place. It was a big truck, modified to achieve unnaturally high road clearance, so when I looked in the rearview mirror, all I saw were headlights and a shimmering grill. I rolled down the left rear window and told Anika to push open the door while staying flat on the rear seat. I got out of the car and dropped to my knees behind the rear door, using the open window as a gun rest. I looked up at the driver of the truck, but saw nothing behind the glaring headlights.

"Don't shoot, you dumb shit," yelled Anderson Track. "I'm here to help you."

CHAPTER 24

Anika and Fey climbed into the cab and I pulled the Mercedes off the road. After once again unhooking the cable from the solenoid, I heaved myself up and into the truck bed, now using the raised tailgate to support the .38. There was little likelihood the sheet metal would stop a bullet from one of the mercenary's high-powered weapons, but it was better than nothing.

Track had hurriedly told me he'd seen us drive by and knew from previous storms that the road was probably cut off by the bay water.

"I could ford Long Island Sound in this baby," he said, slapping the dashboard.

He was as good as his word, plunging headlong into the stream, the engine roaring under low gear, a pair of wakes streaming out behind the rear wheels. Moments later, we were across and headed up the hill. I trained the gun on the bend in the road, the possibility of hitting anything rapidly receding. Right before I lost sight of the racing bay water, I thought I saw some movement on the opposite side of the breach, but it was hard to tell in the stormy darkness.

I fell back down in the bed of the truck and looked up at the sky. There was nothing to see, but I didn't care. I just needed a moment when I wasn't filled with dread, to feel what it was like to be merely anxious and unnerved.

Track stopped at a stop sign and slid open the rear window.

"Where to?" he asked.

"The state barracks," I told him. I wanted to check on Kinuei and be closer to potential communications and fire-power. Though attacks on both Poole and Kinuei had been surreptitious, the attackers going unidentified, I couldn't ignore the possibility that Hammon would risk an all-out frontal assault on the police station, given his desperation and loosening hold on logic and reason.

As we drove around the ferry harbor I could see by my little flashlight that Buchanan's boat was still tied to the dock where I'd left it. It was a relief that someone else hadn't boosted it. Giving the boat back to Buchanan was central to the defense I imagined putting together in the event I got caught.

The harbor was a mass of whitecaps and waves were dashing against the breakwater, sending spumes ten feet into the air. Track took us past the ferry office and up the short hill to the barracks. I slumped deeper into the bed and tried to keep the salt spray out of my face.

When we reached the barracks I jumped out of the truck and stuck my head in the door, telling Kinuei not to shoot me. I walked to the holding cell and into the bright beam of his Maglite.

"How're you doing?" I asked.

"Better now. The coast guard's bringing out a tech to open this thing up," he said, moving the light away from my face. He held the Glock against his thigh with his other hand. "Who's with you?"

I told him, then asked how the coasties could get there in the storm.

"They got a bigger boat."

I went and retrieved Anika, Eloise and Fey, and asked Track if he wanted to hang with us through the rest of the storm. He shook his head.

"I gotta go check on my house," he said. "And get some sleep."

I tried to thank him for what he did, but like Two Trees, he wouldn't let me.

"I still want all of you off my island," he said, before driving off into the night.

Inside the barracks, we made ourselves as comfortable as we could. Those of us not in a cell took half-hour watches, alert for any sign of approach. Kinuei shared his provisions and questioned us on what happened. The Feys let me do the talking, so I told him with as much detail as I could, including the shot to Jock's elbow.

"You held out on me," said Kinuei.

"You asked me for *your* guns," I said. "Not *all* guns."

For whatever reason, he didn't press me on that, though I had a feeling it was a discussion more deferred than abandoned.

❖

After the debriefing we sat silently, kept watch and listened to the storm slowly abate. Kinuei said it was predicted to move out of the area by daybreak, which it did, as if all natural forces were choreographed to achieve a total change in conditions.

And then just to complete the transition, a two hundred foot coast guard cutter sailed into the mouth of the harbor and up to the breakwater below the barracks. Fey and I went outside and offered to grab lines, but they waved us off. With slow precision, the ship eased up against the pilings, which the crew lassoed with massive, braided ropes. A gangplank was deployed and a round civilian in a baseball cap and chartreuse slicker got off accompanied by two enlisted men wearing dark blue uniforms, orange life jackets and sidearms. One carried a little red generator, the other a gas can.

An officer stood at the railing and watched the procession.

"How is it out there?" I asked him.

"Routine, sir," he said.

I followed the three men into the barracks and watched with the Feys while the civilian opened a little hatch on the electronic combination lock, and jacked in a PC on which he tapped for less than a minute before the door snapped open. Kinuei thanked him as he walked out of the cell and the man nodded without looking up from the computer screen. Before he shut down the laptop he popped out a flash drive and handed it to Kinuei without comment. I wondered if he had vocal chords. Throughout all this the young coasties stood at near attention, wordlessly, allowing themselves only the briefest sidelong glances at Anika, who did the same.

After the rescue team left, Kinuei wasted little time hooking up the generator, turning on lights and radios, and firing up his desktop computer. Once everything checked out he sat back and sighed with satisfaction.

"Civilization, baby," he said. "Can't live without it."

"That's debatable," said Anika.

Kinuei turned in his chair to look at her.

"You ready to take a ride, Miss Fey?" he asked

"Back to the Swan?"

"Yup."

"I've got nowhere else to go," she said.

"You could stay here," he said, "but I can't protect you if I'm somewhere else."

"What's your plan?" I asked.

"We go to the Swan. People could be injured. I have a responsibility to assess the situation."

I rode shotgun, literally, carrying the Remington in my lap. Anika and Fey sat in back behind a metal grill. For the first time since arriving on the island I felt completely safe. I didn't know if it was the shotgun or the grill. Kinuei took a southerly route, avoiding the washed-out section of road. It took us past Gwyneth's place, which still stood, though the front yard was full of tree debris and a branch had smashed down through a section of fence.

The sun was now fully aloft and the sky gleamed blue, the leaves still clinging to the trees looking as if washed by divinity. A breeze blew, still out of the north, but now an emasculated thing that could barely stir the hem of a skirt.

The first thing we saw of the Swan approaching from this direction was the ruined SUV, and then the Town Car, not surprisingly where they'd been left behind the low hedge. Then we saw the façade of the hotel. Half the roof shingles were peeled away, and most of the shutters were gone, but otherwise the hotel looked straight and sure, provoking a "Thank God" from Christian Fey.

Kinuei drove his cruiser into the parking lot and stopped next to the dead Fords. He asked me for the shotgun, which I promptly handed over.

"You don't want to wait for reinforcements?" I asked.

He looked at me with a mix of anger and resolve.

"Would you?"

"At least leave the Feys in the car. Doors locked, engine running. It'll be one less distraction."

He did me one better, telling them to drive back up the hill and park somewhere out of the way. He switched on the two-way radio and synchronized the channel with his handheld.

"If I say run, run," he said to Anika as she took the driver's seat. Fey got in next to her. "If you see anything remotely funny, call."

She nodded and drove off. We stood at the end of the walkway to the front door and looked up at the hotel.

"What're the odds these people are stupid enough to fire on a state trooper?" he asked me.

"Anything's possible. This is the Black Swan, home to rampant anomalies."

"You got that little peashooter handy?" he asked.

"I do."

"Okay, I don't know about that. Officially."

"Okay."

He led us down the path and through the door into the lobby, calling out, "Police. Come out with your hands where I can see them." He checked the office behind the registration counter, repeating the same line. Which he did several more times as we worked our way through the first floor, finally arriving at the hallway that once connected the kitchen and bar with the restaurant, which had mostly disappeared.

There were a few sticks of lumber, a small pile of bricks, some broken bottles and a tangled mess of sodden draperies. And that was about it. Beyond the wreckage the narrow patio lay intact, and beyond that stood the docks. Two heavy wooden lounge chairs, apparently salvaged from the storage shed, were on the first dock off the central passageway. Sitting there, facing the Inner Harbor, were Del Rey and Bernard 't Hooft.

I guided Kinuei back through the hotel and around the west side along the brick path and out to the docks. The Harbor Yacht Club was also still standing, though what looked like a piece of wall from the restaurant lay over one of their floating docks.

"Good morning," said Trooper Kinuei as we approached the sitting couple. "How're you folks doing?"

Del Rey shaded her eyes when she looked up at him.

"Pretty good shape for the shape we're in," she said.

't Hooft looked at Kinuei's shotgun, then up at Kinuei.

"You won't be needing that," he said.

"Where are the others?" Kinuei asked.

"Where exactly? I have no idea. The last I saw Derrick he was sliding with a piece of wreckage across the patio toward the water and Pierre was sliding along with him, trying to catch Derrick before they reached the water's edge. I lost track of them as my focus was on Del Rey, who I was able to carry to the relative safety of the hotel."

"He's not kidding when he says carry," said Del Rey. "The man's a bull."

't Hooft enjoyed that, celebrating with a show of clenched fists and bunched-up shoulder muscles. Del Rey swatted at him as if embarrassed.

"What about Jock?" I asked.

't Hooft shook his head.

"We found him in the bar sewing up a wound in his arm. I offered to help but he told me he was fine. He said it like he was changing a tire or shining his shoes. Jock is one tough son-of-a-bitch, but a little this," he said, twirling a finger around his ear in the universal sign language for nuts.

Kinuei had more questions to ask, so I excused myself and walked back on to solid ground, over to the pathway that connected the Black Swan with the yacht club.

The blocky little club building looked mostly undamaged, with windows unbroken and roofing only slightly scarred. But for an overturned picnic table and ravaged message board, the club had come out nearly unscathed. I looked around the grounds for a few moments, then went out on the docks.

With no boats to be hurtled through the air, or into each other, there was little evidence of the storm, except for the huge slab of devastated building from the restaurant next door, lying like a stricken whale astride one of the docks. I walked out there, mindful of the awkward pitch underfoot, with the dock bent under the weight of the rubble.

I didn't know why I knew he'd be there, but I did. Face up, arm trapped inside a tangle of framing materials, his head shifting with the gentle wave action, Derrick Hammon looked less like a titan of high technology than the tragic recipient of random bad luck. Tragic but for his role in putting himself there.

I went back to the Swan to break the news.

CHAPTER 25

The electricity came back on in the early afternoon. I stayed with Del Rey and the Feys while Kinuei and 't Hooft, later joined by Anderson Track, extricated Hammon's body and wrapped him up in plastic. They finished just in time to greet an ambulance sent over from the mainland, the ferry now up and running again.

The distant sound of generators was replaced by chain saws and the roads were filled with service vans and pickups stuffed with fresh firewood.

Two more state troopers came over to relieve Kinuei, who did little to hide his pleasure at their arrival. We gave them descriptions of Jock and Pierre, though it was a little difficult to come up with an offense for which they could be apprehended. By any objective reckoning, the only provable violations of the law since I hit the island were all committed by me. I'd broken into a house, assaulted Derrick Hammon and two security guards, stolen a boat and a revolver, and vandalized two motor vehicles. And shot Jock in the arm, though for that I had a decent defense.

There was also the matter of Trooper Poole's attack, and Myron Sanderfreud's death, though both had occurred before the mercenaries arrived. They were probably the ones who locked Kinuei up in his own jail, but proving that would be next to impossible. Anyway, the odds were good that Jock and Pierre were already off the island, if not out of the country. Kinuei put out an alert to hospitals within a hundred miles of the island for a young male Caucasian with a bullet wound to the elbow, but had little hope that anything would come of it.

The Feys had spent the morning assessing the damage to the Swan, most of which was concentrated along the rear wall facing the docks as a result of the restaurant blowing off. This came as no surprise to me, since I'd seen where the sill was heavily reinforced back in the thirties when the Swan got a new foundation. The restaurant, added much later when the hurricane of '38 was a distant memory, was built of far weaker stuff. It was a rough calculation that included wind speed and direction, shoddy joinery and the effects of the wind pressure pushing up under the crawl space, but I had the hope that at least a big diversion had been in the offing.

What I got was a bit more than that.

◆

It wasn't until the power was back on and the cops had left that I found myself alone again with Anika. She asked me to help her roll up a carpet in one of the back bedrooms that had seen some water damage. Her father had left to buy lumber and other building materials to begin repairs. After some more questioning by Trooper Kinuei, Del Rey and 't Hooft had left with Hammon's body. Kinuei hadn't asked my opinion, but if he had, I would have told him that 't Hooft wasn't in the game for Hammon, he was in it for Del Rey. That he might be a thug, but he wasn't the one who beat up Trooper Poole. It was Hammon himself, a man whose ambition and self-regard had leached out whatever meager humanity he might have once possessed.

Anika and I brought the carpet out to the docks where we hung it over a clothesline strung between the piers.

"I haven't been up to the attic yet," she said. We both looked up at the roof, which had lost a lot of shingles, though the old tongue and grove roofers were all still attached. "I'd like it if you came with me."

"I'd like that, too," I said.

I followed her back inside and up to the second floor. She opened the door to the attic and I let her hold my hand as we walked up the steep stairwell. She snapped on the lights and we walked over to the painting. It was dry to the touch, unaffected by the water that had seeped in between the roofers. Anika nearly cooed with relief. I was glad the thing had survived, and told her so.

"That's 'cause you're an art lover," she said. "Or is it because you love me?" she added, turning toward me.

"I admit you've made an impression," I said.

"I got to you. I knew I would." She took my hand again and led me over to the bed. "Don't you wonder what it would be like?"

"I do," I said. "I admit that, too."

"We've got the place to ourselves," she said.

"I noticed." She started to pull me down toward the bed, but I stopped her and had her stand in front of me. I put my arms on her shoulders, dug my hands into her luxuriant black hair and drew her face close to mine. "I just want to know one thing."

"What?" she whispered.

"Why did you ditch your father the first time I tried to get you out of the Swan?" I whispered back.

She pulled her face back, and I pulled away my arms, bringing with me the flash drive that had been hung around her neck, having snipped the string with my miniature Swiss Army knife.

She clutched at her throat, as if the gesture would restore the drive to its former place.

"What are you talking about?" she asked.

"I can put everything else together, but I can't figure out why you'd abandon him like that."

"Maybe it wasn't about him. Maybe it was about you," she said.

"Maybe."

She put out her hand.

"Please give me that back."

"No. You've got the original. This belongs to Grace Sanderfreud, assuming she now controls Subversive Technologies."

"You're speaking like a crazy person," she said.

"I probably am crazy, but that comes in handy around you people."

She backed further away from me, her eyes narrowing with unease. I sat down on the desk chair and dangled the flash drive from the end of the severed tether.

"Axel's not the only savant in the family, is he? Only your genius comes in a much more colorful package."

"I think you're about to disappoint me," she said.

"Synesthesia. Your brain perceives numbers and letters as colors. That isn't a painting, it's a formula."

She sat down on the bed and crossed her arms, looking equal parts frightened and defiant.

"That's the silliest thing I've ever heard," she said.

"Your brother called you color head, which was a confirmation of sorts, but I suspected it since you told Amanda and me that you assigned numbers to the flowers in your garden. And then there's your tattoo."

"Even if something like that is true," said Anika, "you can't prove it."

"I can't prove anything," I said. "I bet your brother is the only person who knows. Synesthetes often don't reveal their abilities, and considering your gift for conspiracy, you'd never give up such a powerful advantage."

"Gift for conspiracy? Now that's insulting."

"You didn't drop programming to take up painting. You took up painting to help you code. It was better and safer than backing up on storage media. Plus, what a hoot for you. Your cleverness out there for all to see, yet no one had a clue what they were looking at."

"A secret's not a conspiracy," she said.

"No. A conspiracy takes at least two. During the day, while your brother worked on N-Spock inside Subversive, you took over your father's computer in the basement. You'd trained Axel and worked together as a team since childhood, so your development style, your signatures, are so similar they're indistinguishable. But naturally, the attention was all on Axel. And that's how you wanted it, what you reinforced at every opportunity, even distorting the facts to portray him as more fragile and dissociated than he truly is. It was your shield. Always keep the focus on Axel and away from you."

"Axel loves me," she said.

"Yes he does. Not like your mother, who abandoned you, who so hurt you that you killed her off in your mind. Or your father, who neglected you when you needed him the most."

"You must know a lot about neglect," she said. "You're good at it."

"I was. I'm trying to reform."

"Not with me you aren't."

"I've been paying a lot more attention to you than you think. Just not the kind you want. That work of art is a synesthete representation of the algorithms that cause N-Spock 5.0 to crash itself during data transfers. You wrote the original code, and have kept it alive from here, continually changing its characteristics and thwarting all efforts to save the application. Why?"

A bolt of sunlight came in through one of the gable windows and tossed a splotch of yellow on the dark wooden floor. The air inside the attic felt clean, freshened by the cracks between the roofers and the hurricane-washed atmosphere beyond. Anika flopped down on the bed, rolled over on her back and stared up at the ceiling.

"I'm not going to tell you anything about anything," she said. "You know that."

"Fair enough. So I'll tell you. You wanted to bring down your father's company. It was a hated thing, an obsession so consuming that he lost all sense of boundaries between work and home. Programming was the only game his kids knew how to play, his software colleagues their only playmates. But revenge isn't only better served cold, it's best cooked over decades. You kept your synesthesia and coding skills secret from your father, and held your brother completely in your thrall. Not hard to do when you're his surrogate mother. You and Axel have had the run of Subversive's servers and enterprise systems since you were kids. You've got back doors and secret passageways all over the place. When Subversive made the big gamble on 5.0, you were ready. A golden opportunity to both destroy the company and have your father all to yourself on the equivalent of a deserted island."

She rolled back up to a sitting position and waved a finger at me.

"For a stuffy engineer you have an amazing imagination. And what did I do next, create global warming and crash the world economy?"

"No, but you did use the crash to cover another gambit," I said. "Your father never touched the company's assets. It would have never occurred to him. You're the one who hacked into accounting and finance and started playing around, learning the ropes. And making a little money in the bargain. You left bread crumbs around that led somehow to your father, in case you got caught. But eventually, when the timing was right, you hung Subversive's cash and working capital on a collapsing investment fund. It was perfect. Your father gets blamed, but they can't prosecute him for fear of revealing a financial catastrophe to go along with the catastrophe that 5.0 was turning out to be. And he can't fight back, because he sees Axel's handiwork all over the caper. Only it wasn't Axel, it was you. As Hammon said, clever, clever techie."

Anika gathered a thick strand of black hair in her hand and began to run it through her fingers, stopping momentarily to wipe her nose and rub tears off her cheeks, which I hadn't noticed until that moment. She bounced her feet on the edge of the bed, as she'd done before. I suddenly remembered it was something my daughter would do, especially when the threat of punishment was in the air.

"You kill people and get away with it," she said. "I knew you would kill Derrick Hammon. And you did. So there."

"You must know a lot about killing people," I said. "You're good at it."

I had to endure another wag of the finger.

"Talk like that will get you nowhere, Mister," she said, and then jumped off the bed and ran down the staircase. I followed her, unhurried. I heard her go down the next flight of stairs, her footfalls heading through the lobby toward the ruined back of the hotel. I went that way and found her out on the docks, at the end of the central walkway where we'd tied up the *Carpe Mañana*. She embraced herself as if warding off the cold, though the temperature was near perfect, as the weather reverted to glistening autumn, the deep blue above reflected in the rippling surface of the Inner Harbor, the storm now a mirage, a forgotten disturbance in an otherwise temperate continuum.

I wrapped my arms around her from behind, the side of my face half buried in her hair, where the smell of her, the dense feminine smell invaded my consciousness.

"It was inevitable," I said. "A vulnerable, motherless kid, ignored by her father—secretly brilliant, but bored—adrift, with adolescent hormones in full bloom. A powerful figure takes an interest, someone who filled the lonely vacuum, who seemed to understand, who lavished fatherly attention, kindness and good humor. Irresistible."

Anika let her head fall to my arm. I gave her a gentle squeeze.

"But something happened, didn't it? It went too far. You were betrayed. Another adult, someone you trusted, whom you admired, maybe even loved, had proven yet again to be merely selfish and cruel. Interested only in his own fulfillment, the gratification of his own sick obsessions. Maybe out on his boat, where you learned how to tie bowlines. Again, the clever conspirator that you are, you waited patiently for the opportunity to set the matter straight, to bring the world back into harmony."

She started to rock back and forth, and I rocked with her.

"You suggested he take an outdoor shower, something you knew he liked to do. You turned on the water, and while it heated up found the nylon line and rigged it so you could slip it over Sanderfreud's neck from above, and because you needed the extra weight, you recruited Axel to jump off the step ladder with you, each with a foot in one of the loops, which made for just enough weight to counter Myron's bulk. From there it was a simple matter of cleating off the line and waiting for Grace to discover the tragedy."

"You tell such beautiful stories," she said languidly, pressing back into me. "You should be a professional storyteller. People will come from all over the land and sit at your feet to be mesmerized. I'll handle concessions. Popcorn and Diet Coke and T-shirts."

I gave her one more squeeze and let go, then turned around and headed back down the docks toward the hotel.

"No two color heads see numbers the same way," she called. "The painting is worthless to anyone but me."

I turned around, but kept walking.

"It's just a code," I said. "They'll break it. Maybe in time to hit Q1, maybe not. It's worth a go."

"I don't hate you," she yelled to me as I moved relentlessly out of earshot.

My backpack was where I'd left it in the hall. I slipped it on my back and headed west toward the ferry dock. Along the way I tossed the .38 Smith & Wesson in the bay, along with a handful of ammunition. A pair of sea gulls landed on the water's surface, curious over what had just gone kerplunk. Wisely, they quickly flew away, in search of less treacherous prey.

◈

I spent a few hours with Ashton Kinuei, telling him everything I knew, suspected, guessed or imagined about Derrick Hammon, Subversive Technologies, Anika Fey and her family, and what probably happened to Myron Sanderfreud and why. I said I'd gladly give unwavering support to any subsequent investigation and prosecution. Kinuei had the look of a man ready to take on a crusade, and I didn't try to dissuade him, but for me, I was done.

The woman at the ferry ticket counter exuded curiosity, but her Yankee reserve kept her questions to herself. Exhaustion, of all kinds, pulled at my limbs and hung around my neck. I rode over to New London unmolested and mostly asleep, lulled by the gentle rock of the boat. One of the ferry crew woke me when we arrived and helped me to my feet.

"I bet you want to get off," he said. "Unless you want to take a ride back."

"That's the last thing I want to do, brother," I told him, groaning to my feet and stumbling off the ferry.

A cab took me to the marina that served the mooring field where I'd left the *Carpe Mañana*. I could see her from the outer docks, rocking calmly at the end of the two mooring lines. Nearby, men were loading gear, ice and long, limber poles onto a small fishing boat. I asked them if they could drop me off at my boat and they readily agreed. Helping one another was the common law of the sea. You never knew when it would be you who needed the help.

On board the *Carpe Mañana*, I flicked on the batteries and ran through the electronics, all of which checked out perfectly. I started the motor and turned on the freezer, which was woefully short of ice, the only depletion in resources I could categorize as grave.

I dropped down on one of the settees, and in the womb of the big cruiser, let my body finally come to rest, and closing my eyes, allowed my mind to drift airborne into the soothing void of deep, unaccountable sleep.

CHAPTER 26

I'd been in cell phone contact with Amanda and Burton Lewis during the time it took me to launch from the mooring in New London and make my way across Long Island Sound, through Gardiners Bay and into the middle of the twin forks of the East End, finally coming to rest against a floating dock at a tiny private marina off the Shinnecock Canal.

Eddie got there first, having been released from the car well in advance of his human escort. I barely had the bow cleated off when he jumped up into my arms, lathering me with his long, rough tongue and making strange, anxious dog noises.

"Knock it off, you're embarrassing me," I said, gently lowering him to the grey dock, where he bounded off, looking to retrieve the rest of the party.

Amanda wore sunglasses, a long dress that nicely defined her contours, and a huge woven hat, decorated with a fluttering, feathery plume and welded to the side of her head. Burton was all in whites, as he often was, his weathered, tired face alight with glee as he beheld his sensuous new yacht, her recent sea trials invisible to the eye.

I hugged Amanda, shook Burton's hand and officially relinquished command of the *Carpe Mañana*.

"Permission to take a shower and stick my face in a vat of vodka," I said to Burton.

"The shower most definitely," said Burton, leaning back. "I'd be surprised if the health department wasn't on the way."

"So I guess Axel Fey is on his way back to Fishers," I said.

"With an escort," said Burton. "The fellow who's been watching over him. They've grown close."

"Must be an interesting fellow."

"Sometimes opposites attract," said Amanda.

"So you're sure it's safe for the boy?" asked Burton.

"The only people who might do him harm are dead. The hired help have already moved on. 't Hooft's got the girl, a dubious prize, though the only one he cared about. The only threat to Axel now is Ashton Kinuei."

Burton drove Amanda, Eddie and me over to our peninsula jutting into the Little Peconic Bay in the North Sea area of Southampton. The unexpected freshness of such a deeply familiar place clutched at my chest. We bypassed the cottage and walked across the uncut lawn to three Adirondack chairs stationed above the breakwater, strategically placed to allow observation of the infinite variety of natural wonders that played across the mercurial bay.

Eddie broke into a full-out run across the lawn and leaped down to the pebble beach, appearing moments later, legs wet and tongue unfurled, only to race off again for another pass. I was struck by the realization that, being a dog, he had no way of knowing that he'd ever be back home again. For all he knew, his life was now centered on a big custom sloop, which meant long periods underway, punctuated by visits to foreign locales. That this turned out not to be the case was reason enough for an extra display of rapture.

Once settled, the need for refreshments became immediately apparent, a void promptly filled by Amanda, who drew the goods from a secret cache held in deep storage.

Burton had politely ignored the cuts and bruises covering my face and the Ace bandage wrapped around my right hand until it seemed impolite not to ask. I said I'd gladly tell him the whole story, in relatively short order, but right at that moment, I really just wanted to sit and stare slack-jawed at the Little Peconic Bay.

"Fair enough," he said, turning his attention to the half-decayed tennis ball Eddie had dropped unceremoniously in his lap.

So we idled for the next few hours, relishing the waning afternoon, for the moment unencumbered by earthbound attachments or obligations. It was a lovely interlude, utterly violated by the arrival of Jackie Swaitkowski, whom I was nonetheless happy to see.

"Oh good," she said. "You're all here. Maybe we can have an adult conversation."

Jackie was a midsized woman with an unruly mass of kinky red hair and a freckled face that rarely expressed anything short of relentless determination. Nearing forty and the victim of an unforgiving excess of natural energy, she still looked a little like the fallen captain of the cheerleading squad.

I told her if she wanted to sit with the grown-ups she'd have to drag her own Adirondack out of the storage shed at the other end of the property, which she did with surprisingly modest complaint.

"I've been back and forth with the Con Globe attorneys a few times and I think we're close to a final figure," she said, clenching a bottle of white wine between her thighs and pulling out the cork. Amanda handed her a glass which she filled to the brim.

"Nice to see you, too," I said.

"Oh, right," said Jackie. "Hi, Sam, how're you doing? Fine? Good. How about you, Amanda? Okay, too? Great. I've written up the papers, so all I have to do is drop in the end figure. Which won't be insubstantial. Burton's been involved throughout the whole process, so you know the legalities will be bombproof. Please feel free to weigh in at any time," she said to Burton. He lifted his glass in acknowledgment.

Entranced by Jackie's arrival, Eddie generously offered her the next chance to toss a sodden, mangled tennis ball. She knew there'd be no refusing.

"Okay," she said, wiping her hands on her tan jeans, "these are Sam's instructions. Are you ready for this?" she asked Amanda.

"I'm never ready for anything," said Amanda.

Jackie read from a piece of legal paper she'd taken out from the inside pocket of her leather jacket and unfolded on her knee.

"'Eighty percent of the proceeds from the settlement of the intellectual property class action case against Consolidated Global Energies and its successors shall be put in an irrevocable trust. The trustee shall be Burton Lewis. The sole beneficiary of the trust is Allison Acquillo. At the sole written direction of Ms. Acquillo, the trustee may also make such disbursements as shall be specified by Allison Acquillo to her father, Sam Acquillo.' I've got to work on the legal language a little, but you get the gist," said Jackie.

It took Burton and Amanda a bit to absorb the gist, but after a respectful lapse of time, Burton said, "Interesting."

"It's nuts," said Jackie. "He's put no stipulations on how the money's to be spent."

"However, it is specified that she may spend whatever she wants on Sam," said Burton, "if she wanted to."

"Or not," said Jackie.

"That's the point," said Burton.

"If he did that to me, I'd kill him," said Jackie.

"I'm familiar with the impulse," said Amanda.

"I love it when people talk about me in the third person when I'm sitting right here," I said.

"What about the other twenty percent?" asked Burton.

"Sam wants to keep ten, and make another foolish gesture with the other ten," said Jackie.

We sat in silence, waiting for Jackie to explain what she meant.

"He wants to give it to me," she finally said, relenting.

"Not give, compensate," I said. "For all the legal help over the years. The dollar retainer was generous, I agree, but I think it's only fair to clear the rest of the ledger."

"Nuts," repeated Jackie, an assertion neither contradicted nor endorsed by the others.

"At least you're retaining ten percent for yourself," said Burton. "What are your plans for that?"

"For some reason, I've been thinking about sailboats," I said.

The evening was finally allowed to slip all the way into darkness, but for the moon painting the jittery bay waves in its meager light. And with the cool breeze swinging toward the northwest, where it would persist until spring, and surrounded by one dog and three people for whom my heart literally ached with love, I let go of all that wanton anger and remorse, and sailed unfettered toward the end of days.